# THE INSIDE PASSAGE

JONATHAN HAUER

*For Smelly Tramp, Boo, and the former Night Terror*

# PART I

# Lois MacReary

"It was a shit night, Bill MacReary."

Those were the last words that I or anyone else spoke to my husband. A rough send-off, I know, but at the time I was pretty certain I was done loving him. I loved almost everything else about our relationship. I loved our little house in Lutak, Alaska. It was simple: two bedrooms, a den, a small kitchen. It was so close to the mountains and so close to town. I loved the security of having him here. I knew I wouldn't have been comfortable there alone.

But I just don't think I loved him anymore.

I was used to him. Used to him coming home in a bad mood, never asking me how I felt. Used to him grumbling about his funding difficulties. Used to him complaining that his assistant had betrayed him, that she had gone behind his back and let a snake into his hometown Eden — his Lutak. Every night he said the same thing: that goddamn cruise line — NordStar — was going to destroy Lutak with its souvenir-loving tourists, its cell-phone towers, its disdain for all things good and natural. Then he would go to sleep, wake up, and head to work. The next night, the cycle began anew. And I put up with this.

And he was used to me, too. I didn't care about his research anymore. I stopped asking about his funding problems. I could care less what his assistant had done wrong this time or what great evil NordStar had unleashed on his childhood home. I just nodded when he talked. I said, "That's too bad, dear." I know it didn't satisfy him, and secretly it made me a little bit happy. And he put up with me.

That isn't love, I don't think, it's just existing.

The sex dried up years ago, replaced by arguing. But we couldn't even sustain that kind of passion for long. I couldn't even bait him after a while. If there was something uncomfortable between the two of us, he just got quiet. He would leave. He would go camping alone. I never wanted things to be this way, but I learned to accept it. This was my life. And while it wasn't sexy or fulfilling, it was comfortable.

But, tonight, Bill did a funny thing. He remembered our eighth anniversary.


Bill hadn't remembered our anniversary for years. It just never seemed important to him. We never celebrated. I would just put a gift on his nightstand at night and wake up to find flowers on the kitchen table. And I didn't mind too much. It was just Bill, and we weren't in love anymore.

But tonight when I came home from work, he was right there, smiling his stupid smile by the kitchen table. He had a heart-shaped Russell Stover assortment in his right hand and a daisy bouquet in his left. His shirt was tucked in and his unruly brown hair slicked back. This was a Bill MacReary I hadn't seen in a long, long time.

Asshole.

Then I remembered the gift I bought for him this year: a cell phone. It was a functional, thoughtless thing. It wasn't even wrapped. I stopped buying romantic gifts for Bill three years ago when I found the edible underwear from five years ago and the body paint from four years ago in the bottom drawer of his nightstand. The body paint was dried out and the edible underwear was brittle and smelled awful. Looking back, it's almost funny: shattered edible underwear and unopened body paint meant our love was dead. Now anniversary gifts just marked the date, a way to keep track of time out here where time never really changed things much.

So, tonight all I had was this stupid cell phone. The cruise company that Bill so despised had just put up cell towers along the ridge. I thought the GPS built into the tiny device would spark something in his scientist brain. Maybe it would encourage him to check back in if he thought better of storming out some night.

But him with the flowers and candy, smiling like a moron — just like when we met. I didn't know what to make of that.

The first time I saw that sweet idiot smile was a cool October night in Pasadena. Bill was a great student and my Dad, a soil scientist, took a special interest in him. He thought Bill had a great future. In Bill's junior year, Dad had grown close enough to Bill to bring him home for Sunday supper.

I opened the door that night and didn't know what to make of the smirking fool in front of me. His big, goofy smile made him look like one of those chimpanzees trained to flash its pearly-whites in the commercials. If he had been the slightest bit self-conscious about it, I don't think it would have worked. But he couldn't help it, you knew just by looking at him. At least the smile softened that Cro-Magnon brow. And it brought out his almond eyes. That smile didn't make him handsome –it made him lovely.

He had a bottle of wine. He wore a blue denim shirt tucked into jeans and his signature walking boots. He was easy to laugh, and when you saw that stupid smile you had to join in. The strangest thing about Bill – maybe the thing I liked most – was that he wasn't too keen on impressing me. Most boys went out of their way to make an impression on me. But he couldn't care less. He was easy, approachable and aloof.

I decided to make him mine.

Asking a boy out was new for me. I was a pretty professor's daughter, every freshman's fantasy. It took me three weeks to get up the nerve, and when I finally asked him, he said no. He said he didn't have time for dates yet. He said that school came first, that he was the first in his family to go to college and couldn't afford a distraction. Me, a distraction. That was new, too. The rejection made me want him even more.

I flirted with him for years, but he never gave in. I went through a string of boyfriends. They were cute, friendly, and never quite right. Never quite Bill. As far as I could tell, Bill never dated anyone. He still came over for regular Sunday suppers, but I was so frustrated with him that I started ignoring him entirely. He didn't seem to mind. He just carried on as if nothing was wrong. That drove me crazy.

The year I finished my Bachelor's degree, Bill was getting his Master's. I decided to have another go at him. The time was right. What could stand in the way? But he said no. Again. He was going back to Alaska tomorrow, he said. He had a project lined up in Lutak, his hometown. His research would help him finish up his doctorate. He didn't see the point in starting a relationship only to leave. He said he didn't want to start anything that would make it difficult to leave California. But I couldn't let him go. Sometimes that happens. Sometimes you just know who's right for you.

I convinced him to have a beer with me. I told him that I would follow him to Alaska. I told him I wouldn't get in the way of his research. I told him that I loved him and that I didn't care if he loved me back. I told him I wanted to be his wife. He smiled that stupid chimp smile and said okay, I could come along. And that's how I ended up in Lutak, where Bill got his doctorate and forgot about me.

Until tonight.


Tonight, Bill said he wanted to take me to the Lutak Burger 'n Shake, where we had our first official date. I flew out to Lutak a few weeks after Bill left California, and the Burger 'n Shake was our first stop back from the airstrip. He bragged about the fresh-brewed root beer, the chilidogs, the Lutak-ness of it all. I was enchanted. It was simple. It was Alaska. It was for me.

So it was fitting that we went there tonight. Sure, we went there every few weeks over the last eight years, but it never tasted so good. The chilidog was never so spicy or the root beer so cold. It was amazing. More importantly, it was us. Somehow, and I don't understand why, we were getting back to the us that we forgot to remember year after year. We laughed, and ate, and threw each other mischievous little looks. Bill smiled that stupid smile a lot.

Then I gave Bill his gift.

He turned red. He said that I was undermining him. He said I knew how he felt about mobile phones. He said the cruise line brought them and he cursed the "goddamn NordStar deal." He complained about his research assistant and how she had gone behind his back. He called her a "red-headed Judas." He wanted to know why I didn't listen to him. Why I didn't understand him. Why I didn't support him. Why I couldn't see his side of things, just once.

I asked him to tell me when he stopped loving me.

He stopped talking.

We drove home in silence. When we got inside, I told him he might as well leave, like usual. And he did. And I let him. He grabbed his tent and his shotgun, Enid, and loaded up the Chevy. I shouted after him. I yelled, "It was a shit night, Bill MacReary!"

He just got in the pickup and drove away.

About an hour after he left, it dawned on me. We argued. A great hole opened in my stomach, a great longing and sadness that I had stuffed in there and forgotten. Maybe I made a mistake. Maybe I shouldn't have expected to get back to the old us all at once. But I remembered arguing had replaced romance, and silence had replaced arguing. Maybe this was his move. Maybe he wanted us back as badly as I had forgotten that I did.

So I followed him.


This was not the first time I followed Bill. Three years ago, my curiosity started getting the better of me when he fled after a fight. I thought he was seeing some whore in town. Or maybe all that "red-haired Judas" talk was just a cover, hiding the true nature of Bill's relationship with his assistant.

So I followed him. And it turned out he was camping, just like he told me he was.

He was out there all alone, silent. He would find his spot — the overlook just past the rusted oil-derrick — always the same spot. He could see the whole town from there if he chose. Or he could move further in and face the blackness of the mountains rising up behind him. From there, a moonless night would be so dark that it was as if the town didn't exist.

Once he got to the overlook, he'd put Enid down and take a long pee, like he was pissing away all of the day's troubles. When we were in love, we'd go camping, and he would do that same peculiar thing — leaving Enid by the tent while he took a leak. When I asked him about it, he said it was the only important thing his father taught him. He taught him that "when your little gun needs cleaning, don't bring your big gun." That made me laugh.

When he was done peeing, he'd head back to his tent, jump in his bag, and fall sound asleep. It took just a minute. The next morning, he'd be back home for breakfast. And life would go on. The same routine, over and over. It would have been better if he'd been cheating.

I stopped following. Until tonight.


Tonight I drove my Wrangler to the foothills and made the long trudge to Bill's overlook. I moved quietly. I wanted it to be a surprise. More importantly, I wanted to tell Bill that the cell phone was not a message or a rebuke of any sort. It wasn't a way to attack his personal philosophy, at least not on purpose. It was just a stupid habit cultivated by years of loneliness. It was a functional gift.

I couldn't find Bill on the bright side of the overlook, so I walked towards the rising rock. I was amazed by how quickly the town disappeared when I moved in towards the mountainside. The air up there was so crisp that I felt like I'd swallowed a mint each time I inhaled. The stars and the quarter moon, reflecting off the snow, seemed brighter than day. It all seemed so special, so right. This was the place to rebuild my relationship with my husband, to wash ourselves clean of the grudges of the past. I needed to see Bill.

Back in Pasadena, when I was 18 or 19, I watched my Aunt Suzie's house for a weekend while she went on a cruise. She left early in the morning and I showed up at her house that night. I unlocked her front door and walked into her living room. Everything seemed normal at first, until I noticed the TV stand. The TV was gone from its usual perch, leaving only a dusty outline. I couldn't understand why she took a TV with her on a cruise. Wouldn't the ship provide that kind of thing? How had she carried it into her cabin?

Then I noticed the mess: things strewn everywhere, drawers opened and closed haphazardly, lots of dust circles where things had been. I followed the dust and mess until I reached the back door. It was open just a crack, but the wood was splintered where the lock once held the door to its jamb. When the police arrived, they told me that I had probably walked in on the burglar. They told me the perp made a hasty exit, and said I was lucky that he left when he did.

Sometimes the guy didn't, they said, and that was always worse.

When I finally reached Bill's tent, I felt like I did that night at Aunt Suzie's house. I just couldn't understand why he would make such strange choices.

His tent was torn. No, not just torn. Destroyed. Ransacked. Tent poles pierced grey canvas, a Rorschach of dark stains dotted the fabric inside and out. I knew that we had argued, and that we hadn't had such an exchange in a long time. But, as much as Bill loved me, I think he loved that tent more. It was a tent he'd been using since he was a boy. Why would he destroy the thing? Why did he vandalize his own tent?

And why had he buried himself up to the neck in snow?

The light reflecting off of the snow made it look like Bill was holding a flashlight to his chin, like a camp counselor telling ghost stories. His eyes were closed and he looked calm. I tried to wake him up — I even shouted at him — but I couldn't rouse him from that deep sleep. I looked for his canteen. Maybe I could give him some water, maybe even splash it on him. He couldn't sleep through that.

Then I saw the ribcage.

It was half-covered in snow but its shape was unmistakable. It gleamed white, mostly picked over, nearly matching the white powder underneath. Raw white bones with small bits of meat still clinging. And I wondered why Bill brought food here. There was plenty in the house.

Then I heard Bill.

He whispered to me about bears, some arcane bit of information he picked up when he was in the Boy Scouts. He whispered that animals were very protective of carcasses, that they were most dangerous after a fresh kill. I told him that I didn't care about that. We had important things to discuss. We had us to think about. We could discuss the Boy Scouts and bears some other time.

*Please honey*, he whispered. *Listen.* The hushed, almost imperceptible tones, buzzed in my ear. *There's something bad here, something that will hurt you. I don't want this for you. I'm sorry that I led you here, but you have to go now because it's dangerous here – deadly dangerous. You have to go because I love you.*

*I can't leave you here*, I told him. *Not like this. We argued, Bill. Don't you see? I'm going to fetch a shovel and some blankets. We can fix this. I can bring you back. We can be us again. We argued! You get it?*

He didn't respond.

I knew somewhere inside that he had never actually said anything in the first place. I knew that I needed to go. I needed to abandon Bill to the snow, to move past his severed head, beyond his ribcage, beyond his leaf-covered arm and his mangled leg. I needed to go.

But I was already too late. The roar was incredible. A confusing soup of Bill's survival lessons boiled in my head.

*Be still.*

*Put your hands over your neck and lay down.*

*Be big.*

*Make noise.*

*Don't back down.*

I had almost closed my hands over my neck when it hit me. The world spun. Every few rotations, I saw my cell phone flying through the air in an arc towards my still-standing, headless body. When I landed, I was facing Bill, close enough to kiss his lips. Death didn't take his beauty. His almond-shaped eyes beneath a strong brow. His high cheekbones. His pursed lips, capable of the stupid grin that stole me from home. I could have kissed him, but my lips didn't work anymore.

It was a shit night, Bill MacReary.

# 1

She was beautiful.

Seth Sterling winked one eye at the Diana. Afraid to take her in all at once, he took his time scanning her curved white sides, the rows of pristine balconies and spotless glass windows, and the unspoiled smokestack with NordStar Cruise Line's famous blue anchor. Seth anxiously pulled the Beast — a black ballistic nylon suitcase the size of a small refrigerator — across the gangway and onto The Diana's boarding ramp. Trolleys full of luggage flew past him as he made his way into her belly, onto the elevator, and to a small hallway on the port side of the Admiral deck where he was told he could find his cabin-with-balcony.

Occasionally another passenger looked at Seth with either curiosity or disdain, Seth wasn't sure which. He was, however, certain that they wondered what kept him from handing The Beast over to a porter to be whisked to his room, why he bore his own burden. He could imagine their questions: What was wrong with him? Why was he bucking the trend? Did he have a problem with tipping? His lip was damp with sweat. He told himself to stop worrying so much about what other people thought. He might be alone, he might be pulling his own luggage, he might be a little harried from the long coach flight from Phoenix — but he was here. He was here to accept his rightful reward.

He slid his key card into the slot, waited for the green light, then pushed wide the cabin door. A cool rush of air-conditioned bliss washed over his face. The lights were on inside his small room, the window shade open. He could see the Vancouver harbor lights through the sliding-glass door. He inhaled and closed his eyes. Everything was right in the world. He stepped into the room and headed for the bed. He deserved a nap.

Before he could reach the bed, his arm was rudely jerked back towards the door. He turned and saw the Beast, its blocky body filling the doorjamb. He pulled again, but the Beast refused to move. Seth climbed over the Beast and back into the hallway. He put one hand on the Beast's wide carrying handle and another on its front pocket. He pushed. It did not move. The Beast was spoiling Seth's first vacation in two years.

"You damned, dirty…"

No matter how hard he pushed, it would not roll through the narrow doorway and into his cabin. A drop of sweat rolled over Seth's eyebrow and into his eye. He blinked, forcing the salty, stinging solution under his eyelid. He rubbed at his eyes frantically and bent over, groaning.

A man next door — dressed in Tommy Bahama from his logo Relaxer Cap down to his Rum Cay boat shoes — cocked his head. Seth guessed the man was in his early 70s. "Why don't you let the porters give you a hand with that thing?" he asked.

"Because," Seth said, trying not to be irritated by the intrusion, trying to take himself back to the calm he felt just minutes ago, "they just won't." He returned to pushing.

Tommy Bahama's eyebrows lifted. "Now why would you think something like that? You have a big bag. They lift big bags. Look around." Porters in shiny blue NordStar crew outfits raced up and down the hallway, helping other passengers with their luggage. Just not Seth.

"Look, they—" Seth gritted his teeth and calmed himself. He pointed frantically to the porters. "They don't like me, and they won't help. And, you know what? If I was them, I don't think I'd be so fond of me either." He pushed again. The Beast growled, its plastic corners straining against the door but refusing to move through.

"You shitty little…" Seth told the Beast.

Tommy Bahamas rolled his eyes. "These porters like everyone. Look, son, they like you or they don't get tips." He rubbed his fingers together. "It's that easy."

"Like strippers," the man's Chico's-wearing wife said.

Seth stopped pushing and stared at Chico's. Tommy Bahamas did the same.

"Charlie," Chico's said, "I know how the world works. Just like on the Sopranos. Strippers pretend they like you for the cash. So do the porters. Same idea."

"Not now, Nan." Charlie said.

Nan folded her arms and huffed.

"Seriously," Charlie told Seth, "why don't we just flag someone down? We can do it together."

"It's pointless," Seth said, "just trust me on that." He groaned and pushed again, but the Beast did not give. Suddenly, a smiling porter and his luggage cart appeared.

"Yeah," Charlie said, "obviously pointless."

The porter was short and thin. He had Asian features and a name tag that said "Cliffy." Seth smiled at Cliffy. Cliffy's smile disappeared.

"Your bag is in my way," Cliffy said, matter of fact. His cart needed an inch or two of additional clearance, precious floor space where the Beast now sat.

"Yep," Seth smiled at Charlie, "pointless."

"I can't get it inside," Seth told the porter. "Unless I can get a little help here, you're going to have to find another way round."

Cliffy frowned at Seth and the Beast. He abandoned his cart and walked to the giant suitcase. He turned it around a few times, finally settling on its original position. He gave a great shove, the veins on his ropy arms standing at attention. The upper corners of the Beast edged their way through the door, but the Beast would go no further.

"You," Cliffy said to Seth, "there." He pointed to the Beast. Cliffy placed his hands on the upper portion of the bag where he wanted Seth to push. With Seth in place, Cliffy contorted his body like a circus performer. He had his hands on the Beast and his feet flat against the wall opposite. The rest of Cliffy was suspended in mid-air. "On three. One… two…"

Seth pushed and cursed. Cliffy shoved in silence. The upper corners of the bag again entered the room. Soon, the lower corners edged their way into the doorjamb. The Beast's metal teeth bit into the wooden doorjamb, but moved no further. It was still stuck in the doorway, but no longer blocking Cliffy's cart. The little Asian man pushed his cart past the Beast and left the scene. He flashed a big smile as he passed.

Charlie laughed. Nan slapped his arm.

Seth was stuck. He eyed his bag and looked at the spot where Cliffy's cart had been. He got on all fours, and, mimicking Cliffy, put his brown loafers against the hallway wall and his hands against the bag. He pushed, suspended in the air between the hallway and the bag, and grunted. To his surprise, the Beast started to move. Suddenly, the Beast's lower corners freed themselves from the jamb, sending Seth and the Beast speeding towards the cabin's interior. Seth opened his eyes, found his feet, and raced after the bag into the small room. Past the bathroom/shower combination on the right and the small sliding closet to the left, the Beast hit the cabin's queen bed and came to a stop. Seth did not. He flew over the bed and towards the sliding door.

*The Vancouver lights are particularly beautiful in the early evening*, Seth thought, then collided face-first with the door glass.

Seth stumbled to his feet and begged the room back into focus. He touched his nose, then looked at his hand: a few dots of blood, nothing serious. He smiled at his reflection. No dark spaces where teeth should be. His clothes were crumpled and his cheek had a red mark where it connected with the sliding-glass door handle. Seth's dark-brown hair remained perfectly coifed. He turned his attention to the Beast.

"You and me," he told the Beast, motioning with the "vee" of his index and middle fingers. "We're not talking."

The cabin phone rang. Seth cursed and put the phone to his ear. The voice on the other end was cool and familiar.

"My bitch," it said.

# 2

Seth was not surprised to be called a bitch.

The voice on the other end of the line was Thad Wilson, a young-for-his-position partner at Radley & Associates, Seth's firm. Thad called all of the young lawyers who worked for him his bitches. They were, as Thad had often explained to Seth, part of a successful bitch farm. They even had softball jerseys that had the word "BITCH" stenciled across the back in the place of their names. They put up with this treatment because Thad had a proven track record of quickly and effectively grooming his bitches into successful partners, then encouraging them to move off the farm and start their own. After several years on Thad's farm, Seth was now a seasoned hand.

"Glad I could reach you, bitch. I have news." Seth pictured Thad at the window of his 23rd floor office, his sleepy, feline eyes taking stock of downtown Phoenix. "I just got back from a partner meeting, where I reported on the NordStar project." Seth's heart pounded. Thad's report, Seth knew, would have a huge impact on Seth's partnership review later that year.

"You were a good little bitch on this one, Seth. You put in the hours. The executive committee — even Guy Radley himself — is impressed. They'll all remember your work. Things are looking very good." Thad was probably looking at his well-manicured nails now, probably rubbing them against his lightly starched white oxford shirt.

"Wonderful, Thad," Seth said. "Just fantastic. Thanks." Everything was falling into place as planned. Seth was feeling euphoric, triumphant even. The pain from his encounter with the door vanished.

There was no response from the Phoenix end of the line. Thad was weighing Seth's words. Seth was familiar with Thad's habit of analyzing even the simplest phrases, scanning for tells, double-meanings, possible slights. Seth held his breath. Finally Thad spoke, as if there had been no awkward pause.

"I also wanted you to know that Buddy was happy that we bought the cruise tickets for you. He was very impressed with you and thrilled that you'll be aboard the maiden cruise to Lutak. So that doesn't have to be awkward, okay?"

Buddy was Scott "Buddy" Tennison, the brains behind NordStar. Strangely, Buddy was not NordStar's CEO. That title fell to Buddy's more charismatic brother, James "Lord" Tennison. But everyone at Seth's firm knew that Buddy pulled the strings, not Lord. NordStar was a major client, and if Buddy was happy with Seth, it would buy even more leverage when the partnership review came around.

"Thanks," Seth said. "I appreciate that."

Thad waited a few seconds before responding, "I want Buddy — I take that back, I want all of our clients — to think of you as a senior associate, a future partner here. Less bitch, more equal. Got it?"

"I don't know what to say."

"A 'thank you' will do."

"Thank you."

Thad paused. "You might want to hold off on that. I might have just fucked you. We'll have to wait and see."

"I'm not following."

Another pause as Thad scanned for meaning.

"Oh, I think you are," Thad said. "You could have turned down the cruise tickets. It probably would have been the smarter move. The humble one, anyway. This is the most important year of your career, bitch. You could have said, 'thanks but no thanks, I'm too busy for a cruise.' That always impresses the partners. But you accepted the tickets. Why do you think you did that?"

"Because," Seth said, "I was honored that the firm would do this for me." He was beginning to feel exasperated by this conversation.

Pause. "Bullshit."

"And you, you recognized my work in such a generous way. I couldn't say no to that."

Pause. "Double bullshit."

Seth felt cool sweat trickling under his armpits. Nervousness flushed his already overtaxed pores. Seth was relieved to be having this minor breakdown thousands of miles away from Thad's all-knowing eyes. "Because," he tried again, "you basically sanctioned a vacation after what we went through for the past two years?"

Pause. "That's a triple. You're smart enough to figure this out. Think about it. You know the crew will hate you for what you did — you negotiated pay decreases for all of them in order get NordStar into Lutak and get The Diana launched. And, as nice and pretty as she is, they will be awful to Melanie, too. You know that."

"Actually, that's not—" Seth protested.

"And you know that I would never expose my loved-ones to such treatment. My family's more important than my career, I'll tell you that much. Bitch, the crew is going to go out of its way to make the trip miserable for anyone from Radley."

"But, I think—"

"Seth, stop. I know the truth. You want to be there in case anything goes wrong. You think that if this thing doesn't go off without a hitch, you won't make partner. You don't see this as a vacation. This is control."

It was no use fighting. Thad was right.

"Maybe." Seth said, wedging hand towels under his arms. "I guess it's possible. I mean, I want you to know how much I appreciate you thinking of me. But I also think it's the responsible thing to do."

Thad said nothing for what felt like a full minute. Then: "Good. That's good, Seth. But know that this is on your shoulders now. If you're there to field problems, you're also responsible if something goes wrong." Seth pictured Thad's cat-eyes popping wide open, electric ping-pong balls, and his irises wide with easy prey. "The whole firm will know it's your fault. I'm taking myself out of the loop. So, like I said, you might be fucked. We'll just have to wait and see."

Seth had no idea how to respond.

"So, changing subjects, how's the cruise going so far?"

Seth took a few breaths. "The boat's nice," he said.

"It's not a boat, bitch. Rule of thumb: if you stand in the middle of the top deck and can't pee over the side, it's a ship. The Diana is well over 1000 feet long, weighs 80 tons and holds 2500 passengers. It's a ship. Don't make that mistake around anyone from NordStar, or you're definitely fucked. Totally fucked."

"Ship, right," Seth said.

There was a pause.

"Okay. Now, you know, have fun," Thad said. "Call me if you need anything."

"Of course. Absolutely."

"Oh, I forgot to ask," Thad said coolly, "is your fiancé enjoying herself?"

A shiver ran down Seth's spine.

"Melanie's not here," he replied, his jaw tight. "We're through as of this morning."

Thad paused. "Can't say I didn't see it coming. Anyway, call me if you need anything. I like to keep tabs on my bitches, bitch."

The line went dead on the Phoenix side.

Seth licked his lips. He was exhausted. The cabin's queen bed called to him. He sat on it, unbuttoned his wrinkled blue oxford, then removed his shoes. He spread his toes, eager to forget the cramped flight, the Beast, Thad, even Melanie. He shoved a pillow over his eyes and sprawled diagonally across the mattress, simultaneously enjoying and fearing having an entire bed to himself. As he felt himself let go of the waking world, he heard a voice, squawking, parrot-like from his nightstand.

It was his cabin intercom. "Attention all passengers," a vaguely European accent said through a crackling speaker, "please proceed to the Starlight Theater for a Welcome Aboard drill."

"Really?" Seth said. He pulled the pillow from his head and sat up. "Really?"

**3**

Emergency lights flashed outside Seth's cabin.

Seth stood at his doorway watching NordStar crew using orange flashlights to direct passengers to the Starlight Theater. Cliffy, now in an orange emergency vest, stood immediately opposite Seth's door, signaling to his right. Seth made the turn and immediately collided with Charlie. Seth turned back to a grinning Cliffy, who now directed passengers in the opposite direction.

Seth did not look back at Charlie or Nan as they made their way to the mutual gathering point. But he heard them.

First Charlie: "What's wrong with this guy? Who doesn't check a bag that big at the gate? And is the cursing really necessary? I know he thinks no one can hear him, but I can. Should we talk to the captain? Who goes on an Alaskan cruise alone?"

Then Nan: "Maybe he has problems. He obviously has a connection to that suitcase. Not healthy. And no normal person would go out in public looking the way he does. All that sweat! Maybe he needs a friend, Charlie."

Then quiet. Seth pictured Charlie red with fury — angry with Seth, angry at Nan for empathizing with his new nemesis, angry that the gods had put him on a cruise next door to a crazy person. The silence was intolerable. Seth contemplated apologizing to the couple, assuring them that he was neither insane nor an asshole. He was just an attorney.

Then he heard a female voice with an Australian accent call his name. "Sterling? Mr. Seth Sterling?"

Seth snapped back into the moment. He was at a set of doors leading to the cruise ship's premier entertainment destination, the Starlight Theater. The young woman next to him wore a perfunctory smile, looked from Seth to her clipboard and back. She looked familiar, somehow.

"Y-yes," he said. "Seth Sterling."

The woman's grin disappeared. She checked something off her clipboard, then reached behind her into a stack of yellow, inflatable life jackets. Seemingly not finding what she was looking for, she walked away. Behind Seth, a long line of impatient cruisers stood staring at him, frowning. All except Charlie. Seth knew men who only smiled when they were furious. And Charlie was definitely smiling. Fresh sweat beaded on Seth's brow. Seth had no desire to get into a beef with a cruiser twice his age.

"It'll be okay, big guy," Charlie said, still smiling. "Don't you worry. The nice lady will be back real soon with a special jacket for you." Seth was shocked to find that Charlie's smile had been entirely sincere. Nan was equally sincere, offering an exaggerated nod, her eyes wide with empathy.

The woman with the clipboard returned. "Sorry about the wait, Mr. Sterling. I didn't think any of these jackets—" waving to her pile of life preservers "—would, uh, fit someone of your obvious importance." She handed him a yellow rubber jacket with a neck hole. It looked like a big, limp version of a Do Not Disturb hotel door hanger.

"What do you mean 'obvious importance?'" Seth asked. He slipped the floppy jacket over his neck.

"Please, Mr. Sterling, there are a lot of other passengers waiting."

Before he could respond, Nan slipped her arm around Seth's and led him into the theater. "Don't you worry, honey," Nan said, "My husband Charlie here and I — I'm Nan Jenkins — have been on a hundred of these cruises, and this is how they all start off." Arm in arm, Charlie trailing, they followed a path of gesturing flashlights to their seats.

Tolerating his newfound friend, Seth took in his surroundings. He was impressed. Designed to seat the ship's entire population in one shot, the Starlight consisted of an orchestra level, a mezzanine, and a third deck, unheard of on cruise ships. More astounding than the size of the theater was the stage backdrop, an enormous window offering a panoramic view of the back of the ship and the open water beyond. It was nearly dark outside now, the remainder of Vancouver's skyline twinkling against an obsidian-blue sky.

A pre-recorded fanfare erupted from giant speakers framing the stage. A man in a tuxedo ran through the theater aisles and jumped onto the stage, a familiar yellow door hanger around his neck. The stage window went opaque, causing the Vancouver skyline to disappear entirely. A spotlight came on.

"Ladies and gentlemen," the man said. "Welcome aboard NordStar's newest ship, the Diana!"

The crowd applauded.

"I'm Stevie Bruebecker, your cruise director." He bowed to more applause. Stevie was younger than Seth expected a cruise director would be, maybe mid-twenties. He wondered how someone found that line of work. What high school counselor tells you that you'll make a good cruise director? "As you all know, this is our maiden voyage aboard the Diana, and we don't want to keep you from enjoying this magnificent ship or your voyage any longer than necessary." He sounded sincere.

"Before we set you free for a week of indulgence, relaxation and pristine, Alaskan nature — including our newest port, Lutak — I need to read you a note I've just received from the Alaska Department of Fish and Wildlife."

"You'll love this," Nan said, "he does it every year."

Stevie continued, brows furrowed: "The department is advising our guests to take extra precautions and be on the alert for bears while in the Juneau, Lutak, and Skagway vicinities. They advise people to wear noise-producing devices such as little bells on their clothing to alert the bears to their presence. The department advises you to carry pepper spray in case of an encounter with a bear. Most importantly, people should be able to recognize the difference between black bear and grizzly bear droppings.

"Black bears are far less dangerous than grizzlies, so the department wants you to keep the following distinctions in mind. Black bear droppings are smaller and contain berries and possibly squirrel fur." He scanned the crowd, his expression barely masking a face clearly meant for yuk-yuk antics.

"Grizzly droppings, on the other hand, have little bells in them and smell like pepper spray." Stevie dropped the faux-solemnity and allowed his smile to re-emerge. The audience, even those who had heard his routine before, laughed and clapped enthusiastically.

Seth did not.

"But seriously, folks. I want you to have a great time on board. We have some fabulous activities for you during the cruise, including our brand new port in Lutak!" The crowd applauded. "Now, for actual ship's business I will hand you over to our ship's head purser…"

The woman with the clipboard took the stage. Seth was finally able to take a good look at her. She was petite and attractive in a short haircut, soccer-player way. She wore white nylon pants with white sneakers and a navy NordStar blazer over a tight white top. Like Stevie, she had a floppy yellow bib suspended from her neck. He swore he knew her from somewhere.

"Please welcome," Stevie bellowed, "the lovely Tammy Wurser!"

That did it. The name and the face came together. Seth's firm had handled one of Tammy's discrimination charges against a NordStar captain. Something about partner swapping, Internet sites, perhaps a string of pearls? Seth couldn't be sure about what had happened, but he knew Tammy Wurser was definitely involved. Radley's attorneys traded these stories like inmates trade cigarettes.

"Hello ladies and gentlemen," she said, "I am Tammy Wurser, the ship's head purser. I know, sounds kind of like a Dr. Seuss rhyme. I get it all the time." Tammy offered an embarrassed smile. Cruisers laughed politely. "I am here for your safety, and I can be reached at any time via the Diana's telephone system. Just dial 911 — for our American passengers, your government stole that number from NordStar cruises." A few more laughs.

"Now, should something more serious happen — something more dastardly — something that puts this beautiful ship in so much danger that we need to evacuate, you're going to go through precisely the same drill you went through tonight. No worries, right mates?

"The ship's intercom will instruct you to go to a designated gathering point, and my crew will lead you to tenders that can get you off the ship. When you get to your tender, you'll be handed one of these life preservers." Tammy pulled her yellow plastic life preserver out from under her chin. "You all have one of these on right now, so it can't be too hard to get in and out of them, right?"

Nan elbowed Seth and smiled.

Tammy continued. "Now, these little jackets automatically inflate at the touch of a button. Here." She held out a tiny red button at the end of a yellow handle sewn to the life jacket. "Now I want you all to locate your button, but be careful not to push, it's very sensitive."

While the cruisers checked their jackets, Seth noticed that Tammy was staring directly at him. Her hand fumbled with something in her right pocket. Something in her blue eyes told him that the next few minutes were not going to be pleasant. Seth closed his eyes and felt fresh sweat explode from his pores.

POOF!

The jacket inflated violently around his neck. Other cruisers looked around for the noise and spotted Seth, red faced and sweating in an inflated yellow life jacket.

"Good on ya, sir," Tammy said over the crowd's laughter, "but next time wait until we're at the tenders." The crowd continued laughing at Seth while Charlie and Nan discouraged those closest with disapproving frowns.

"Mr. Sterling?" A deep voice behind Seth asked. Nan and Charlie exchanged uncertain glances. Seth turned around to face a tall man with a short grey beard. He wore a sharply pressed uniform, and, piercing through the coarse facial hair, a hard slit of a mouth. "I am Captain Michael Kelly."

Another familiar name. Wasn't he mentioned in Tammy Wurser's complaint? Yes, Seth was certain he was.

"Would you follow me, please?" the Captain asked.

# 4

Seth followed the Captain into the hallway beyond the Starlight, then into an elevator bound for the Promenade Deck. Captain Kelly — dressed in a navy blue tailored suit with bright ribbons and medals advertising his vast accomplishments — looked just as a Captain should. The only thing marring the Captain's gleaming, streamlined look was a slight bump under his right pant leg that Seth assumed was a small gun strapped to Kelly's ankle. Guns had become ever-more popular accessories for airplane pilots and ship's captains after 9/11.

Kelly caught Seth looking at his leg. Seth looked away. Kelly reached over and pushed a button on the inflated donut around Seth's neck. It deflated with a whoosh.

The elevator doors opened and the two entered the ship's vast promenade. Kelly looked at Seth, smiled and winked. They were now standing in the middle of what appeared to be a picture-perfect American town. Maybe somewhere in Nebraska or Indiana. Surrounding them were wide avenues and blocks of pristine redbrick buildings. They looked like they had been constructed in an early-20th century heyday. Stores and cafes filled the buildings' first floors, and what appeared to be apartments — actually pricy guest suites — filled the two or three levels above. There was a town square in the middle of the faux Mayberry, complete with grass, trees, rows of benches, and an enormous stone fountain. Above it all was the night sky, brilliant stars visible despite a glowing quarter moon.

For the second time tonight, Seth was impressed. He had seen various concept sketches back at the office, but nothing prepared him for its unfaltering reality. With the other passengers still in the Starlight Theater, Seth was the first cruiser to see Diana's town square. His mouth hung open. There were no other crewmembers present, busy as they were with tasks below decks, in the theater, and on the bridge. It was here, without prying eyes or ears, that Captain Kelly first spoke.

"Buddy told me that you would be aboard," the Captain said. "I thought you might appreciate being the first to see this."

The Captain's tone was soft, almost quiet, but easily understood. Seth was amazed by people who didn't need to speak loudly to be heard. His co-workers acted as though they had perpetually left a rock concert. These were people who lived to argue over telephones and conference tables. The Captain was a refreshing change of pace.

"I'll admit," the Captain continued, "I'm surprised that you actually agreed to come. Took some guts. I don't know if you noticed, but people here don't exactly like you."

"Hadn't noticed," Seth said and crammed the yellow life preserver into his pocket. A thick welt rose where the preserver had hugged his neck, an angry red collar testifying to his earlier humiliation.

The Captain chuckled. "Well," he said quietly. "I, for one – and probably the only one – am happy to have you on my ship."

Seth realized that Kelly had another motive for bringing him to the top deck before the crew were done with their tasks: the Captain didn't want the crew to see him with NordStar's hated outside counsel. It was a savvy move and Seth didn't fault him for it. He pictured a mutinous crew parading with pitchforks, torches and a noose, intent on hanging him and Kelly from the enormous elms circling the ship's town square.

"Thanks, Captain," Seth said. "It's good to finally see, in person, what we've been wrangling with for the last two years."

"Two years for you. I've been pushing for this for most of my career. Well, not this," he said, gesturing to the faux town square, "but Lutak. And now, because of you, we're doing it. Don't get me wrong. The window dressing is wonderful, but Lutak was always my goal. These ships become bigger and fancier, but Lutak has always been the jewel. The last unspoiled bit of the passage, and it's ours. Exclusively." The Captain winked.

Seth nodded. For Seth, Lutak was a very different kind of jewel. In its facets, Seth saw his future. A partnership at Radley. A high six-figure income. Then seven. Stability. A family maybe. He could handle that. After all he had been through, he was ready for a brighter future. The last two years had been a pain in the ass. 16-hour days. No movies. No poker games. No trips. Too many fast-food meals and too much bad office coffee. Worst of all, he had no time for Melanie. He had let their relationship die in the interest of furthering his career. But he had survived. And now the Diana was on its way to Lutak, with him on board. The crew might not like him, but nothing would keep him from seeing his jewel, his Lutak, his future come to life in the Alaskan wilderness.

"Besides," the Captain said, "Lutak is the only reason NordStar's still operating. It's the line's last chance to avoid bankruptcy. Without Lutak, I firmly believe we'd all be out of jobs. You should be proud of that." The Captain winked again. That winking was wearing on Seth. Why was Kelly so intent on putting him at ease? "Come, let's have a look around."

Winking aside, Seth wondered why the ship's Captain was treating him to a private tour. While he had been instrumental in getting the Lutak cruise off the ground, there were certainly more important people aboard and more important jobs to be done. He hoped that it was simply the Captain's way of thanking him for a job well done. Experience, however, suggested otherwise.

Kelly walked Seth through the town square, explaining the watering systems, the building materials, explaining the glass barriers that ringed the promenade to curb wind while preserving the town's uncanny calm. He showed Seth the various shops, the clever way the engineers used forced perspective to make the buildings look taller than they actually were. He was clearly pleased with his ship.

"I can't wait to see our passengers sitting on park benches with a view of Mendenhall glacier towering over the cafe across the street. Can you imagine? We're a traveling town. We can make the wonders of the world into our scenery. Now I'm going to show you my favorite part of the ship. Maybe it's the Irishman in me."

He led Seth through Restaurant Row – a block of storefronts promising everything from filet mignon to tikka masala – and to a magnificent glass tower at the end of the row. The tower had to be at least five stories tall. At first, it was difficult for Seth to see what the monolith held. It looked as though it was filled with rows and rows of metallic polka dots. As he neared the tower, it became clear. The structure housed countless bottles of wine and other exotic looking liquors stacked upon one another in clear glass rack after clear glass rack.

"So, in addition to this marvelous setting, we now offer the finest wine selection in all of Alaska. Indeed, one of the largest selections in the world. The engineers put all sorts of fancy machinery underneath the tower to regulate the temperature in there. So, no matter how cold our Alaskan nights get — or how hot our Caribbean nights, once we move her down south — this wine cave will remain perfect. And this thing is basically an impregnable fortress. The whole structure is reinforced by three layers of security glass and coated in a shatterproof window film. Really a marvelous bit of work."

Seth patted the thick glass. Kelly walked around the tower, then stopped and put his right hand against the glass. It responded to his touch, bright light forming a circle around Kelly's splayed fingers. He removed his hand to reveal a numeric keypad projected between the tower's glass panes. Kelly tapped what seemed like 30 digits into the pad. Seth hadn't noticed it before, but there was a small gap between the floor pavers and a door-sized glass panel to the Captain's left. The panel slid open and Kelly motioned for Seth to enter.

The tower's center was hollow, with enough room to hold a decent cocktail party. Seth and Kelly stood in the middle of the space, surrounded by the tower's glass wine racks. Just above them was a swing seat.

"For accessing the upper-levels," Kelly said. "The expensive stuff. Now, where did they put it?" Kelly bent down and fumbled around for a bit, then found what he was looking for in the glass rack opposite the door. "Ah, here it is."

He straightened, holding a full bottle of Jameson whiskey.

"Shall we?" Now it wasn't just a tour, it was a drink with the Captain; the same Captain who had just piloted the Diana out of Vancouver on its maiden voyage; the same Captain who had a million other things to do besides walk around with NordStar's outside counsel.

Seth chewed his lip.

Why was Kelly being so attentive?

# 5

Kelly's cabin was exactly how Seth thought a captain's quarters should be. Dark, wood-paneled walls, sailing miscellany everywhere, a free-standing globe, a bronze telescope on a wooden tripod, a small bunk, and a heavy wooden desk covered with charts and pictures of his handsome Captain's wife and burly Captain's sons. What Seth did not expect was the view: the fore and aft of Kelly's cabin was all glass. Seth could see over the promenade's brick buildings to the open waters in front of the ship. To the rear, Seth saw the bridge, towering high above the aft decks.

There were a few crew members standing on the bridge, blank expressions on their faces. It looked like dull business. They sat around on raised stools in front of banks of machinery and watched the front of the ship. Occasionally, one crew member would turn to the other and say something. But they never actually pushed a button or turned a dial. After a few moments staring, Seth noticed that one of the bridge crew was staring back at him. The crew member mimed looking through the viewfinder of a camera as if to say, "take a picture, it will last longer." Seth looked down.

"Not much privacy," Seth said.

"You'd be surprised," Kelly said. "Actually, you will be surprised. Watch this."

Kelly, still holding the fifth of Jameson, pushed a button on his wooden desk, causing the heavy wooden desktop — charts and all — to slide neatly into the table. From within the table, a large touch screen arose. It came alive, emblazoned with NordStar's logo and a menu of options. After two taps, the glass facing the bridge became opaque. The bridge crew could no longer see into Kelly's quarters.

"Neat trick," Seth said. "Like in the Starlight Theater. How does it work?"

"Electrochromic glass," Kelly said. "Something to do with suspended particles activated by a surge of electricity. We use it on the wine tower, too. Can't have the sun hitting that old booze. And it impresses the hell out of the cruisers. Now watch this."

Kelly smiled and pushed a few more buttons. "It just gets better," he said.

The bridge-facing window cleared as the forward window-wall blossomed with a number of dials and instruments. Like the wine tower's touchpad, these instruments were made of bluish light projected between the window's glass panes. In the middle of the virtual instrument stack was a large, classically styled captain's wheel. The Captain pulled out a pair of gloves with "WhitespaceTM" written across the backs of the hands.

"Put these on," he said. "This is great. Nobody else has this."

Seth slipped the gloves on, and found that some sort of tension cable in the glove molded the fabric to his hands.

"One size fits all," the Captain said. "Now, put your hands at ten and two. Just like driving a car."

As Seth put his hands in position, two cartoon hands made of blue light appeared on either side of the virtual wheel on the window before them.

"You ever played a Nintendo Wii?" Kelly asked. "You know, virtual bowling, tennis? Navigating this ship is liking playing a super Wii." Seth stared at the Captain, not sure what to do. Seth brought his hands to rest against the virtual wheel's spokes, and – as he did so – the gloves limited his finger movement so that he felt that he was actually holding a wheel.

"Go ahead. Grab it. You're not going to break anything. Now give it a good turn. Pretend that you're on the Price is Right."

Seth looked at the Captain, then towards the bridge where an alarmed crewmember jumped to his feet and waved his hands wildly.

"Ignore him," the Captain said.

Seth shrugged and scanned the space around the ship to be sure that he wasn't going to hit anything. He threw the virtual wheel to the left and watched it spin in a wild, blue blur. The view through the front window shifted and Captain Kelly braced himself against his desk. Behind Kelly, on the bridge, the formerly lax crewmembers jumped into action mode. They pushed buttons, turned dials, and ran from one side of the ship to the other. The scrolling scenery slowed, reeled left a touch, then came back to what felt like forward. The Diana was back on course.

"I like to keep them on their toes," the Captain chuckled.

"They must love you," Seth said.

Kelly smiled and winked, the flesh around his left eye folded into myriad tiny valleys.

That winking again.

*That man thinks a wink will solve anything*, Seth thought.

Another tap on the touch screen and the view to the bridge was again obscured, made opaque by millions of tiny, suspended particles. The Captain found a latch on the side of his freestanding globe. He opened it to reveal a chest of ice and two glasses.

Kelly handed Seth a healthy serving of Jameson, then proceeded to pour one for himself. Both drew long, slow sips from their glasses. For a short time, neither said anything. Seth disliked silence almost as much as he disliked drinking whiskey neat. Silence signaled contemplation. As an attorney, Seth liked others to talk without thinking. Hurried conversation resulted in blurting — the blurting of truths, hopefully. A pause, on the other hand, meant that something important was coming. Kelly's silence, paired with the Captain's unusual desire to spend time with NordStar's outside counsel, caused Seth's neck hair to stand on end.

"It's been a lovely tour of the ship, Captain, and I always appreciate a drink. But I've got to admit that I'm a bit surprised you wanted to take out time from this beautiful ship's maiden voyage to hang out with me. I'm just a rank-and-file attorney."

The Captain looked to his whiskey, then to Seth, but said nothing. Seth took another sip of his whiskey, the Jameson burning the back of his throat, numbing him against what he sensed could only be bad news.

"Captain, I am NordStar's attorney. I want you to feel comfortable sharing anything that's troubling you."

The Captain remained silent. Seth's mind turned to the worst. Maybe Lutak backed out of its agreement with the cruise line. Maybe the Captain said something inappropriate to the Lutak Town Council, a famously prickly bunch. Maybe he had a dalliance with someone inland, and NordStar was no longer welcome. Seth's firm had dealt with such mistakes before. Seth just needed to know. Needed to be sure that the cruise would be a success. Anything else would damage all the hard work he'd done. His future. His mind backed off the ledge. No, it had to be something smaller, some internal shipboard matter that was troubling Kelly. Clients always overreact.

"Is it the Tammy Wurser thing again? I know we told you that you couldn't fire her, but our settlement also meant that she can't harass you, either. And I know you've stayed clear of her. You have stayed clear of her, right Captain?"

The Captain smiled. This was not a happy smile. It was the dreaded male anger smile. He took a sip of whiskey and tightened his eyes against the burn.

"It's not Wurser," he said. "And I'd appreciate it if you didn't mention that name again for the duration of this voyage." The Captain shook his head and frowned, then took a larger draw of whiskey. "No, Mr. Sterling. What I'm about to tell you is worse."

Kelly steadied himself against the desk, as if the ship was again spinning out of control.

"Much worse."

# 6

Captain Kelly was right, the situation was far worse than Seth could have imagined. It was so far outside of his area of expertise. If this cruise — his career-capping work — was going to succeed, he needed help. He thought of Matt Schott, a litigator who specialized in union work and had a predilection for Spanish slang. The two formed a quick friendship when they interned as summer clerks at a local firm during law school. Matt was the only one that Seth trusted under the circumstances.

"Seth Ozymandias Sterling!" Matt shouted. The Pixies' "Monkey Gone to Heaven" blared somewhere in the background of Matt's Tucson home.

Seth hated that Matt continued to call him by his full name — mainly because of the embarrassing middle one. The name came from Jeanette, Seth's mother. Shelley's Ozymandias was her favorite poem: "My name is Ozymandias, king of kings:/Look on my works ye mighty, and despair." This, she decided, was an amazing thing for Seth to say if and when other children would ask him why he had such an exceptional middle name.

What she didn't know was that Ozymandias was just another name for an Egyptian pharaoh named Ramses II. The same Ramses II who enslaved Jews in Egypt and suffered the Ten Commandments. This made for tense times for young Seth Sterling during Hebrew school, and made him reluctant to speak his congenital catch phrase. On the other hand, he enjoyed saying it to his little sister, Shelley, when he left the bathroom after a particularly satisfying bowel movement.

"Matt Schott!" Seth yelled back. People often mistook Matt's loud speech for gregariousness. It was not. Instead, Matt suffered partial hearing loss following an unusual accident in his first year of law school involving a bark scorpion and a pair of over-the-ear headphones. Since then, Matt liked his music loud and his conversations louder.

"How's it going, Seth Ozymandias Sterling? It's been a long time."

"I know. I've been busy. Not an excuse. But I've had zero time and I've been meaning to call. Totally sorry."

"No big deal. Just two years without so much as a 'hello.' Whatever. Just leave the little people behind, right? Out of sight, out of mind, I always say. Such is the cost of moving up in the world, huh?" Matt's voice was playful as always, but Seth knew that there was hurt lurking behind the facade. Luckily, Seth knew that Matt was generous with his friends, willing to forgive past slights in favor of lasting friendships.

"So, I'm not going to bullshit you," Seth said. "I'm calling because I need your help — your expertise. But, because we haven't spoken in a while, we can do the perfunctory catching up thing if you want."

Matt giggled. Schott had two laughing modes. He either tittered like an amused schoolgirl or he laughed himself into a weepy delirium. Seth was thankful for the giggle. If Matt really got going, he would be useless.

"Okay," Matt said. "Let's be perfunctory. How's Melanie?"

Seth knew the question would come, but it hurt just the same. "Melanie left me this morning."

"I saw that coming."

"Why does everyone say that?"

"You've turned into a total *pendejo*."

"*Pendejo*? Asshole? Thanks, Matt."

"It's true, Seth Ozymandias Sterling. You've gone from nice guy to sleazy corporate lawyer. Where are you?"

"I'm on a cruise ship."

"*Ay dios mio*! Seriously? A cruise ship? You remember that you make a living negotiating contracts for the travel industry, right? The crew is going to treat you like its *puta*, homes. *Cuando barato el Diablo vende, él bien se entiende*. You know what I mean?"

"When the devil sells…something…he understands it?"

"It means that when the Devil sells on the cheap, he knows it. It means that the all-inclusive world is off-limits to you – especially now that you're a party of one. Remember that story about Gorman accidentally checking his luggage at LAX?"

Dale Gorman was a partner at the firm where the two had clerked. Gorman – Seth's hero and mentor for an entire summer – showed Seth the ropes of contract negotiation in the airline industry. He was one of the greats. He taught Seth the importance of perfection: You slip up, even once, Gorman told him, and you end up with a suitcase full of dog shit.

Gorman told that story to all the new clerks, kids in their second year of law school. Each year, after Gorman's lecture, the clerks turned to one another and told each other that Gorman was just trying to scare them. But Seth knew better. Gorman knew that a defeated opponent, even in an area of law as innocuous as contract negotiation, would remain forever bitter. Yet here he was, aboard The Diana, willingly submitting himself to the same abuse.

"You want to end up like Gorman?" Matt asked. "Or even worse? I mean, I wouldn't eat any prepared food, I wouldn't have the cleaning service in your room — I wouldn't trust anyone." Somewhere in the background, the Pixies switched to Black Sabbath's "War Pigs." "So, where you headed?"

"Alaska."

"You're not on that new ship, are you?"

"I am. How did you know about that? Cruise lines aren't exactly a major interest of yours."

"You remember Evie Kramer? That wacky, paranoid *chica* with the Kool-Aid red hair from law school?" Matt asked.

He did. That's how most people remembered Evie. But Seth remembered much more. He remembered thinking that he could build a life with her. He remembered that she had dumped him just before first semester finals. She told him that they'd "always have Paris." And then she disappeared. In the years since, Seth's memories fashioned Evie into the lost love of his life — his Ingrid Bergman. He was surprised that Matt didn't remember—

"Oh shit!" Matt giggled. "You dated Evie! How could I forget how broken up you were over her?"

"It's been a while. How did you know she was in Alaska?"

"How do I know anything? Facebook. It fucking rules. So you aren't with Melanie any more, and now you're on a crash course with Evie!"

"Watch it," Seth said.

"Does she know you're coming?" Matt giggled.

"Yeah. We've been working together off and on for the last two years. She helped me get NordStar into Lutak."

"Wow. She clearly wants you. That *mujer loca* is drawing you in, *esse*. She wants to mack on some old law school chum!"

"Enough, seriously."

"Okay. But *a buen sueño no hay mala cama*, you know?"

"I don't have the slightest clue. You wanted to catch up? Your turn. How's Lynne?"

"She's cool. We're biking more. I'm shaving my legs like a pro – and I like it. So that's pretty much the deal. On to business, then?"

"Thank god. Okay, ground rules, I need you to keep this to yourself. I mean, you can't even tell Lynne."

"You know me! I'm like a Swiss vault. This won't go past me."

"Okay, second, I just need to know if what I want to do is possible, legally-speaking. I don't need to know whether it's morally permissible. I just want to know what the courts say about it. You'll have your personal opinions, but I need you to keep them to yourself. Okay?"

"Ooh. This is intriguing."

"Okay?"

"Okay, but I get to do both."

"Both what?"

"I get to tell you whether its legally permissible, and then I get to tell you how stupid you are for advising a client to do it. Fair?"

"Fair enough."

"So what is it?"

"Well, I told you I'm on a cruise. I want to pull a total Burma here. Like we did in the Auto Workers of America case when we were clerks. Something big is happening here, and I need to keep it on the down low. The cruise line's future may depend on it."

"You mean the Burma where we basically turned a 24-hour plant with workers' dormitories into a strict dictatorship where employees had no access to Union representatives? That Burma? Yeah. You can't do anything like that where you are. You're aboard a floating city filled with filthy rich American white people."

"You're positive?"

"No, I'm not positive. It's just a really bad idea."

"I thought you advised your clients to do this all the time."

"Well, yeah, I do. But on a much smaller scale, and not with civilians. Especially civilians that can afford their own attorneys."

"Well, it might be worth the risk. Can you at least look into this for me and get back to me as soon as you have something? I need to act fast."

"How fast?"

"Tonight fast."

"It's nine o'clock here. And Lynne and I were going to do a few laps around the campus."

"I really need your help. Matt Schott, you're my only hope."

Matt giggled. "So you want me to start doing research for you at this hour, forgo time with the beautiful Lynne, and probably give you an answer that will permit you to engage in behavior that I find personally reprehensible and ethically irresponsible?"

Seth did not respond. Matt hummed along to "Waterloo," now playing in the background. There was a hollow pounding on Seth's cabin door.

"You need to get that?" Matt asked.

The sound made Seth's belly grumble. It was room service. He hadn't eaten anything, and was feeling a bit nauseous from his drinks with Captain Kelly.

"Look, Matt, I appreciate your help."

"Of course you do."

"And I know it's a lot to ask."

"Yes. It is."

More pounding.

"I will owe you. Big time. Whatever you want, I will do it."

"Might involve leg-shaving."

"Okay. Seriously. But I have to go now. I'm guessing that's my dinner, and I need to get in good with at least one crew member here. Just spend a half hour on this thing, okay?"

"I don't represent you. Whatever happens with the information I give you doesn't come back to me. This is a favor for a friend and nothing more. Got it?"

"Promise," Seth said.

The Arizona end of the line went dead. Seth hopped up from the bed and answered the door. There was no one there, just an unattended room-service cart. On top were a white linen tablecloth, a white linen napkin, freshly shined silverware, and a bone china plate under a silver dome. Seth looked left and right, but there was no one else in sight. Just the dinner cart.

Seth turned back into his room, lifted the Beast, and worked it into the space between the bed and the sliding balcony door. He returned to the hallway and pulled the cart into his room. He knew Matt was right to question his plan of action. But drastic times called for drastic measures, right? He had worked too hard to let his career fall through his fingers. He didn't want to have to start all over again.

He also knew that Matt was right about needing to be cautious on the cruise. Gorman's was not the only property that had been vandalized by angry airline employees. Seth had not heeded Gorman's advice on the way back from a tense meeting with the Air Line Pilot's Association and wound up with a bag full of airport slippers. And that was just for sitting in on negotiations.

Here, in order to keep NordStar in the black and make the Lutak stop a reality, Seth successfully downgraded United Crew Engineers and Stewards' – basically the whole crew's – pay scales. Sure, he padded it with employee options and bonus plans, but it was still an obvious attack on the crew's bottom line. And the crew was powerless to stop it. Radley was on good terms with the union after it convinced major players in the industry that it would be best to shorten the crew's workday. In actuality, maritime law already mandated the shortened workday, but UCES's general counsel didn't know it. In return, UCES agreed to lower pay on the Diana. It was all very tidy and went a long way towards making Lutak a reality.

"A win-win for the cruise industry," Thad had said. "It's now in compliance with legal requirements, and our client has a favorable environment for its Lutak venture. Be proud, bitches!"

Seth's stomach groaned. He knew the Diana's crew was out to make up for that pay decrease. He knew he was depriving families back in god-knows-where from badly needed resources. He knew better. But he needed to eat.

Fearing poisoned food, feces, maybe insects — something horrible — Seth cautiously lifted the silver dome. But there was nothing on the plate. Well, not nothing exactly, just no food. Instead, there was a 4x6 inch glossy Kodak photo with a yellow sticky-note obscuring the faces. Seth read the sticky first. In neat, almost feminine handwriting, the note said, "Chew on this." It was signed "Cliffy." Seth removed the sticky. Underneath was a picture of a much younger Cliffy surrounded by five similar-looking girls and an older woman missing several teeth.

Seth sighed and picked up the phone. If he was going to make it through this cruise, he was going to have to make peace with at least one crew member.

# 7

Four cabins away, Ceejay Brecht stared at her new iPhone. The 17 year-old All-Region hurdler with the long blonde hair did not want to be on a cruise with her parents, Doug and Linda. She wanted to be back home in Ann Arbor, Michigan. She wanted to be with Laura.

It will do you good to get out of Michigan, her father told her. Her mother said that she'd benefit from learning a thing or two about the great outdoors. But the only nature that Ceejay cared about right now was human nature, something about which her parents had no clue. They certainly had no clue about Ceejay's nature, her needs, and her feelings. About Laura.

So, while her parents enjoyed their first shipboard meal, Ceejay stayed in her cabin, staring at her iPhone, waiting for Laura to call, e-mail, something. It had been at least half an hour since Laura last texted. Is it over? she wondered.

Ceejay met Laura outside Zingerman's Deli on a cloudy day two weeks before the Brecht family left for Alaska. Laura was collecting signatures for a cause that Ceejay didn't understand.

"Hey sister," she told Ceejay, "you want to be part of the next big thing?"

Laura was older, 20, practically a woman. She wore the standard issue Ann Arbor lesbi-uniform: DC sneaks, tight jeans, white wife-beater under a white tee, and a DC hat cocked towards ten o'clock. But she had something that most Ann Arbor clones didn't: a sense of humor. More importantly, she dug Ceejay's sense of humor.

"You selling Tupperware?" Ceejay asked. Her tongue flicked her lip ring in fast, nervous loops. Doug and Linda hadn't wanted Ceejay to pierce her lip. But when she came home with the thing the previous spring, they decided to compromise. She could keep it, they said, as long as she stopped playing with it when she spoke to them. All the flicking was grossing them out.

Now, before this attractive stranger, Ceejay relished her tongue's ability to move the ring so fluidly. She believed it sent signals of rebellion and sexuality. The flicking made her feel confident. It gave her something to do. It took the edge off.

"No, man," Laura laughed, "I'm changing the world. And I think you might want to help." She winked and thrust a pamphlet Ceejay's way. Something about inflated judges' salaries depleting Michigan's public funds.

Ceejay glanced at the pamphlet and pushed it back at Laura. "Yeah, see, I kind of like this world. I don't need a pamphlet."

Laura put her hand in front of her mouth so that only Ceejay could see her lips move. "Me too, but don't tell anyone." She leaned closer. "Can I tell you a secret?"

"You can tell me your secret," Ceejay whispered in Laura's ear, "but I can't promise to keep it."

Laura wrinkled her nose. "I'll take the chance."

Ceejay now flicked her piercing involuntarily, wildly, her stomach doing little turns in time with the lip ring's rotations.

"Well, here goes," Laura said. "I only collect signatures to meet girls."

Ceejay smiled as she pushed away from Laura. "You shallow bitch!"

"Hey," Laura winked, "it worked, right?"

It did. For the next week, Ceejay and Laura were inseparable. They took long walks along the Huron. They drank coffee at Common Language. They even met one another's families. Ceejay, however, did not introduce Laura to her parents as a romantic interest. They weren't ready for that, she was sure. And things were going too well with Laura to introduce unnecessary drama.

Laura was perfect. She took no offense at Ceejay introducing her as a friend. She didn't pressure Ceejay to do anything with her until she was comfortable. She was patient and caring. After only a week, Ceejay felt something for Laura, something like love.

And that's when she remembered that the cruise was coming up. She didn't really want to take the cruise in the first place. Her and a thousand old couples on a boat for a week did not sound like her idea of a good time. In one week, everything would change. She was not just going to be away from home, she was going to be away from Laura. And what had only a week before seemed like a mere week quickly became an eternity away from love. Hell on the water.

Before beginning an outright protest against the Alaskan hiatus, she tried alternatives. Could Laura come with her? After all, Ceejay was going to have her own cabin, there had to be room for one more.

"We're stretching the budget as is," her Dad told her. "And airfare is going to be outrageous with only a week left. Sorry, hon. Maybe she can come with us to Mackinac in October." He mussed her hair.

Maybe Laura's parents could pay her way? Laura's parents said "no." Against their wishes, Laura hadn't looked for a job that summer. They certainly weren't going to foot the bill for a cruise. Ceejay was crushed. She refused to go to Alaska without Laura.


Doug was flummoxed.

Ceejay had plenty of other friends, but she wasn't throwing a fit just because they couldn't come along. Ceejay had never been a difficult teenager. She was his little sweetheart, his pride and joy, and a disciplined All-Region hurdler. He would bend time and space to see her smile. But he could not let her stay back from the cruise. In time, she would treasure the trip. He was sure of it.

But that did not mean that Doug did not sympathize with his daughter. He remembered being young. Being pulled from his friends during precious high-school summers. There had to be a compromise. Three days before the trip, Doug made Ceejay pencil him into her busy schedule. They would meet at three o'clock on neutral ground: The Crazy Wisdom Tea Room, just blocks from their house. He was determined not to leave the meeting without some sort of mutual understanding.

Five minutes before the scheduled meeting, Ceejay saw Doug's rear plopped in a seat facing away from the stairwell of the second-floor tearoom, where she now stood. Anger welled in her. She waited until 3:00 pm, sharp. Then she snuck up beside her father, pulled out a chair, and collapsed so abruptly that she thought her seat might break. She wanted Doug to know that she meant business. She would not make this easy for him.

"Look," Doug said, "I love you, but you're coming with us. We've put too much money and thought into this to go without you. So, let's find a way to make this work."

Ceejay would not look at him. She checked her fingernails. She played with her lip ring. She kicked the table legs. He needed to bring more to the table. This would not buy her compliance.

"I know you want to stay here," Doug continued. "I know you want to hang out with your friends. I know you're reluctant to leave Laura, even for a short period of time."

"Short? Hardly."

"Okay, remember, I haven't been your age for a while. So, time passes a lot more quickly for me."

Ceejay nodded.

"Another thing about being old and all, other than time passing quickly, is that things have changed since I was a kid. People act very differently now than they used to. Do you understand me?"

Doug stared into Ceejay's eyes. She returned her own cold stare.

"Do you understand me?" Doug repeated.

He kept staring. Ceejay thought she saw something else in there. Something besides his and Linda's determination to rip her from Ann Arbor, the core of the summer, and Laura. Some flicker of true understanding.

Ceejay's heart skipped a beat. Was he saying what she thought he was saying?

"People interact, well, differently today," Doug said. "I know this, and I accept this. So, I think I have a solution."

Ceejay felt nauseous. She hadn't expected to do this here, now. She wanted Laura's hand for strength. She was afraid to speak. She flicked her lip ring in fast circles. Her Dad flinched with each quick loop. She stopped flicking. Doug put his hand on the table between them, palm down. He was accepting her as a lesbian, and she hadn't had to say a thing! She put her hand on top of his.

"Oh, honey," Doug said, "I think you understand what I'm saying."

"I think I do, too, Dad." She wanted to leap up and hug him.

He pulled his hand out from under Ceejay's, and away from the table. With Doug's hand gone, she could feel that Doug left something on the surface of the table. Something smooth. A little larger than a deck of cards. She pulled her hand away.

Then it registered.

"An iPhone?" she asked, incredulous.

"Yes," he said, "your mother and I thought it was time."

Her jaw dropped. She was furious. "A cell phone? Is this a joke?"

"I know you're excited, but it's no time to forget your—"

"I'm not excited, Doug," she insisted. From now on, he would be forever Doug.

"Your mother and I realize that there are so many other ways to keep in touch with friends now. Myspace, Facebook —"

Ceejay stood, kicked her chair from the table, and left. Later that afternoon, Laura had talked Ceejay down. She told her that her parents loved her and were simply trying to make the best of a difficult situation. They didn't know any better. The iPhone was a nice thought. And it would only be one week, after all.

"Absence makes the heart grow fonder," Laura said.

Reluctantly, Ceejay agreed to accompany her parents to Alaska.

Now aboard The Diana, Ceejay checked her iPhone's wi-fi status. She had four concentric semi-circles stacked atop one another that indicated full reception. And then she heard a tone indicating that an e-mail had arrived. She opened it hungrily. It was Laura with a one-liner: "HOW R U?"

Ceejay spent a half hour formulating a response. It had to be witty, romantic and sensitive. At first, it was too wordy. Then too simple. Finally, she erased the whole thing and wrote a two-sentence response: "I MISS YOU. WHAT RU DOING?"

"ABOUT 2 GO OUT," Laura wrote.

"IM JEALOUS," Ceejay typed. "WHERE RU GOING?"

"2 BEYOND."

Beyond? Everyone in Ann Arbor knew Beyond was a total meat market. Worse, it was a hetero meat market, a place where breeders slobbered on one another then took each other home for sleazy one-nighters. What would Laura possibly want with that?

"BEYOND? WHAT 4?" Ceejay asked.

"CJ - I DIDN'T WANT IT 2B LIKE THIS."

# 8

Seth's clothes were still a mess. He checked his watch. He had just enough time to change and have a bite to eat before his midnight meeting with the Captain, Thad, and Buddy.

The Beast hissed at Seth as he loosened its zippered restraint. Musty air, tinged with the smell of Seth's unwashed wardrobe, escaped from its belly. The Beast regurgitated what was left of Seth's life. His 34 years amounted to these things: a Gore-Tex rain jacket; a leather Dopp kit; three suits and five blue oxfords; khaki pants and polos; two pairs of dress shoes; a bunch of underwear; several pairs of socks; a set of slip-on Vans, checkered with skulls; a pair of white running shoes; ties; two belts; three diplomas; one photo album; one laptop; and an iPod.

But that morning, before Melanie left him, there had been so much more.

"Can't happen," Melanie said, sitting at the kitchen's granite counter and nibbling on her usual breakfast of whole-wheat English muffin and peanut butter. "We can't stay together. We can't get married. It just can't happen."

The two lived together in a two-bedroom condominium overlooking the Tempe Town Lake – less of a lake than a huge man-made puddle amid strip malls and desert, really. But it was water. It wasn't too far from the university or work. Seth assumed it would fetch a decent amount if they needed to sell it, even after the real estate collapse.

Melanie would not look at him. Instead, she stared at Matt Lauer interviewing Lindsay Lohan for the Today show. A droplet freed itself from Melanie's left eye. In retrospect, Seth understood that she was trying to hold it together for his sake, to make it okay for him to leave her, to go to work, to move on with things. But at the time it just seemed precise and cold.

"Look, I know that the last couple of years have been difficult, but we can fix this," Seth told her. "The NordStar project is over. Mission accomplished. And we've got the cruise tonight. We drive to the airport in, like, three hours. Then we get to spend the time we need alone. You'll see."

The droplet freed itself from Melanie's eyelid, slid down her face and stopped on her upper lip. Melanie licked the tear away with the tip of her tongue.

"It's too late, Seth. Can't happen. After the cruise, it will be something else; some other job will pull you away. You're far from finished."

Seth got up from the counter and looked out the window of their condominium. The Tempe Town Lake was still. It was early September, and, at just past seven in the morning, already too hot for people to be outside enjoying the water.

"Okay, I'll give you that. There's more work ahead. But I promise I won't be as stressed as I was. I won't have to work as hard as I did. They know I'm capable now. They'll make me a partner. It's as good as done!"

"Good! I'm glad. Really glad." Now tears flowed freely from both of Melanie's eyes. "But I'm glad for you — not us. You can't have both. You can't work for Radley and maintain this relationship. Can't happen."

"Listen, Melanie, this is your first day back. You've been gone. We haven't been together. Give us some time together. This cruise lasts a week. You'll feel the way you used to. We can get back to who we used to be."

Melanie had just returned from visiting family, or something similar. He had stopped keeping track of her travels. She began taking little weekend trips by herself, or with friends, a couple months after he disappeared into the NordStar project. Her little weekend trips soon became weeklong sojourns. Seth was not bothered by Melanie's absences. In fact, it gave him more time to focus on his work. It gave him the time to become successful partner material. This was what he wanted.

"That's what I'm afraid of," Melanie said. "I don't want to feel for you again. I don't want to be hurt again. It can't happen." She shook her head. "Can't happen."

Those words. Can't happen. She kept coming back to them. Can't happen was how Seth knew Melanie would never change her mind. Can't happen meant she did not want to share a life with him. These two simple words were carefully rehearsed. They were a deceptively powerful mantra, an incantation she would speak if Seth got close to convincing her that they could be together. Can't happen had been discussed with family and received the support of friends. Can't happen meant that he was going to have to let her go.

"Okay," he said. "Okay." He put his arms around her. "I don't want you to hurt. I don't want to hurt you." He gritted his teeth, tightening his face against a wall of emotion that could undo him. He walked into the bathroom, cried, washed his face, and left.

The Beast had been a hasty pick.

Seth had just three hours to go to buy luggage, go back to the condo that – as of this morning – was no longer home, pack up his belongings, and head to the airport. The only thing between him and his new future was a place to put the things he would take from the apartment. He drove straight for Dmitri's Luggage Emporium, an overpriced bag seller in Phoenix's posh Biltmore area. Seth pulled into the store's lot. Dmitri himself stood at the door. He was a short, thin man dressed in Euro trash finery: a green silk button-up with a tattoo-like print crawling over his right shoulder, black slacks, black belt with silver buckle, and pilgrim-toed black leather shoes.

"Good morning, sir," Dmitri said with a slight Russian accent.

Seth was embarrassed by the task at hand, and did not immediately answer Dmitri. He worried, as the recently-dumped often do, that others would immediately guess his predicament: that Dmitri would immediately guess that he was purchasing luggage because his fiancé was calling it quits; that he needed to pack quickly to minimize the discomfort. Dmitri stared at him, waiting for a response to his greeting. Seth's forehead became damp. He felt like a teenager buying condoms for the first time.

"Sir?" Dmitri said. "Just browsing?"

"Uh, no. I need to buy something…a bag," Seth said. "Something durable…something that can carry a whole lot. But, you know, maneuverable. Wheels on it."

Dmitri smiled. "I have just the thing." He walked to the Tumi display to his left, and came back with a small leather rolling bag that looked like it could fit within an overhead compartment with plenty of room to spare.

"It's surprisingly large inside, sir. Great for a weekend. And you don't need to check it!"

Seth shook his head and wiped his brow. "Uh, no. It's going to have to be bigger than that. I need to carry more than that."

Dmitri turned back to the Tumi display and retrieved the next largest bag. A black nylon piece. Very classy. But before Dmitri could speak, Seth shook his head.

"Bigger," Seth said.

"How long do you plan to be away?" Dmitri asked.

"Forever."

Dmitri shook his head. "A tall order," he said.

He walked towards another, larger Tumi bag, then turned. Seth's forehead was shiny with sweat. His jaw was clenched. His fists were balled. Dmitri put his hand on Seth's shoulder and squeezed. Seth looked down at the luggage salesman's paw, then looked into Dmitri's eyes. Seth's jaw-muscle loosened, and his eyes became wet.

"Do you want to talk about it?" Dmitri asked.

"Yes." Seth was shocked by the forthrightness of his response. He was a proud attorney, a person who played emotions close to the vest. But, here he was, opening up to a complete stranger.

"Come in the back," he said. "We'll have some tea."

Seth looked at his watch. He needed to be at the airport in an hour and a half. He needed luggage. He needed to pack. But the need to talk was more powerful still. And so he followed Dmitri to the rear of the store.

Dmitri already had a pot of tea going. Seth smelled cinnamon and something harsher — more pungent — that he couldn't quite identify. Dmitri poured a cup, added some sort of clear liquor with a Cyrillic label, and passed the concoction Seth's way. He guided Seth to a small wooden stool. Seth sat and sipped the tea. Its strange herbs and bracing edge helped almost immediately.

Seth spoke for a half hour straight. His nose and eyes leaked steadily. Dmitri listened without interrupting. Seth began with Melanie, then turned to the last two years, and the sacrifices he had made in the name of career. He talked about being a bitch in the name of future partnership. He talked about the cruise, and how he had wanted to be an attorney since he was small. How, in the third grade, he had come to school dressed as a lawyer for a full week. When he finished, Dmitri said nothing. Then he opened his mouth, and closed it again.

Dmitri got up, leaving Seth in the back room. A minute later, he returned, wrangling with the Beast, its refrigerator-sized bulk knocking over the teapot. The spilled substance filled the back room with the wonderful and pungent fragrance.

"It's a display model," Dmitri said, ignoring the spilled tea, "not meant for sale. The manufacturers make these giant bags for our windows. But they're fully functional, I promise."

"Okay," Seth said, laughing through his tears, "that's a bit big."

"No, it's what you need. A man your age shouldn't need such big baggage. But here we are, aren't we? Anyway, a good piece of luggage can be a lifesaver, you'll see. A gift from Dmitri."

Seth wiped his nose. "Are you sure?"

"Yes. Take it, go. You have some packing to do and a plane to catch."

Seth looked at his watch. He had only an hour before he needed to be at the airport. He jumped out of his seat.

"Go," Dmitri said.

"I have to give you something for this."

"Send me a postcard from your Lutak. Tell me how your giant bag worked for you."

"I can do that. I will do that, I promise."

"Good," Dmitri said, giving Seth another comforting shoulder squeeze. "You'll get through this. I know it."

Seth nodded. He grabbed the Beast's gigantic handle and dragged it outside and into his new future.


Seth stared at the Beast's empty belly, its contents now emptied onto the cabin floor. His own stomach complained sympathetically. He took a deep breath, shoved his wrist into a clothes pile and retrieved a wrinkled blue polo shirt and a pair of khakis. He stripped out of his sweat-stained button-up, pulled off his dress slacks, and stood for a minute in his underwear, wondering at the strange path that led him here.

A pounding at the cabin door brought him back into the moment.

# 9

Seth saw a funhouse version of Cliffy, the Asian porter, through the cabin door's peephole. Cliffy had a determined grimace on his tight-skinned face. Seth thought about how to win him over, what he could say that could possibly turn the tide. He nodded. If he was going to make it through the cruise, he had to make Cliffy like him. Had to. He opened the door.

"You called — " Cliffy said, his bottom lip dropping in apparent shock.

Seth followed Cliffy's eyes as they scanned up and down Seth's body. And then it registered. Seth was wearing only his underwear and socks. He backed towards the bed, where he had put his khaki and polo.

"Mr. Sterling," Cliffy said, "this is definitely a new low." He walked away.

Seth pulled the khakis over his left leg. "Whoa, there. Cliffy, right?"

Cliffy kept walking. Seth hopped down the hall after him, his right leg still pants-less.

"You don't understand," he said. "I just wanted to get to know you."

"Oh, I think I understand all too well, Mr. Sterling."

Seth paused, pulling the pants over his right leg, then continued after Cliffy. "No. I didn't mean 'get to know you' the way you're thinking."

Cliffy kept walking.

"I don't care to get to know you in any way," Cliffy said. "I know who you are. And now you're trying to seduce me? No thanks."

"No! It's been a crazy night. My mind was elsewhere. I didn't want to do anything other than tell you that I understand."

"Understand what?"

"I understand that the pay cut hit you. I understand that you have a big family. A mom that, apparently, could use dental care."

Cliffy stopped, turned to Seth, and scowled.

"Okay," Seth said, "that came out wrong. A beautiful mother, you have a beautiful mother. And I understand what you're going through, with the pay cut, being away from home. I understand."

"You can't possibly."

"Then explain. Tell me about you. I'm all ears. I just need you to know that, ultimately, we're on the same team. Please, Cliffy. We don't have to go back to my room. We can go somewhere public. I just need someone on my team."

"Why would I want to do that? You're not on my team. You're not on a team with anyone on this ship."

"You're wrong, Cliffy. This ship's going to have some trouble, and if you're going to continue to be able to send any money back to that family, I'm going to need your help."

Cliffy thought it over. "Okay," he said. "We'll talk. But this better not be a trick. No more funny stuff with you in your underwear."

"It's no trick, Cliffy. It's serious. And no more underwear, I promise. But first, can you grab me something to eat? I can't concentrate if I haven't eaten." His belly grumbled its agreement.

Cliffy grumbled something in return.


Cliffy and Seth sat on small plastic seats on either side of the tiny plastic table on Seth's balcony. It was dark and cold, but food made everything better. Seth chewed on a stale peanut butter and jelly sandwich that Cliffy had scrounged from the crew kitchen. It was glorious. Between bites, he gulped clean-tasting water from the small glass that NordStar provided each cabin. Cliffy glared at Seth, taking the occasional drag off of his State Express 555 cigarette.

"So," Seth said, pointing a triangle of PB&J at Cliffy, "first things first. You don't look like a Cliffy."

"No?" Cliffy said, sending a long stream of vaporized tobacco Seth's way.

"No. I'm guessing that it's either short for something difficult to pronounce, or just an assumed name for the sake of the passengers. Stupid Americans, right? I mean, can't even take the time to learn a proper name. Got to force some American name on you, something as dorky as Cliffy. Am I right?"

Cliffy frowned. "You are wrong."

"Okay, okay. So it's Cliffy. But, it's got to be spelled differently. You're Vietnamese, right?"

Cliffy was surprised. "Yes, Vietnamese. How'd you know?"

"The cigarettes. State Express 555s. Vietnam is the only country I know so obsessed with British cigarettes. Everyone had a pack on them."

"So you've been to Vietnam. Good for you. So very privileged. So worldly, Mr. Sterling." Cliffy inhaled deeply and blew another cloud into Seth's face.

"Please, call me Seth." Seth reached for the crumpled pack that sat on the small table between them. "May I?"

"Two bucks."

"Can I open a tab? You know where I live. My wallet's always on the nightstand. You can take the cash whenever you like."

Cliffy nodded.

"So, like I said," Seth reached for the crumpled cigarette pack adorned with a royal blue circle, "can't be spelled C-L-I-F-F-Y. Nobody in Vietnam has that name." He lit a densely packed paper tube and took a long drag.

"I do."

"What's your last name? Smith? Because I met loads of Vietnamese Cliffy Smiths when I was over there."

Seth laughed, but Cliffy only stared at his dying cigarette, its embers burning dangerously close to his slender index and middle fingers. He switched position, now holding the cigarette between his thumb and forefinger as though he were writing with a small piece of chalk.

"The last name is Clay-Phan. It's hyphenated."

"Well that's unusual." Seth ran the name through in his mind. "Wait a minute. Cliffy Clay-Phan. You say that fast, it kind of sounds like that mailman from Cheers. Hey there, Normy. You know? You ever see that?"

"Yes. My parents, too. They loved it. A little too much, I would say." Cliffy stubbed out his dying cigarette and reached for a new one.

"Explain."

"Well, you saw my Mom in the picture I left for you. The one who needs the dental work? She met my dear father in the mid 1980s. He was kind of like you. A traveler. From America. Stanley Clay. My mom, Hy Phan, had more teeth then. He met her in a noodle shop. He saw her slurping up pho and knew he had to have her."

"Who knew noodle soup could be so sexy?"

"No one but Stanley, I don't think." Cliffy snorted and smoke escaped his nose.

"So," Cliffy continued, "Stanley extends his stay for a while. They are hot and heavy, right? Mostly, they sleep together and watch bad American television. Cheers reruns were particularly popular at the time. They especially liked that their names, when combined, were the same as Clifford Clavin's."

"Clay-Phan. Love it."

"Of course you do. Stupid people love silly names."

Seth sucked a particularly harsh drag from his cigarette, draining much of its remaining tobacco. He picked an errant fleck of tobacco from his teeth.

"Anyway. One night, after a 'special' hour-long Cheers, the one where Rebecca Howe is trying to decide between Sam Malone and Evan Drake, they made me."

"Excellent. Little Cliffy."

"Right. But then Stanley found out that I was coming. He went home. His vacation was over. For my Mom, though, all of her vacations were over. Still are."

"Wow. I'm sorry, man."

"Don't be. I came into being. I'm happy about that. And Mom did a good job with me. She met Tran Lac, and he was a good father. I wish he was still here. He gave Mom four more daughters. Wonderful sisters. And he left us enough money to attend school. I am a doctor of electrical engineering."

"Then what are you doing cleaning up after old rich people on a cruise ship?"

"A lot of people in my country have advanced degrees. We have many doctors, lawyers, and engineers. There's just no work and very little hope of emigrating to first-world countries. So we take on whatever jobs we can find. Many of us take jobs where language is important, so that we can stay sharp."

"Stay sharp for what?"

"For the day that our country can support its wealth of educated citizens."

Seth pushed his cigarette into the ashtray, scattering black sand across its glass bottom. He reached for another cigarette, but Cliffy grabbed his wrist.

"Four bucks now," Cliffy said. "Don't think I forgot. Now, why did you want to talk to me? What's this trouble you mentioned?"

Before Seth could answer, his cabin telephone rang. "Hang on a second, Cliffy. I've got to take this."

The phone rang again. Cliffy stood and headed for the cabin door.

Seth put out his hand. "Seriously, Cliffy, you let me talk to my friend and then I'll be able to tell you much more. I need to take this. Just a couple of minutes, I promise."

Seth ran back into the cabin and lifted the handset.

"Seth Ozymandias Sterling!" the voice on the other end shouted, loud enough for Cliffy to hear.

Cliffy offered a quizzical expression as he attempted to pronounce Seth's middle name. Then Cliffy smiled. "Seth Ozymandias Sterling? S.O.S.? Sounds about right."

# 10

Seth reached Captain Kelly's quarters at 11 p.m. As he entered the Captain's room, he saw Kelly seated at his desk. He was no longer wearing his neat jacket, and the bottle of Jameson was nowhere in sight.

A familiar mustache was projected in blue light across the cabin's front-facing window. It was Buddy Tennison, NordStar's de facto leader, running the company in place of the charming, absentee CEO, his younger brother Lord. Try as he might, Seth always saw Wilford Brimley when he looked at Buddy. Like Brimley, Buddy kept his snowy eyebrows in equal proportion to his epic white mustache. He wore horn-rimmed glasses, granny-style, on the tip of his nose. Whenever they video conferenced, Seth half-expected Buddy to advise everyone to buy Liberty Mutual Insurance.

Kelly pulled a second chair close to the desk. "Seth Sterling is with us now, Buddy," he said.

"I see that. Good to have you here, son." His voice was weary; an occasional sip from his coffee mug accentuated his obvious fatigue.

"Hey there, Buddy." Seth waved to the window and took a seat. "Glad I could be here to help with this."

"As am I," Buddy said. "Is Thad on the horn?"

"I'm right here, Buddy," Thad said, his voice loud and clear through a speaker on the Captain's desk. Unlike Buddy, Thad sounded like he just stepped out of the morning shower. Seth knew that Thad had already had quite a long day. Thad had taken two depositions and appeared in court to argue a summary judgment motion. But Thad's voice betrayed nothing. He sounded well-rested, energetic, and ready to clear away obstacles. Seth hoped that one day he would learn Thad's trick.

"Good. Okay, Michael, go ahead," Buddy said, looking at Kelly.

"Well, gentlemen, I'll cut to the quick," the Captain said. "We now have three dead in and around Lutak. On average, there are two fatal bear maulings per year in all of Alaska. But all three of these occurred near our new port in Lutak. This is news, bad news, especially with that thing still at large."

"Three dead?" Buddy interrupted. "I thought we were talking about two. Not that two is great, but did we know that there were three?"

"Sort of. The press is only aware of two."

"I guess that's a bit of a relief," Buddy said.

"At least until the press connects the dots," Kelly said. "I wouldn't be surprised to hear them say three or even more. They might inflate the figure to make better news."

"Who's the third?" Buddy asked, defeated.

"Well," Kelly said, "He's actually the first, chronologically-speaking. It's Pierre Rambeaud."

"Christ," Buddy said.

"Who's that?" Seth asked.

"Rainbow Bear," Kelly said, then handed Seth a newspaper clipping. Seth examined it:

*Environmental Activist Eaten By "Brother"*, **May 23, 2008, Anchorage Daily News:**

Early this morning, the remains of Pierre "Rainbow Bear" Rambeaud were found near his campsite in the mountains outside of Lutak, Alaska. The coroner has not released an official cause of death but sources believe that Mr. Rambeaud was the victim of a bear attack. A source who refused to be identified told us that he was, "surprised it didn't happen earlier. That lunatic was just asking to get chomped."

Mr. Rambeaud, often compared to Timothy "Grizzly Man" Treadwell, achieved fame in the late 1990s for his Wall Street Journal column and regular appearances on "Oprah's Favorite Tech Things." In recent years, however, Mr. Rambeaud achieved celebrity by changing his name to Rainbow Bear and announcing that he would commune with brown "grizzly" bears of Alaska's famed Inside Passage.

In the year leading up to his death, Mr. Rambeaud posted entries to his Rainbow Bear blog detailing his efforts. He often complained about isolation, but wrote that the wild bears that frequented his campsite were his "brothers" and that he envisioned that one day he would no longer need the "company of men." Recently, Mr. Rambeaud's blog responded to criticisms about what many experts believed was inappropriate contact with the wild animals by calling such accusations "elitist" and "removed."

Mr. Rambeaud also became a vocal opponent of cruise industry expansion in Alaska's Inside Passage, arguing that it destroyed the state's unique ecosystem and led to the destruction of grizzly habitats. He caught national attention by criticizing Alaska's Governor's opposition to adding several varieties of Alaskan wildlife — including the moscat skink and the polar bear — to the endangered species list.

Mr. Rambeaud was 42 years old.

"Didn't they find that wacko more than three weeks ago?" Buddy asked.

"Yes," Kelly continued, "early August. But nobody got too worked up about it then. Most people considered it a foregone conclusion that he would end up dead. So, it was more a joke than a concern."

"Got it," Buddy said, "but, again, that happened last month. Old news, right? Isn't the usual procedure to put a bear down once it kills?"

"Usually," Kelly said. "But the Alaskan officials either couldn't, or wouldn't, determine which bear did it. None of them were guarding Rainbow's carcass. And, frankly, no one was inclined to destroy a bear because of Rainbow's stupidity."

"So they just let it drop?" Buddy asked.

"If you'll permit me," Thad offered, "it's an election year, Buddy. Stories like that capture the public interest for only so long. As I recall, the day after they found Rainbow, Senator Hollister lied about his Vietnam experience. Hollister said he was shot more times that he actually was. My guess is that the searchers let it drop once media attention drifted."

Buddy shook his head. "And now, here we are. So, who are two and three?"

"Bill and Lois MacReary. Discovered last night."

"Bill MacReary?" Buddy's image looked at Seth. "Christ. Wasn't he our man in Lutak?"

"Close," Seth said. "Our contact is his research assistant, Evie Kramer."

"According to my man on the ground," Kelly said, "Ms. Kramer discovered the MacReary's bodies, such as they were."

Seth couldn't believe his ears. Out of the corner of his eye, Seth registered shock on Buddy's face as well. But whatever surprise had shown in the old man's face quickly disappeared.

## 11

Seth met Evie as a first-year law student at the University of Arizona.

She was part of Seth's first study group, but she didn't seem like a law student. She didn't have the usual pre-law or poli-sci bachelors degree. Instead, she had a doctorate in geology. And she was far too cool for law school. While the other students spent their free time sweating over hardcovers in the law library, she sat on benches outside reading for personal pleasure. This was totally unheard of, and made her a sort of envied pariah.

She didn't look like an average law student, either. She was tall and slender with short, spiky hair dyed an intense Kool-Aid red. She had tattoos: a black Celtic cross at the nape of her neck, a Superman symbol on her calf and the word "MAINTAIN" printed in gothic text on the inside of her upper-right thigh. Seth learned about the last tattoo on their third date.

After dating for two weeks, Seth knew he wanted to be with Evie forever. In retrospect, it was obvious to Seth that this relationship could not work. Unlike Seth, whose calm conservative demeanor practically pre-ordained that he become an attorney, Evie had signed up for law school on a lark. She was, as Seth told his parents, a "free spirit."

And so, one night halfway through the first semester, Evie's announcement should not have come as a total surprise. The two lay on Seth's queen bed, reviewing the day's Torts lesson, something about the necessity of walkie-talkies on boats.

"Hey, Ozzy." Besides Matt, Evie was the only person permitted to use Seth's horrendous middle name. And, even in its abbreviated form, hearing it was like tin foil on fillings.

He ignored her, engrossed in a photocopied case summary.

"Hey. Ozzy."

He pulled his face away from his photocopies and focused on Evie.

"What up, Harriet?" Seth responded. He believed this was a particularly humorous and accommodating way to respond to Evie's normal salutation. Thankfully, she always responded with a laugh.

"Ozzy," she said, closing her Torts textbook, "I'm done with law school."

"Well, Harriet, I think I am, too." He cocked an eyebrow and smiled as he dropped his case printouts and leaned towards Evie. Evie's hands stopped his chest.

"No, Ozzy, not just for tonight. I mean I'm really done. I'm quitting law school." She mock-pouted, her eyes and lips dramatizing the difficulty she had endured reaching this decision. One look at her eyes and Seth knew she was serious about leaving school. He knew that her exciting and unpredictable persona also led her to rash decisions.

"But we've only been in school for a handful of weeks," he pled. "You can't know you're through with it. You've barely given it a chance."

"I've given it all the chance it needs, Ozzy. It's not my thing." She bit her cheek and squinted her left eye. Seth knew there was more still.

"You've already made plans, haven't you?" he asked.

She nodded. "We'll always have Paris," she muttered, and nudged her fist against Seth's chin.


Two days later, she was gone. Seth pined for her at first, but his demanding law school course load soon filled the void. He didn't speak with Evie again until the NordStar project landed on his desk.

During one of his many negotiations with the town, Seth learned that Evie was in Lutak, working as a research assistant to Bill MacReary, the primary opponent to NordStar's new port. Seth reached out to Evie, and she agreed to become Radley's — and his — in-road to making peace between NordStar and Lutak. Seth had Evie to thank for cementing his future at Radley.

Over two years, they consulted frequently from afar — Seth in Phoenix, Evie in Lutak. They resumed a sort of relationship. It was not romantic, Seth wouldn't do that to Melanie, but he knew it was more than just work. Eventually, Evie came forward and supported the new port even though that meant breaking ranks with Bill MacReary. Despite their rift, Bill remained Evie's hero and personal mentor. She went on about him constantly when they spoke.

Seth had looked forward to seeing Evie when he reached Lutak. Though he wanted to be sad that Melanie was gone, he realized that the timing couldn't be better. Maybe, just possibly, Evie would see him and want things to be like they were for those few weeks in law school. Seth certainly did.

But this latest news — the news that she had discovered MacReary and his wife's mauled corpses — was going to make things difficult.

# 12

Kelly resumed his briefing. "CNN is flying a team to Anchorage as we speak. The roads are closed, so they want to dock at our port sometime early tomorrow morning. They plan to make the maulings their big story tomorrow with live coverage from Lutak for most of the day."

"Well," Buddy said, "we can't let that happen. Tell them that they can't use our dock."

Thad's voice arose from the speakerphone in the Captain's quarters. "Sorry to interrupt, Buddy, and I obviously don't know your business as well as you do, but I guess I'm not certain why these maulings are so ruinous."

Buddy looked like he couldn't believe what he was hearing.

"I understand," Thad continued, "that these attacks might make excursions less popular in Lutak this time around — and it might keep cruisers from getting off of the ship altogether — NordStar will have several more opportunities to recoup its investment. And you can't turn down press access. If you do that, you will have a real shit storm on your hands. And I don't use the phrase 'shit storm' lightly."

Buddy huffed, but Thad continued calmly. "Mr. Tennison, CNN will still find a way to get into Lutak and they'll say that NordStar tried to block access to the story. That's bad news. I've seen it time and again. I don't want to see NordStar's good name tied to these attacks any more than necessary."

"If I may," Seth said, "Captain Kelly gave me a run down on the situation earlier this evening and I agree that press coverage of these attacks will have a much greater impact than I understood at first blush."

"Go on," Thad said.

This was Seth's opportunity. His first year in law school, he had learned that getting your way had less to do with how well you sold a solution than how you framed the problem itself. Now that he had the floor, he could frame the situation any way he liked. And, after speaking with Matt Schott, he felt certain that he had a solution that would satisfy everyone involved.

"Basically," Seth said, "we have two problems. First, as you mentioned, we have the current cruise to worry about. Cruise excursions provide the bulk of any cruise's profits, alcohol being a distant second. Most excursions are booked on the first full day at sea. Tomorrow. If we lose those non-refundable bookings because passengers learn about the attacks, this cruise bleeds money. With the operation costs sky-high and NordStar heavily leveraged on the Lutak project, there is legitimate concern that lost business from this one tour could bankrupt the cruise line."

Buddy's projection looked even angrier. It was a hard thing to see him so exasperated. It was like having Santa mad at you. And it was a cardinal rule among attorneys to avoid painting a negative picture of their client's business. But it was no secret that NordStar was treading on thin financial ice. This, coupled with Thad's already frank language, opened the door to completely frank discussion about the attacks' impact on the cruise line. If he was going to buy into Seth's solution, Buddy needed to know how dire this situation actually was.

"Second," Seth said, "even if the loss of money on this one cruise isn't enough to destroy NordStar, the second problem probably will. It's the Trip Advisor effect. The old adage that old folks don't use computers is no longer true. Everyone is online these days. Cruise passengers — especially the older ones who make up the majority of Alaskan trips — click right over to online travel websites and go on and on about their negative experiences. They won't even wait until the trip is over, they'll do it from the comfort of NordStar's nicely appointed cabins. And if those reviews label Lutak as dangerous bear country, negative reviews might sink the Diana, and this cruise line, for good. So, Thad, I can see where Buddy and Captain Kelly are coming from."

"But," Thad said, "I still don't think we can cut off press access. I think that's shooting ourselves in the foot."

"It's either the foot or the head," Buddy said. "We need to delay press access until we can fix this thing. We're done if we let them into the port. I don't see how we have any other choice. "

"But," Kelly piped in, "what if there's no fix? We keep the press out, they give us a black eye. The bear news gets out anyway, and we lose the income from this tour. And, as for a fix to the bear situation, I have it on good authority that we can't get an Alaska Animal Control team in there until the end of next week. We get to Lutak on Tuesday. So, delaying the press does nothing for us. I think we just maintain our current course and take our lashes. We can't control nature, Buddy. That's always been a burr in our side. It's part of the cruise industry. Besides," Kelly added quietly, "I agree that CNN will find a way in anyway. Lutak is not an island. If we block the port, they'll try the roads. If we block the roads, they'll get in overland somehow."

"So," Buddy said, "no matter what we do, we're screwed. No good option here."

"Gentlemen," Seth said, proud that the others argued their way into his arms, "I think there is a third way."

## 13

"You want to allow the press into Lutak, but keep any of their coverage – and all communications that might reference the coverage – from reaching our passengers?" Captain Kelly asked. "Ridiculous! We're not some third-world dictatorship that can cut off access to information coming in and out of the ship."

"Actually, I believe we are," Seth said.

Kelly fumed and Thad remained silent. Finally, Buddy spoke.

"It's brilliant," he said, his glassy image obviously thrilled by the possibility of a way out. Santa was happy again, and the world was back in order. "I knew there was a reason we brought this young man on board. Seth, make it so."

Thad jumped into the mix. "Buddy, Captain Kelly, may I talk to my associate in private for a moment?"

"Absolutely," Buddy said.

Seth knew Thad wouldn't be thrilled by the plan. It was risky, and putting it out there without vetting it through him first was going to be a problem. But, just like NordStar, Seth's future was at stake here. If the cruise line failed, even for reasons beyond his control, it was on him. Like the Trip Advisor effect, failing here would generate negative reviews from the Radley partnership that would ruin his future.

Kelly tapped the screen on his desk a few times and gave a telephone receiver to Seth. "Go ahead," he said, still red. Seth looked at the receiver, took a deep breath, then put it against his ear. Without Buddy and Kelly in the loop, Thad would tell Seth exactly what he thought of his plan.

"Okay, it's just us now," Seth said.

"How are you doing there, bitch?"

"Good, good. Pretty good. I think we have a shot at bringing this thing under control."

"No, I mean. How are you, Seth Sterling, doing? You feeling okay? You've certainly had a rough day."

"I know, but I think I'm okay."

"You nervous?"

"Not really. I mean, I just want to work hard and solve this problem for our client."

"Oh, you're lucky, because this would all make me totally nervous. And floating that plan of yours to the client – without discussing it with me first – would freak me out. I'd be nauseous right now. I'd absolutely need to throw up."

The PB&J and 555s coursing through Seth's gut reminded him that they were still down there. His stomach lurched as Thad-induced waves of nausea flowed over him. He fought to hold himself together.

"Do you have any idea how irresponsible it is, bitch," Thad continued, obviously angry but not raising his voice, "to tell a client — a cruise line with elevated duties to its passengers — to do this? Does the phrase 'appearance of impropriety' mean anything to you?"

Thad wasn't going for it. Seth should have known that he wouldn't. He would easily convince Buddy and Kelly, he knew that. He was telling them what they wanted to hear. But getting Thad on board was going to be a different game. NordStar paid Radley attorneys like Thad because they offered objective, conservative advice. Seth's plan, he knew, sounded dicey. But it was Seth's only shot at saving this cruise — and his future. He pressed on. "Thad, I know where you're coming from, but I don't see any other way."

"What if a relative dies, or there's an emergency back home?"

"That doesn't change our duties to the passengers. As long as we don't endanger them, we're probably not going to be liable for any negligence here. Besides, we're just talking about one day here. Once we have the non-refundable excursion bookings in hand, the cruise is secure. And if the bear is still out there when we reach Lutak, we can reroute the passengers to something else. Or give them a discount on a future cruise. We have a ton of options. We're not putting anyone in danger's way here."

"You'll have a mutiny."

"Not a mutiny," Seth insisted, "we can ply them with free booze. Change the odds in the casino. We can keep the passengers happy."

"The crew hates you, you know. You think they'll willingly go along with this, this East German, GDR bullshit?"

"I think Burma is more analogous."

"Watch the sass, bitch. I bet you anything that The Diana's crew won't let you get away with this."

"They don't need to," Seth said. "At least, they don't all need to. I lucked out. I've got someone who is perfect. And even if the word did slip out somehow, I don't think the crew will purposefully do something to sink the cruise line. They'd be out of jobs. But we can deal with that situation if it arises."

Thad digested for a bit. The pause was welcome. Unlike Seth's attitude towards clients, Seth loved to get partners lost in the wrinkles of their own brains. A good attorney will dismiss obvious problems out of hand, but when an unusual plan might just work, it requires serious thought. Seth let Thad think. The tide was turning, he knew it.

Finally, Thad spoke. "Okay, boy genius. What about your Trip Advisor effect? Don't you think that refusing to refund aborted bookings in Lutak will bring on the dreaded negative reviews?"

Questions meant consideration, and consideration meant that Thad just might let Seth's plan go forward.

"Those are only problems," Seth replied, "if the bear is still on the loose when we get to Lutak. This plan buys us the time to get our own team into Lutak and find this bear without losing the excursion bookings."

"And how do you get a private bear-hunting team into Lutak? I thought that the whole attraction of the place was that it has tight hunting regulations. 'Alaska's last unspoiled destination,' the brochure says."

"I have a way around that."

"I'm sure you do. I'm guessing her name is Evie?"

"That's right."

"You're a user, you know that? You use people. But you do it effectively. I like that about you."

Thad paused again. Seth had him.

"You've done the research here? We're on solid ground legally? Tell me you know that the law is solid."

Seth smiled. "It's solid. And I think it's arguable that we're on fine ethical ground, too. These are desperate times, Thad. Look, I know this plan doesn't guarantee success. But it gives us a shot, and we can't just go down without a fight."

"Maybe you can't, Seth. But I can. This is not my ass on the line, it's NordStar's. And I'm not gong to be responsible for leading NordStar to ruin. Your plan smells bad. I don't like it, bitch."

That was it, then. Seth's solution was sunk, along with his future. Thad wouldn't let the advice stand.

"But I don't have to like it. This is your gig, I told you that before. If it works, you get the glory and NordStar becomes a life-long client. If it doesn't, I don't mind finding a replacement. I like you, but I won't be associated with the huge turd I see this becoming. As I told you before, I will put all of this on your shoulders. You believe me, right?"

"I do, and I'm willing to accept that responsibility."

"Okay, bitch. Tell Buddy and the Captain that we're good to go."

There was a *click*. Thad was gone.

## 14

"Everything okay?" Buddy's image asked.

"Just fine," Seth replied. "Just handling a few details. Thad apologized for having to run. Family obligations. I'm sure you understand."

"You mean," Buddy corrected Seth, "that he was double-checking your work."

"Can't put anything past you, Buddy," Seth smiled with confidence. "Thad gave us the final go ahead."

"Okay," Buddy's image said, "Seth, you said you have someone — someone who you won't disclose — who can disrupt the telecom without tipping off the entire crew. Let's put your magical elf to work."

"Will do," Seth said.

"Michael?" Buddy asked.

"Yes, Buddy?" Kelly responded.

"Can you think of anyone on board that has serious hunting experience? We need to put a party together straight away."

Captain Kelly looked astounded. "Shouldn't we hire specialists to go out and take care of this thing?"

"Who knows how long that'll take, or how much it will cost. You and I both know that NordStar's money is tight enough as is. People have been hunting these grizzlies with shotguns for as long as I can remember. Hell, even before that — and before guns even arrived on these shores — the Indians used bearskins for food and warmth. I'd hate to have to tell the board that we spent thousands of dollars just to take out a fucking bear. No specialists. Just the ship's best shooters and me."

"You?" Kelly stared at Buddy's image. "This is absurd."

"It's not. I've done my share of hunting. This is a sink or swim proposition and I want to be along to oversee the whole operation."

"I'm not questioning your hunting skills, it's just that..." Kelly trailed off.

The blue Buddy in the glass gazed directly at the Captain, his giant projected eyeballs vacuuming the air for words left unsaid.

"Damn it, Michael," Buddy said. "There's more to this, isn't there?"

"Always is," Kelly said. "It's about how we know that the same bear attacked all three victims."

"Make with it," Buddy insisted. "What do you know and how do you know it?"

"The ranger who surveyed each scene is a friend of a friend. He classified these incidents as fatal bear maulings. He didn't see how anything else could cause such a mess, or why. Besides, he measured nearly identical bear tracks at each site. But there's something else about the scenes that bothered him. He didn't spot it until they found Bill MacReary and his wife."

"What is it?" Buddy asked impatiently.

"MacReary's gun was empty, just like Rainbow Bear's. At the Rainbow Bear site it wasn't really an issue. All the rangers thought Rainbow was a lunatic. So when they saw that Rainbow's gun wasn't loaded, well, it didn't come as a surprise. Nobody thought he was equipped for Alaska anyway."

"Right?" Buddy said. "And?"

"Well," Kelly hesitated. "According to the ranger, MacReary was an experienced camper. Hell, he grew up right by the attack site. He said MacReary always had a loaded gun with him when he camped on the range, said that MacReary gave it some awful name – Ethel or something. But when they found MacReary's shotgun in that torn up tent, the chamber was dry. MacReary didn't even load the thing. So, we have two victims with dry guns – guns that probably would have saved their lives."

"This doesn't leave the room," Buddy said.

Santa was mad again.

## 15

Seth left Kelly's quarters at half past midnight. He shivered, not against the cold of the night — Seth expected the northern night to be colder — but because of the uncertainty that lay ahead.

So many questions.

*It had to be a bear tearing these people apart, right?* he mused.

Kelly said so. He said a person couldn't make that much of a mess of another person without a gun or explosives. And, even then, the cuts were too precise. But a bear can't unload a weapon, right? So, maybe it's some sort of lunatic out there with a machete or something, maybe something the park ranger couldn't figure out? He could be like the killer on the Appalachian Trail a few years back. Could they have a serial killer on the loose?

Stepping off of the elevator, Seth realized that he was scared. Scared to be all alone. Scared that he might be dealing with a human killer. Scared that his well-trained, analytical mind could react to violence in such a pragmatic manner. More than anything, Seth was scared that years of hard work could so easily be dashed.

At least he was finally getting his shipboard bearings. Seth made a right, winding around the buffet building. Next to the buffet building was a set of stairs that, one flight down, let off right in front of his cabin door on the Admiral Deck. Seth's cabin was situated, he now realized, almost directly beneath the Captain's. This was no coincidence, he was certain.

He should have known this was going to be a working trip.

His mind wandered back to the killer haunting Lutak. He cursed himself for wasting precious brain time on this stuff. He was neither a bear expert nor a criminologist. Besides, Seth became paranoid when he was tired. Allowed to wallow on the subject in this state, he knew his mind would produce stranger and stranger possibilities. But Seth was unable to shut the flow of ideas. He needed to calm down. Even though there wasn't much left to do tonight, he needed to be fresh for the morning. Things had to go perfectly or The Diana project would go down in flames, taking NordStar and his career along for the ride.

It was surprisingly quiet on the promenade. He thought the first night aboard would encourage cruisers to let loose, partying until the early dawn. But, aside from a few stragglers still sitting on barstools in what looked like sidewalk cafes, there was little noise or celebration. It was as though this ship, this floating city, knew it had a grim task ahead of itself and was batting down the hatches for a difficult passage.

Beyond the drinking holes, Seth's red eyes could just make out the Diana's sentinel, Captain Kelly's treasured wine tower. The glass obelisk advertised the Diana's elegance and NordStar's daring. It told its onlookers that no matter how brutal the outside world — whether the searing heat of the Caribbean Sea or the brutal cold of the Alaskan North — the Diana can always do nature one better.

Seth skulked down the carpeted stairs towards his room. When he reached his floor, he noticed that the door was slightly ajar. Light poured through the crack, defining clouds of smoke billowing from somewhere within the cabin. Seth knew that the crew hated him for the salary reductions, but this was taking it too far. How could they burn his things? This was outrageous. And wasn't it dangerous to have an open fire on a ship at sea? Didn't they know that the Captain would probably fire them for this, that they might even be prosecuted?

"God damn it!" Seth shouted, and then covered his mouth.

The Jenkins's cabin door opened. Charlie popped his head into the hallway, his face a street map of lines left by his bed sheets.

"Everything okay there, buddy?" he croaked.

"Oh, yeah." Seth stood in front of his own cabin door, blocking the growing cloud from Charlie's glassy eyes. "Sorry about the noise, Charlie. Nothing I can't handle, thanks."

"Okay, just keep it down. Okay, son?"

"You got it, Charlie. Thanks for your concern."

As Charlie disappeared back into his next-door cabin, Seth heard him say, "I don't know, Nan. I think he has Tourette's. Go back to sleep."

Seth turned back to his task. He wanted to put something over his mouth to keep the smoke from suffocating him. Seth felt his pockets and found the remote-controlled life preserver. He smashed it against his face and made his way to the door. Seth wanted to test the cabin's door handle, see how hot that fire was. He removed his left loafer, slid his sock over his right hand, and tentatively turned the metal lever.

It was cool. Maybe the sock material was too thick. Seth looked at the door crack and saw that the smoke was getting thicker. There was no more time to mess with the door handle. He would simply have to burst in. Seth lifted his right foot, the one still in sock and shoe, and kicked at the door, violently shoving it open. He heard a gasp from within. He could not quite see through the haze, but sensed that there was one person, maybe two, trapped in the room.

*The idiots who did this got themselves stuck in there?* Seth wondered. *Serves them right.*

With the preserver covering most of his face, he charged the room. His bare left foot immediately struck the Beast, still wide open, sending him flying. Seth lay on his back on the queen bed, looking up at two shadowy figures smoking State Express 555s.

"And this," Cliffy explained to the other figure while pointing a lit cigarette Seth's way, "is Radley's attorney, Seth Ozymandias Sterling."

Seth squinted at the second figure, and nodded his head.

"Ozymandias," Cliffy continued, "this is Zoran. He's from our telecom cabinet."

"Hello, Zoran," Seth said, confused. From his prone position, he offered a hand to Zoran, but Zoran ignored him.

Zoran cocked his head and examined Seth. "Does he always dress so strangely?" Zoran asked Cliffy, a Slavic accent that Seth did not recognize muddling the words.

"Seems to," Cliffy said. "Earlier tonight he was parading around without pants on."

Zoran shook his head. "Americans," he huffed.

"Americans," Cliffy repeated, exhaling a long stream of blue smoke.

Zoran tapped his cigarette into an overflowing ashtray and made a disgusted face. He then pulled a flat, green cigarette box from his pocket. Seth did not recognize the label, but assumed they were some sort of Eastern-European favorite.

"Well," Cliffy continued, "I'll leave you to do your business. I have to run an errand a few doors down. Be back in a few."

Understanding dawned on Seth's sleep-deprived brain. Cliffy had brought the telecom officer to his cabin. Seth's cabin was not the telecom cabinet. Therefore, Cliffy was off to do Seth's bidding in an empty telecom cabinet.

"So," Zoran said, "Cliffy tells me you like to buy Croatian cigarettes."

*Brilliant*, Seth thought, *Cliffy is absolutely brilliant.*

# 16

Ceejay Brecht sat alone in her cabin, keeping silent vigil over her iPhone. After hours of argument, Laura simply stopped messaging. Ceejay shut down the iPhone and restarted it. She had rebooted the iPhone every half hour since Laura's last message with the superstitious belief that a fresh start would grease the rusty virtual gears that kept her from responding. The iPhone came back to life. This time, however, the word "searching" blinked on the top left of the phone's display. The iPhone was not talking to the ship's wireless network.

Incredulous, Ceejay shook the cell phone. No change. She got up from the bed and walked a few paces away. Still nothing. She held the phone high in the air, then put it on the floor. Still nothing. She threw herself back onto the bed. She rebooted again. Fearing that she would scare away the elusive signals by staring at the phone, Ceejay shut her eyes. Behind closed eyelids, she could still make out neon outlines of the iPhone's virtual buttons dancing in the darkness. Ceejay waited thirty seconds, then eased her eyes back open. Her light-deprived corneas looked past excruciatingly bright Mail, Maps, and Notes icons. She still had no signal, no wi-fi, and no way to stay in touch with Laura. Five restarts later, the grey signal bars on the iPhone screen were magnified by a single, salty teardrop.

# 17

Seth sat on his bed in a nicotine-induced daze. Three cartons of Croatian cigarettes were neatly stacked on his cabin dresser. The brand name included lots of Js and Zs and Seth didn't remember how Zoran had pronounced it. The only thing he knew about the cigarettes was that the three cartons had cost him 75 dollars. The telecom officer had left fifteen minutes ago, smiling and counting his money.

Cliffy bounded into Seth's room. "It's done."

"That fast?" Seth asked

"I'm a doctor of electrical engineering, Ozymandias. You have no idea what I'm capable of."

Seth was thrilled.

"The ship's navigating and emergency systems are intact, but all passenger communications are down."

"Marvelous."

"I can restart the passenger telecom whenever you want. But you may have to buy a few more cigarettes."

"Not a problem." Seth smiled. "And I'll be sure to sell any extras back to you just before they ship you off to jail for messing with the ship's equipment. I hear you can buy anything with cigarettes in the clink."

Cliffy frowned for a beat, apparently realizing that Seth was chiding him. "Don't think I won't take you down with me. I will tell the authorities everything. You know that, right?"

"I expect nothing less, Clay-Phan."

"Oh," Cliffy said, smiling sheepishly, "I also have a surprise for you." He went out the door of Seth's cabin and returned with a room-service tray, topped by a white china plate covered with a sterling silver dome.

"Please," Seth said, "not again. I don't need the guilt of someone else's sad photograph. You lift it."

"But of course." Cliffy wheeled the tray in front of Seth and removed the silver dome with a sweep of his arm and an elegant bow.

"You are a god," Seth said.

The plate had a short glass of milk and five puffy chocolate chip cookies. Salivary glands burst in Seth's mouth. He dipped a cookie in the creamy milk. The cookie's pores greedily soaked up the liquid. The warm chips melted against his tongue and lips. He chewed, swallowed, breathed, dunked, then repeated.

"You get some rest. You've got a big day ahead of you tomorrow," Cliffy said.

Seth tried to wish Cliffy a good night, to say thank you, but his tongue was mired in the rich cookie-milk mixture. He simply waved at the back of Cliffy's head as Cliffy slipped out of the cabin and shut the door behind him. Cliffy now gone, Seth instinctively grabbed his cell phone and entered Melanie's number. By the time he cleared his throat and went for the phone's green "dial" button, he stupidly realized that the phone would not be able to get a signal.

*Just as well. It's not like she tried to call me, either.*

Melanie was out of his life. Truly gone. A sad lump slowly worked its way from Seth's chest to his throat. He stuffed it back down with another cookie. After three more cookies, Melanie was a distant memory, replaced by sugar and the satisfaction of a plan well executed. The cruise line would survive – and all because of Seth and his crafty Asian friend. He lay his head against the soft queen pillow and let the day's troubles melt away.

# PART II

84 Hauer

# Chuck Tucker

I've covered a lot of bad shit in my time. After 'Nam, I realized that I was more comfortable living in a war zone than at home. How fucked up is that? FUBAR. That's about right. Thing is, after Nam, I was done with death and destruction. Despite my love of the war zone, the smell and excitement of a constantly shifting environment, I fully realized that war is the great scourge of the Earth. Nothing good comes of it. War, can't live with it, can't live without it. I figured the best compromise was carrying a camera, not a gun. And that was it, that was a career.

For the last thirty years I've successfully documented the best and worst of humanity in as many wars as I have fingers: nine. Yes, I suffered a few injuries along the way — a bullet in the butt covering a Shining Path rampage in Peru; shrapnel in my cheek getting exclusive shots of "president-for-life" Saparmurat Niyazov dealing for oil in Turkmenistan, and a missing pinky finger getting video of the Saffron Revolution in Myanmar — but I was always careful, and I credit that for my survival. And though I loved every minute of it, my wife, Susan, told me that she had had enough. Transferring to the domestic desk was her idea.

"Sorry we won't be seeing you around The Safahi anymore, Chuck," Chrissy Amanpour told me.

This was a running joke among the network's senior correspondents. Turns out there are actually two Safahi hotels in Mogadishu, Somalia. I chose the wrong one. 24 hours and one firefight later, UN peacekeepers pulled me out of the trunk of an old Mercedes. I still haven't lived that one down. I grunted, punched Chrissy in the shoulder, and reported for duty at the new desk. I steeled myself for a boring ride to retirement, ten years of squirrels on skis and greased pig contests. But when I saw the Lutak card on the assignment board I thought, *at least here's something a little bit interesting, something that won't give your wife the runs.* You'll get little bit of time in the bush, maybe see some nice wildlife, breathe the unprocessed air of Alaska. Might not be so bad after all.

We left for Juneau that night. The flight from Atlanta covered about 3200 miles, a long trip for most, but for me it was just another workday. The trip got more complicated from there. We took a turbulent ride aboard a puddle-jumper from Juneau to Haines, which is about ten miles southwest of Lutak. From there, most people would drive to Lutak. The local route normally takes about 20 minutes. Unfortunately, the only roads leading into Lutak were under repair — mudslides, we were told — and closed for the week.

This left us three options: we could fly a private pontoon plane to Chilkoot Lake and hike in from there, we could boat in to the new port, or we could hike through the night. With the ridiculous amount of gear CNN required us to take, both hiking and flying the crew into Lutak was out of the question. So we settled on a boat ride. But then we found out NordStar didn't want us docking at their new port. They said it had to remain open for their cruise and supply ships. I'm guessing that, in truth, they simply didn't want the bad publicity. This was turning out to be like the time I snuck into Myanmar. I felt right at home.

It was chilly but not cold, and we were stuck. After waiting for a half hour on the tarmac, I had an epiphany, which coincidentally is the same epiphany I've had on every assignment in my long distinguished career. It went something like this: "Fuck it." I was there to get the footage. I didn't need a sound man. I didn't need a talking head with me. I just needed the three Cs — chart, compass and my camera — and I would get what I came for. So I left. I went guerrilla.

I trudged away from the tarmac. Nobody dared try to stop me.

I've always done my best work on my own. That footage of Kenji Nagai in Yangon last year? The one where he's helpless at the foot of a Burmese soldier? There's no way I would have gotten that footage with a full crew on my back. So, I was impatient to get myself off the beaten track and away from CNN's domestic yahoos with their three Ms - mics, makeup and micromanagement.

Instead of taking the usual walking route along the water, I decided to take the path less traveled. Immediately to my east was Mount Ripinski, a 3600' green helmet rising over Haines. I figured I could cross Ripinski by foot and get to Lutak by mid-morning, well ahead of my colleagues. And, hell, I might get lucky with some workable footage along the way. I knew from my guide book that Ripinski trail was supposed to be one of the prettiest hikes in all of Alaska, a green floor covered with ferns leading up to a snowy top, one of the lowest in the majestic Takshanuk Mountain range, with a view of Chilkat lake and the Chilkat Mountains. An unforgettable view, the guide promised.

Too bad it was still hours until sunrise. There was just a sliver of moon visible through dense clouds and I couldn't see shit. Worse, those adorable ferns tripped me up every step or two. About an hour into my hike, I got caught in one of those little fuckers and turned my ankle. Night passage proved more difficult than I had expected. I had been through worse, though, and a lame ankle wasn't going to stop me.

I limped my ass across Ripinski's face, watching all the while for a good shot. In the near blackness of the night, however, there was little chance I'd find anything usable. I reached the top as morning sunlight silhouetted the frighteningly big mountains to the East. I estimated that I was still a good five hours from town. Now that I could make out my surroundings more clearly, I spotted an open glade surrounded by spruce-hemlock. Beneath the glade, the trees were thicker but not impassable. Beyond that, I could just make out Chilkat Lake, an impressive veil of bluish-white draped over the landscape for miles.

After hours of struggling through the dense undergrowth – it was probably six or seven in the morning by now – my old bones needed a breather and a spot of water. I limped into the clearing and dropped my pack. I lifted a canteen to my lips, sweet water about to pour into my parched throat, but stopped short of drinking. Ferns trembled about 30 yards away. Two brown puffs bounced out of the plants. Without any real expertise to back it up, I guessed the grizzly cubs were no more than a year old. They didn't see me. They were more interested in fighting over a piece of driftwood.

And that's when my shit got real scared.


I only really know one thing about wild animals, something I learned during a run-in with a lioness in Rwanda. It's a rule that we share with every member of the animal kingdom: never get between a mother and her children. And those cute grizzlies' Mommy had to be around here somewhere. Thankfully, the brown puffs kept their distance.

I've been in tense situations before and I have always had a keen ability to think my way through without panicking. I don't know where I get it. My dad was a nervous Nelly and my mom went through electroshock therapy when I was 13. But me, nerves of steel. Doesn't make any sense.

The hairs on the back of my neck stood on end. I stilled myself, slowed my breathing, and watched the trees for a larger, more dangerous looking puff of brown. She had to be out there. I listened, but heard no padding, no heavy breathing. I took a long look behind me, but there was nothing in that direction either. I held my breath.

I reached down and undid a snap on my pack. The snap's metallic release sounded like a gunshot in the silence of the clearing. The cubs still paid me no attention. I pulled my Ikegami from its place in the middle of the pack and flipped it on with my thumb. Drawing the viewfinder to my eye and resting the pad on my shoulder, I zoomed in on the horizon. I found a small puff of steam a small distance from the cubs. I followed the trail down to Mommy's head, low in the ferns, staring away from me. Her body was hidden behind a clump of green.

My heart leapt into my throat. Back in the shit again. Mommy was approximately 50 yards from me and would get to me in no time if she thought I was a threat. I flattened myself against the ground, propped the camera against the pack, and hit the red REC button.

I kept my left eye glued to the viewfinder. The cubs rolled, bit, and scratched for a full half hour. Occasionally I'd pan over to mommy bear's position, but she was content to lay still and send hot streams of grizzly breath into the Alaskan sky. This was so much better than covering a war. It had all of the excitement without any of the soul-sucking ugliness. I lost no faith in humanity here. Instead, I gained an appreciation for the natural world. I resolved to contact Animal Planet as soon as I was done apologizing to my CNN producers for providing them with a monotonous 45 minutes tape of baby-bear play.

Just the same, I figured that Mommy might be the one responsible for the attacks in Lutak. The victims probably messed with the cubs and got what was coming to them. My producers should be thankful for my willingness to leave the crew and capture these shots, shots that would lend some sympathy to the beasts that I was certain NordStar would kill in the coming days. My footage would round out an otherwise blasé story about another Alaskan bear attack.

Mommy's head suddenly entered my viewfinder frame, nodding. Apparently, she agreed with my assessment. She stretched her magnificent neck and sniffed the air. She let out an irritated woof and turned her eyes my way. I calmly pulled myself away from my pack. Ever the consummate professional, I kept the viewfinder against my eye as I pulled the pack onto my shoulders. Behind me, I knew, was a thicket of spruce. I would walk into the forest and disappear. I would not pose a threat to Mommy. I would take my camera and be a ghost.

Mommy was still 50 yards off, staring at me. Her neck began bobbing back and forth, like my wife when she was angry. I had to move faster but my ankle still throbbed from tripping over the goddamned ferns. A slow, measured retreat was probably still the best means of getting off Ripinski alive, to get away without looking like a threat. But I was having trouble convincing my body to take it so smoothly.

Thankfully, despite wrenching her head this way and that, obviously irritated, Mommy still hadn't moved. I was close to the edge of the glade now. I was going to make it.

Another of Chucky's skin-of-his-teeth escapes. Suck it, Amanpour.

That's when I heard crunching in the spruce behind me. I smelled foul breath, a mix of fish and rotting flesh. I swung the camera around, but it was inappropriately zoomed for the closeness of the encounter. In the viewfinder, I was blinded by a white blur. It might have been lens flare. Maybe I was shooting directly into the sun. As I pulled the camera from my eyes, I felt something yank on my chest, as though I had caught my pack on a tree branch. I looked down and saw that the pack was drooping to the left, the strap on my right shoulder torn. I looked down from my right shoulder and saw a large tear in my abdomen. Bloody, spring-loaded ropes of intestine pushed their way through the hole.

I don't remember anything after that.

# 18

The Beast made its own way through the dirt path, tottering from wheel to wheel with little trouble. Its dark silhouette was barely visible — even only a few feet ahead of Seth — in the dim night. Seth did his best to keep up with the Beast's pace, but was slowed by his long, black judge's robe. It was too big for him, and he kept tripping over the hem. He was angry about this, and considered calling his secretary at Radley and yelling at her for ordering the wrong size. He patted himself down for a cell phone, but the robe had no pockets. Seth was naked underneath the dark cloth.

It was imperative that he keep up with the Beast, because It was the only thing protecting Seth from the others out there in the dark, things that snorted and woofed beyond the pines that crowded their narrow path. Occasionally, Seth caught glimpses of the big, hairy others. They would surely seize him if he did not have the Beast to guard him.

Needles and dirt gathered into a thick orbit around the robe's hem. Soon, Seth knew he would be unable to move forward at all. The Beast gained speed as Seth slowed. The monsters in the trees sounded closer and closer. Finally, Seth stopped moving altogether. The Beast disappeared into the blue-black night. This was going to be the end for Seth Ozymandias Sterling. Nothing would stand between him and the monsters that sniffed and snorted in the dark. To his surprise, he got down on his knees and prayed. Though of Jewish descent, he did not consider himself a religious person, and knew no formal prayers in their entirety.

Still, Seth prayed:

"Dear God. Don't let me die here. I don't know why I am wearing a judge's robes. I am not a judge, and don't make a habit of impersonating them. As you can see, my luggage has deserted me and I'm about to be eaten by bears. If you could just step in here and help me out, I think I'd change some things about the way I live my life. I have a lot to offer, I am sure of it. Anyway, whatever you can do. Thanks. Best Regards. Seth."

A woman's voice boomed from beyond the trees. "Request denied!"

Seth sighed. The trees vibrated around him, full of hairy monsters about to strike. Branches fell and trees splintered as hairy monsters toppled the surrounding wood, climbing towards him. Riding atop the monstrous herd was a demon woman with bright-red hair, her naked skin cutting a pale silhouette against the sea of fur. She laughed as her minions tore him apart.

Seth gasped awake, strangely aroused. His eyes were bathed in a thin film of red, the surrounding whites bursting with a roadmap of swollen capillaries. He swept his arm across the breadth of the bed, feeling for the reassuring presence of Melanie's calf, wrist, or thigh. But she was not there. He was alone and, he now remembered, lying on a queen bed in a cabin aboard the largest ship to traverse Alaska's inside passage. He closed his eyes again.

Now he lay on a bearskin rug, stroking Evie Kramer's red hair. She wore a shiny black teddy, so short that the word "maintain" was visible on her upper right thigh. Though he hadn't realized it until now, Seth was completely naked. Embarrassed, he grabbed a corner of the bearskin and covered himself. Hundreds of miniscule bears fled out from under the rug, skittering, cockroach-like, to the corners of the room. He hopped up and smarted smashing the tiny bears with his bare feet.

"Pesky little fuckers," he said. He danced across the floor and squished tiny grizzly after tiny grizzly. Then there was a bang. He looked down and saw a gaping hole in his chest. Evie stood before him, pointing a smoking shotgun in his direction.

He furrowed his eyebrows and shook his finger. "What'd you go and do that for?" he asked.

"Request to step on tiny bears is denied," she said. Her eyes blinked sleepily, reminding Seth of his boss, Thad Wilson.

Evie pumped the shotgun, and then put another hole in Seth.


Seth awoke again in a pool of sweat. Again, he was aroused. His cabin was bright. The clock now showed nine and his cell phone agreed. It took a few seconds for Seth to shake the sleep and remember the crises of the night before. Lutak was at risk. Three dead, each torn to pieces by one very smart grizzly, according to Captain Kelly. Worse, the deaths threatened to ruin NordStar and derail Seth from his partner track.

Panic worked its way up Seth's throat. It tasted like tobacco, stale peanut butter and chocolate. He reminded himself that — at least for now — the situation was under control. Seth turned on the cabin's small flat-panel television. Nothing but snow. More proof that Cliffy had successfully cut off communications to and from The Diana. He had turned it into Burma, as he had said he would. Passengers would be angry over the communications shutdown during this long day at sea, but free alcohol and a presentation on expeditions would solve that. Then the drunk, captive audience would buy enough marked-up side excursions to more-than make up for the cheap alcohol they would consume.

His panic subsided. There was a knock on the door.

"Just a minute," he whispered. He peeked his head around the door and found Cliffy, looking fresh.

"Morning, Ozymandias. You know what time—" He stopped talking when he noticed the pronounced lump in Seth's boxers.

Seth looked down. "I'm just happy to see you, Cliffy." He smiled.

"No time for joking, Ozymandias." Cliffy walked past Seth, studiously avoiding physical contact, and walked to the cabin's small TV. "You need to see this."

Cliffy flipped the set on but the picture was nothing but snow.

"I know, Cliffy. You did a great job. Enough gloating."

Cliffy gritted his teeth. "Not that." He flipped through station after station of snow until he settled on the ship's internal television channel, the only station still in operation. "This."

One glance at the TV and all of the blood rushed out of Seth's nether-regions. Tobacco, peanut butter and chocolate wound back up his esophagus.

# 19

The TV set was a cheap imitation of a 24-hour news desk. The letters "DNN" were stenciled on white poster board next to a sign that said: "Free liquor in the Starlight Deck at 10 AM in the Starlight Theater. Don't miss Dan Feltzer, ventriloquist extraordinaire, in the Goldmine Lounge at 3 PM." Stevie Bruebecker, still wearing a tuxedo, and Tammy Wurser smiled and acted as though nothing in the world could trouble them. But their foreheads were damp and their gestures were a bit too fast. Something was wrong.

"You're going to be just fine," Stevie said, waving and winking. "We are working to fix the satellites right now and can assure you that these bizarre rumors about bear attacks are nonsense."

"I mean," Tammy interrupted, flicking a bang out of her face, "just consider the source."

Stevie nodded too fervently. He echoed Tammy's words, "—the source."

Tammy continued. "We've seen this sort of thing before. A teenager gets a little nervous on their first day at sea and starts telling stories."

"But this is completely out of line," Stevie added.

"Totally out of line. And we don't want someone crying dingo—"

"We say 'wolf,' Tammy."

They laughed heartily at this. The off-camera audience did not.

"The point is," Tammy said, "you don't want some excitable teen ruining your vacation."

"And with so many wonderful activities planned today, it would, well, it would be shame. There are," Stevie laughed, "no crazy bears out there. We're not going to let anything happen to our treasured guests."

He smiled. "Do any of you know how to tell brown bears from grizzlies?"

A loud grumbling came from off-camera.

"Okay, then," Stevie said, and then wiped sweat from his upper lip. "So, we do apologize for the technical difficulties and are working to fix them as soon as humanly possible. In the meantime, we hope you will join us in the Starlight for a wine-tasting—"

"—I'll have some whiskey out," Tammy said, elbowing Stevie and winking. Again, no response from the audience.

"And," Stevie said, "we'll talk about all of the amazing opportunities we have available to make your voyage even more memorable."

The audience grumbled again.


"What is this?" Seth said, turning to Cliffy and raising his arms in exasperation. He turned off the TV and got in Cliffy's face. "What the fuck is this? How could this happen?"

"I'm not sure," Cliffy said.

"What do you mean you're not sure? You're a doctor. You know what happened. Either everything's on or off, right?"

"As far as I know."

"And you made sure everything was off, right?"

"Off. Yep. Everything was off." Cliffy nervously fingered his pack of 555s, fished out a couple of cigarettes, and offered one to Seth.

"Put those things away. What's wrong with you?"

"I thought it would calm you."

"It would, but now isn't the time for calm. Now is the time for damage control. Smelling like cigarettes isn't going to help any. I need to instill trust, here, Cliffy. Come on!"

Seth immediately regretted his harsh tone. He put his hands on Cliffy's shoulders and looked into his eyes.

"Look, Cliffy, you're the only reason things haven't gone completely to seed here, but I need you to think hard. How could anyone have gotten this information? We hit Burma before CNN or anyone else could broadcast the story, right?"

"Yes. I have no idea how anyone got any information. It's impossible that they got it from the ship's facilities."

"And why are Donnie and Marie lying about the maulings on the television? Don't they know that this can come back to bite NordStar? Who told them to do that?"

"I have no idea. Wait, maybe—" Cliffy said. "Maybe they aren't lying?"

"Are you serious? They just told the passengers that there is no bear problem in Lutak. And we both know there is a bear problem in Lutak."

"Is it lying if you don't know that what you're saying is wrong?"

"Okay, I have no idea what you're talking about right now."

"Well, I didn't tell Stevie or Tammy anything. And I don't think anyone else did either. So, maybe they really do think that some teenager is making all of this up."

Seth let Cliffy's words sink in. "That actually makes sense," he said. "And I don't think it's a lie unless it's intentionally false. But what if you don't know that you don't know but assert that you do, just the same."

"I think that's a lie, then. Does it matter?" Cliffy asked.

"Not really. We need to get a hold of this teenager. Do you know who it is?"

"Yes. And she's right down the hall. I take care of her room. You want me to grab her and bring her back here?"

"Good thinking, but I'm not down with kidnapping just yet. And she's a minor, which is bad."

"So what, then?"

"We talk to her."

# 20

"Housekeeping," Cliffy said, knocking on Ceejay's cabin door.

"Go away," Ceejay said through the door.

"I have a morning treat." He smiled at Seth as though he had just unveiled the secret of universal room access.

Seth elbowed Cliffy. "That's creepy," he whispered. "You sound like a To Catch a Predator episode. Why don't you just offer her a candy bar?"

Cliffy sniffed. "I offer all of my passengers a morning treat. I just gave one to Nan Jenkins."

"That's even creepier."

"You two whispering about how to get into my room is the creepiest of all," Ceejay said through the door.

"Now look what you've done," Seth said.

Then, to Seth's surprise, the door opened a crack.

"What do you want?" Ceejay said. A stuffed nose muffled her voice.

Seth couldn't see much of her through the small opening in the door. But what he could make out was depressing. Her eyes were red — redder than his — and heavy streaks of mascara ran from her eyes like black sunrays.

*She must have cried herself to sleep*, Seth thought.

"We just want to talk," Seth said, "about the bear attacks you mentioned." Seth punctuated "bear attacks" with air quotes.

"God, you people are all the same. I'm not lying!"

"Which people? Who else have you spoken to?" Seth asked.

"Where are we, Guantanamo?" Ceejay asked. "I'm not talking to anyone else!" Ceejay slammed the door with enough force to shake the thin walls around her cabin.

Seth winced. Then it hit him. He retrieved his wallet from his back pocket and removed his cabin's key card. He tapped Cliffy on the shoulder, then pointed at the card.

"Good for you, you still have your room key," Cliffy said.

Seth's eyes bulged. He shook his head and put his finger against his lips, signaling that Cliffy should be quiet. He pointed to the key card, pointed to Cliffy, and then pointed to each of the doors surrounding them. Pointing back at Cliffy, Seth mimed placing his key card into the key slot. Understanding lit on Cliffy's eyes. He pulled the universal key card from his jacket's inside right pocket.

"This?" he mouthed, pointing at the card.

"It's the only way," Seth whispered.

Cliffy grimaced. "They'll fire me."

"If we don't do anything about this, there'll be no job to fire you from, Cliffy."

Grudgingly, Cliffy swiped the card in and out of the reader. Seth pushed the door open, accidentally knocking Ceejay from her perch at the peephole. She fell to the floor.

"What the—" she said.

"I didn't mean to knock you over," Seth said. "I just need some information."

Ceejay scrambled backwards, her eyes wide. Seth could see her hands working hard behind her, looking for something to ward off her intruders.

"Look, I just need to know why you're telling people about bear attacks. What gave you that idea?" Seth demanded.

Still retreating into the cabin, Ceejay's searched the top of her dresser and found her iPhone. Instead of answering Seth, she swung the phone at Seth's head. He ducked too late. The iPhone slammed into his left temple. He fell to the floor in dramatic fashion, eyes fluttering, his hand against the side of his head.

"What have you done?" Cliffy asked, dropping to Seth's side.

"The same thing I'm going to do to you if you don't get the fuck out of here."

"You're going to hit me with a phone?" Cliffy asked incredulous.

Ceejay landed a quick blow against Cliffy's brow.

"Ouch! Quit it!"

She raised her arm again and circled the phone threateningly above Seth and Cliffy.

"Okay, okay!" Seth said, shielding his head with his hands. "Look, we didn't come in here to wage war with a teenage girl, or otherwise assault you."

"You had no right to just barge in here!" Ceejay shouted.

"You're right," Seth said. "You're completely right."

"Completely right," Cliffy said, cupping his eye.

"It was a bad move," Seth said. "Please. Just put the phone down. I just wanted to know."

"Know what?" Ceejay said, still threatening to rain terror from above.

"Look, just put the phone down and we can discuss this."

Ceejay stared at the two pitiful men cowering on her cabin floor. Cliffy's eye was starting to swell, the skin around it blossoming with oranges and yellows. Seth held his head as though he was keeping a shattered crystal bowl together. Ceejay eased her grip on the iPhone.

"Okay. Get up. And don't try anything."

Seth nodded and put his hand out for Ceejay to help him up.

"You're just lucky my parents weren't in the other room. My dad would have torn you two apart."

"That would have been a lot less embarrassing," Cliffy muttered.

"Rushing into a young girl's room," Ceejay continued, "what's wrong with you?"

She pulled Seth and Cliffy from the floor. Seth took a seat on Ceejay's thoroughly unmade bed.

"You have any ice?" Seth asked.

"No," Ceejay responded. "I hadn't planned on anyone breaking into my cabin today."

"I'll go get some," Cliffy said. He grabbed the ice bucket from the bathroom and stumbled out of the room.

"Now," Ceejay said to Seth, "talk." She brandished the cell phone as though she would attack if his information didn't satisfy her.

Seth finally removed his hand from the crown of his head. "Look, I can't tell you much. But, well, see, I believe you."

"About what?" Ceejay stepped into the room's small bathroom. Seth heard water running.

"About the bears," he shouted to her in the other room. "I don't think you're making this stuff up. Telling tales. You know what I mean?"

Ceejay came back from the bathroom with a wet towel. "Here."

Seth pressed the wet cloth against his bruised head. "Thanks."

"Look, I don't care whether you think I'm making any of this up. I know I'm not. And I don't care whether it's right, either."

"Then why all of the upset? Have you seen yourself in a mirror lately? Mascara everywhere. You certainly don't look like a happy camper."

"I have other problems."

"Thanks to you, I have problems, too," Seth said.

"Among them, you smell like cigarettes."

"Still?"

"Yup. Got any extras?"

Seth handed her the wet towel. "Wipe your eyes, you look like Tammy Faye."

"Who's that?"

Seth groaned. "How old are you?"

"Old enough to know that a few of your cigarettes would wipe any memory of your intrusion this morning."

Seth shook his head. "Alright, come on then."


Seth, Ceejay and Cliffy sat on Seth's small balcony, smoking Zoran's Croatian cigarettes. The men used their free hands to push ice against their respective wounds. Despite her attempts to remove the makeup, Ceejay's face was still blasted with tear-stained mascara.

"So, you got an e-mail?" Seth asked, exhaling blue smoke that drifted out into the endless seascape.

"Yes," Ceejay said, frowning at the last third of her rapidly diminishing cigarette. She pulled a fleck of ash from her tongue and then spit over the railing. "I normally roll my own, you know."

"Great. That's just what we need, 12 year-olds with rolling papers. Fantastic."

"I'm 17."

Seth shook his head. "Babies making baby cigarettes. What's our society coming to?"

"At least I'm not like 40 and still smoking."

Seth threw his hands in the air. "Why does everyone think I'm so old?"

"You aren't aging well," Cliffy said. His eye was now swollen shut, the skin a deep purple.

"Thanks for the kind words, blinky," Seth said.

Cliffy pointed at his wounded eye. "At least this will go away. You will look like that forever."

"That, Cliffy," Seth pointed at Cliffy's eye, "is an improvement. Once that's gone it'll be back to the old Cliffy Clay-Phan, Phantom of the Diana."

Cliffy laughed, and then winced.

"Cliffy Clay-Phan?" Ceejay asked, her smile throwing curves into the streaks sprayed wildly around her eyes. "Like the mailman from Cheers? That can't really be your name."

"Great," Seth said, "the youth of today know Cheers but have never heard of Tammy Faye. Anyway, you didn't look all that much better just a few minutes ago," Seth said to Ceejay. After a pause, he added, "Zebra face."

"That's the best you've got? Zebra face?"

"I couldn't share my first thought."

"You didn't have a first thought."

"I did. I'm very smart. I just didn't want to hurt your feelings."

"Whatever."

"We're off topic," Seth said, "about this e-mail. When did you get it?"

"Maybe around four this morning?" Ceejay said.

"Okay," Seth said, "problem is that there's absolutely no way you got that e-mail this morning. The ship's comm. system has been down since about midnight last night."

"I didn't get the e-mail through the comm. system," she said.

"Are you sure? How do you know?"

"Well, I was in the middle of an argument with my girlfriend back home when the signal died." Ceejay teared up. "Turns out she had a boyfriend that I knew nothing about. We texted back and forth for a while. I thought we were making some headway. She said something about leaving him for good. Then the thing up and died. No more texting. I kind of freaked out."

"Done. So, you were waiting for an e-mail from your girlfriend, and it magically materialized out of thin air in the early morning?"

"Something like that."

"And you're certain you didn't get it from the ship's Internet?"

"Look. This thing?" Ceejay waved the iPhone at Seth. "It can get onto any network available. At around four, it found a new network called 'Canuck Free-Fi.' The signal was weak, but it was enough."

"She got a signal from the shore," Cliffy said. "Why didn't I think of that?" He turned to Seth. "I can't jam signals coming off-ship, Seth. I only stopped the onboard stuff."

Seth coughed at the mention of their involvement in the shutdown. He widened his eyes, stressing that Cliffy not say anything more.

"Wait a minute," Ceejay said, exasperated. "You two are responsible for the communications shut-down?"

"No," Seth lied.

"But your friend said —"

"We didn't do it," Seth said.

"Yes we did," Cliffy said, almost proudly.

"What is wrong with you?" Seth asked Cliffy.

Cliffy shrugged. "The jig is up. She's onto us."

"Are you terrorists? Like Al Qaeda or something?" Ceejay reached for her phone.

"Oh, put the phone down," Seth said. "Do we look like Al Qaeda?"

"Well, your buddy here looks like that shoe bomber — Richard Reed? — after they worked him over on the plane."

"I assure you he's no Richard Reed. We were actually trying to keep this cruise on track. But then you went and ruined our efforts by blabbing about bear attacks in Lutak."

"I didn't mean to blab it to everyone," Ceejay said. "I just needed to reconnect."

"What does that mean?" Seth asked.

"Well," she said, "that girl I told you about? She was my first girlfriend!"

"Oh," Seth said, looking down at his nicotine-stained fingernails.

Ceejay welled up again, tears threatening to coat her cheeks. When she next spoke, her voice had the halted cadence of a goat. "Sh-sh-she said that she couldn't leave Gary. She wished me well, but she wanted me to know that it was over and that she hoped I would be safe on my cruise. She linked to a CNN story about a mauling spree in Lutak that left three dead. She told me to be careful. Anyway, I needed someone to comfort me – a post-breakup heart-to-heart or something. But then I wasn't getting a cell signal anymore, so I couldn't call my friends. So, guess who was left to talk to?"

Seth and Cliffy shrugged in unison.

"My parents."

"Oh," Cliffy said.

"Oh no," Seth said.

"I woke up bright and early, put on makeup for the first time in forever, and decided to go with good old mom and dad to breakfast. Seems they weren't interested in my little drama. They told me it was too bad, but that was it. They wanted to talk to everyone else at the breakfast table but me. Like they're going to make lifelong friends here." Ceejay snorted with disdain. "So, I figured that the article about bears in Lutak might get their attention. Turns out it got the whole table's attention."

Seth's face sunk, becoming pale.

"Then it got the next table's attention. And the room's. And now it's on TV. Everyone's saying I'm full of shit."

"Right," Seth nodded. "I've heard that."

"And my parents called me a liar. They bought the company line. They think I just want attention. So, I locked myself in the room, threw myself on the bed, and cried myself back to sleep."

"Gotcha," Seth said, handing Ceejay a Kleenex and a cigarette.

"And I have you two to thank for all of this," she said.

There was a knock at the door.

"Seth, you in there?" Captain Kelly's voice boomed from the other side of the door.

"Look," Seth quietly told Cliffy and Ceejay," I need you guys to stay out on the balcony until I give you the all clear."

"This is the worst vacation ever," Ceejay said.

"You've obviously never been to Laughlin," Seth said, then walked into the cabin bathroom. He swallowed a blob of toothpaste from his Dopp kit, then shouted at the door. "Be right there, Captain!"

## 21

Seth threw open the door and blurted, "I guess we'll need more whiskey, huh?"

Captain Kelly shook his head tightly. Buddy moved out from behind Kelly, his giant white mustache wilting at the corners of his mouth.

"Ah," Seth said.

"Morning, son," Buddy said. He pushed past Seth and moved into the small cabin. With the drapes shut, Seth's room was almost completely dark. The only light came from Stevie and Tammy's bright smiles on the small TV.

"I didn't know we gave you a smoking room, Seth." Buddy pointed at the full ashtray. "And I didn't know you smoked. Hell, I didn't know anyone smoked anymore."

"My apologies, Buddy," Seth said. "I know there's a no smoking policy —"

Buddy waved Seth away.

"Son, I could give two shits about smoking. I'm more concerned about the plan – your plan. It isn't working. We've got passengers saying they won't step foot off the ship because of some killer bear."

So it had gotten all the way to Buddy. That was it. NordStar was going to fire Seth and Radley, and it was all his fault. No doubt they would also file a malpractice suit of some sort. Seth kissed his partnership — hell, his whole career — goodbye. Buddy sat on Seth's comforter and smoothed the blanket around him. He pointed at the ashtray.

"You got any more of those things?"

Well, that was something. At least he could share a cigarette with the firing squad. He worked a 555 loose from its pack and handed it to Buddy.

He offered one to Kelly, but Kelly shook his head and frowned, obviously displeased.

Buddy took a drag off of his cigarette and let out an ecstatic moan. "Don't get to smoke at home. Missus number three doesn't look too kindly on it. Not that she wants me to live a long life. None of them have. She just doesn't like the second-hand stuff. She wants to keep spending my money for as long as possible after I'm gone." He chuckled, an unsettling, gravelly sound. He examined his cigarette. "I haven't had one of these since the war. Forgot how good they were."

Buddy wasn't dropping the axe immediately. What was he waiting for?

"You were in Nam?" Seth asked nervously.

"Yup. Daddy pulled some strings, but told me the best he could do was get me stationed in a reporting shed in Saigon. He could have gotten me out of there, though. I know that. He thought the war would give me character. But that didn't work. I just became a hell of a poker player and sucked the smoke out of about a billion 555s."

"Wow," Seth said, unsure how to proceed. "So, uh, when did you get here?"

"Helicoptered in this morning," Buddy said.

"I didn't know the Diana had helipads. That is totally impressive."

Kelly interrupted, "While we do have helipads here, Buddy choppered to his own boat, then took a dinghy to meet us on the Diana. Our pads are for emergency evacuation use only."

"Gotcha," Seth said, imagining the type of personal yacht that carried its own helipad.

"Look," Kelly said, "we need to get down to business."

Buddy looked displeased with Kelly. "The whole thing's gone to shit. We're fucked because your plan didn't work."

"Well," Seth stammered, "from what I'm hearing, a lot of passengers still think the bear attacks are just a rumor, a teenager's wild tale."

"Rumors are worse than facts," Buddy said. "At least with facts you get something concrete to hold on to. Something to laugh at, or at least something to be brave in the face of. Here, people don't know what to think."

"Our excursion meeting is not producing," Kelly said.

Seth checked his phone. Half past ten. Passengers should be in the Starlight right now swallowing free booze and signing up for Lutak's overpriced adventures.

"And if people don't buy the trips, it means that Lutak is a disaster," Buddy said. "I think you know how heavily NordStar leveraged Lutak's success."

Buddy stared at Seth. Seth nodded. Buddy kept staring.

"Son," he said, "we need you to come up with another brilliant idea."

Kelly nodded and squinted at Seth.

Seth was confused. The morning had been a disaster. Passengers were unhappy. Why was Buddy taking another chance on him? It made no sense. Just the same, if Buddy was going to offer him a branch, he would certainly take it. No use in disabusing Buddy's belief that Seth was some sort of Svengali capable of saving NordStar from almost certain doom. He thought for a minute as Buddy helped himself to a second 555 and Kelly stared on.

"You know," Seth said, "how you said that rumors are worse than facts?"

Buddy brightened. "I do."

"Maybe we can still give the passengers a fact, something that builds confidence in NordStar. Something that makes Lutak safe and makes the ship an even more spectacular attraction."

"And how do we do that?" Kelly asked.

"Well, it's pretty simple," Seth said. "But first we have to get off this boat."

"Ship," Kelly said.

"The Diana," Buddy said authoritatively.

"Right," Seth said. "And once we do, we're going to have to make a whole lot more of that wine tower's booze available to your passengers."

"What? Why?" Kelly asked.

"The best thing you can do right now is keep your cruisers blotto. And you're not going to want a drop of Jameson's in that tower when we return."

# 22

Seth stood in an airy concourse that led through a pair of metal detectors and out onto the Diana's outer deck. Buddy walked through the detectors and into sunlight. Seth held his cell phone to his ear. The wind blowing through the concourse made it difficult to hear the phone's tinny speaker. Seth trusted, however, that the man on the other end of the line could easily shout and giggle through even epic gusts.

"Seth Ozymandias Sterling!" Matt Schott bellowed. Somewhere in the background of Matt's Arizona home, Seth heard the unmistakable intro to Black Sabbath's "Iron Man."

"Burma tanked," Seth said in a monotone. "Just thought I'd let you know about the fruits of our labor."

Beyond the metal detectors, in the bright morning sun, Seth spotted the silhouetted forms of crew members preparing the dinghy that would take Seth to Buddy's yacht.

"What, you want my sympathy?" Matt asked. "I told you this would happen. If there's one thing I learned from my time in Mexico it's that *usted no chinga con Norteamericanos ricos*. Know what I mean?"

Seth didn't, but he could guess: Matt thought that he was being shortsighted and perilously ambitious.

"I know," Seth said, "it was a really stupid move."

Matt giggled. "Well, what are you going to do. You win some, you lose some. I've been hearing about your little cruise on CNN today. Something about maulings in Lutak."

Seth did not respond for a bit, then said, "I'm about to do something very dangerous."

"No you're not. You don't do dangerous things. You're a civil attorney, the very definition of risk averse," Matt said, suddenly serious.

"Starting today I do. Anyway, the reason I'm telling you this is that I might not make it back."

"Aren't you being a little dramatic?"

"There's a homicidal fucking bear out there."

"And you're not going anywhere near it, right Seth?"

Buddy looked up from the dinghy and gave Seth a thumbs up. It was ready to go. Seth smiled and returned the sign.

"No, well not alone. I'm bringing an old man with me."

"Sounds brilliant."

"There's one other thing."

"Yeah?"

"If I, you know, if I get hurt, I figured you could pass the news on to Melanie."

"Why me?"

"I haven't exactly kept in touch with anyone. And you have Melanie's number. So, could you just pass on the news for me?"

"I don't think I'll have to. With the coverage this thing is getting, you'll definitely make the news."

"Well, I'm listing you as my next of kin on the emergency contact thingy. You'll get the first call."

Buddy impatiently waved at Seth. Seth smiled and held up a hand, holding Buddy off for a few precious moments.

"You can still back out of this thing, Seth. You're not compelled to do something stupid. You can just come home and call it a loss."

"This is my career we're talking about."

"You're being dramatic again. This isn't the Seth Ozymandias Sterling I remember from law school."

"Maybe. I've got to go. Remember, if I bite it, the first call goes to you."

"Oh wait. You talk to Evie yet?"

"No."

"Because there's some weird shit on her Facebook page nowadays."

"Wonderful," Seth said. Buddy stood with his hands on his hips, his mustache downturned. "We'll talk about it later, Matt."

Seth folded the phone, shoved the Beast through the metal detectors, and boarded the dinghy.


"There she is!" Buddy shouted, pointing to the Diana off in the distance. Seth was confused. He didn't remember making a full circle. He thought they were heading towards Buddy's yacht, not back to his temporary floating home. But then Seth saw a name — The Nellie — advertised in black letters on the ship's immense bow. As they drew closer, Seth realized that The Nellie was a scale replica of its larger sister – a pricey gimmick for a company near bankruptcy.

The tender crept up to The Nellie's dive platform, an enormous plank of white fiberglass spiked with white rubber treads — it had to be at least forty feet wide. Overhead, Seth could just see the outer reaches of a helicopter propeller perched atop the upper-deck. Buddy led Seth into The Nellie's main parlor. He waved his hands across the expanse of the great room. "Welcome to my home away from home."

Had Seth not known that this was Buddy's yacht, if he had been blindfolded and dragged here by persons unknown, he would have thought he had been delivered to a T.G.I. Friday's, maybe a Chili's. The parlor walls were laden with every manner of tchotchke, from team pennants and fishing implements to photographs and license plates. Amidst the junk-laden walls were a bar, a pool table, and an assortment of small wooden booths with seats upholstered in busy patterns that would not be spoiled by a good splash of beer. Towards the back of the parlor was a set of brass-railed wooden stairs leading to what Seth assumed was the bridge.

Buddy smiled proudly. "Make yourself comfortable, it'll be a few minutes before we have the bird fueled and ready to fly."

"Fly?" Seth asked, fear creeping into his voice. "I thought we were motoring to Lutak in The Nellie."

Buddy shook his head. "Lutak is about 650 miles away as the crow flies. The Nellie can only handle about 25 knots. It would take days and we'd barely be ahead of the Diana. We need to get there today. We'll chopper in and nip this thing in the bud by this afternoon, maybe tomorrow at the latest."

Seth gulped. He remembered hearing somewhere that helicopters, unlike fixed wing aircraft, are inherently unstable. If there is any lack of input or control, the helicopter will tip and crash. Buddy walked the length of the parlor, slipped behind the room's oaken bar, and filled two glasses with foamy, amber beer.

Buddy handed one to Seth, then tipped his own glass over his mustache. Seth took a big gulp and felt the ice-cold drink take root in his gut, drowning some of his butterflies. At the back of the room, Seth saw a figure bound down the stairs, fingers occasionally gripping the brass rail for assurance. Even before he saw her face, the aggressive stance signaled that Tammy Wurser, the ship's purser, was aboard The Nellie.

"Wonderful," Seth muttered.

"Buddy," she said in an accent thicker than he remembered from their previous encounters, "the bird's ready to fly."

"Wonderful," Buddy said, casting a mischievous eye towards Seth and draining the remainder of his beer.

"Isn't she supposed to be back on The Diana?" Seth asked. "I mean, she is the ship's head purser."

Buddy threw an arm around her shoulder. "A purser doesn't really do anything anymore," Buddy said. "She's there to keep people happy, keep the crew happy, and give both something to look at." He pulled his hand from her shoulder and gave her bottom a hearty smack. She beamed and swatted him back.

"Besides," Tammy said in her thick Australian accent, "you don't really think NordStar could entrust a successful hunt to this old yobbo and a poofter like you, you poofy piker. Buddy tells me you've never even held a rifle."

"Isn't she a kick?" Buddy asked.

Seth stared at Tammy but said nothing.

"Well," Buddy cleared his throat, "Tammy is also the best marksman for 200 miles. I don't have time to assemble a crack hunting team, so I'm damn well bringing along someone who can shoot."

Seth doubted that this was Buddy's primary motivation. He took a mental note to have a conversation with Buddy about the dangers of romantic relationships with employees. For the moment, however, he was more concerned with the realization that Tammy must have been outright lying to the passengers that morning on the television. If she was this close to Buddy, she must have known that there were bear problems in Lutak.


The three emerged from the parlor onto the Nellie's upper deck. Seth put a hand over his eyes to protect his face from the harsh wind blowing from the helicopter's propeller. The chopper had four captain's chairs and a storage space at the rear for their gear. Buddy pulled a door open and gestured for Seth to enter the back row. Buddy donned a pair of heavy white headphones and clambered up to the pilot's seat.

"Buckle up," Buddy said and winked at Seth, "it's going to be a bumpy ride."

## 23

The ride had been bumpy, as promised.

On several occasions, Seth was certain his stomach would force up the small amount of food he had eaten the night before. But to his surprise, he eventually acclimated to the helicopter's irregular, churning rhythms. The occasional lurch or roll no longer bothered him, and his face returned to its normal pallor. The view, a maze of water and forested shore, finally gave way to a grey rectangle that Seth had seen too many times over the past two years.

To his eyes, Lutak's dock was nothing to write home about, just a ship-sized rectangle of concrete paralleling the shoreline. A small vessel — Seth assumed it was the CNN boat — was tied to the dock, taking up a tiny percentage of its wide expanse. On the other side of the dock, there were two towns visible in the distance. They were bisected by a dense expanse of forest and connected by a single-lane road. The first town hugged the Passage's shoreline. Its metal roofs shined so fiercely that he could not make out the individual buildings. From what he could tell, the layout was everything NordStar had promised, a beautiful, modern community dotted with parks and held together by footpaths. To its southwest, an ice-blue river snaked its way to an enormous lake.

"Chilkoot Lake," Buddy yelled over the thrum of the prop blade. "Excellent fishing. The sweetest sockeye salmon you've ever tasted."

Northwest of the shining town was another, a collection of lopsided clapboard shacks huddled together for warmth against jagged hills that led to snowy peaks. Seth scanned the horizon for a break in these towering, powder-filled mountains, but found none. He could not understand why anyone would choose to live amongst these tatty-looking buildings. *It would,* he thought, *be like eating at Sizzler when there was a Ruth's Chris just across the street.*

"What's that?" Seth asked, pointing to the shacks. "That other town there."

"Other town?" Buddy responded, then shrugged at Tammy.

Seth understood. The second town was Lutak — the real Lutak. The Diana's passengers were never meant to see it. As they approached from the water, all they would see was NordStar's version of the town, the myth of a prosperous modern Alaskan port.

Suddenly, the chopper's tail dipped and they were hurtling down, down, down to the dock. Seth's hard-earned comfort disappeared. He tasted bile in the back of his throat. He drew air through his nostrils and let out short gasps of air. He had made it this far, and was not willing to vomit in his client's helicopter. Seth gasped when the landing skids touched the dock's heli-pad, making his nausea all the worse.

Tammy and Buddy slid easily out of the helicopter's front row, but Seth could not figure out how get out from the rear. He fumbled for a latch, a lever, a handle, a button — whatever thing would get him out of Buddy's tilt-a-whirl and into the open air. His chest heaved involuntarily, sending foul liquid into his mouth. His cheeks expanded and his eyes bulged, like Dizzy Gillespie making sweet music on the horn. Seth struck the wall as if sheer force could save him from defiling Buddy's chopper.

Seth put one hand over his mouth to capture the dribble escaping his lips. Behind him, he heard a whooshing noise, like a mini-van door sliding open. He smelled fresh air — outside air — invading the province of his caustic stench. His mind registered it before his body could: an exit! With hands over his strained lips, Seth spun and lurched for the dazzling swath of outside hanging on the helicopter's opposite wall.

Outlined against the bright opening was a slight figure with feminine features. Seth dearly hoped it would move, but it did not. Instead, its arms spread, Jesus-like. The words "bad timing" echoed through his brain as he sent a stream of hot grey soup its way.

# 24

"You always did know how to make a girl feel special, Ozzy," Evie said. She squeegeed spew from her cheeks and shoulders. To Seth's amazement, her Kool-Aid red hair was untouched.

"Oh, man." Seth peeled off his windbreaker and handed it to Evie. Though covered in his sick, he couldn't help but notice that she still had the lean body and lusty curves he remembered from law school. He admonished himself for even thinking about her body after the awful thing he had just done. He yanked the Beast through the helicopter door and across a splotch of sick on the dock's concrete heli-pad.

Apparently frustrated by the windbreaker's inability to absorb any of the mess on her face, Evie dropped the stained jacket onto the Beast. She grabbed what she could of Seth's blue oxford and wiped her face against his poly-blend wrinkle-free dress shirt. The resulting stain reminded Seth of a Discovery Channel special he'd seen on the Shroud of Turin. Her face now free of puke, Seth could tell that her eyes were rimmed with a red as intense as her neon locks. Then it all came back to him. Evie found her mentor and his wife — or at least significant parts of them — in the snowy slopes outside of Lutak just the night before. He reached for her. "Evie, God, I'm sorry about all of this."

She backed up a step and shook her head. "Not your fault," she sniffled. "We all know the risks out here. Bill knew better than anyone. And Lois was as big girl. Truth is, we're just guests here." She waved at the mountains. "The more we pack people into these remote areas, the greater the probability of attack. Pure statistics."

Seth was surprised by her bluntness. She seemed to accept the MacReary's deaths as natural, expected even. Seth had never lost anyone particularly close to him. The closest he could recall was a grandparent's death when he was much younger.

Before he could try to comfort her again, she crossed her arms and changed the subject. "I thought we weren't going to see you for a few more days."

"That was the plan," Seth said. "But then that happened." He pointed to the small tug bumped up against the dock, a magnetic CNN placard covering the boat's real name.

"So you're here because CNN's about to make NordStar's P.R. a bitch, right?" she asked.

She was getting right to the point. "Going to? Already have. You should see the media access on these cruise ships. Cable, Internet, cell phones. It's a nightmare, like the cruisers never left home. They sit around watching CNN coverage all day while we're at sea."

"Probably makes you wish you could just shut it all down. The ship's communications, I mean."

"Tried that," Seth said. He was surprised that he was comfortable telling Evie what they had tried on the Diana. But then again, there had been a time not so long ago when he trusted Evie with all things intimate. Why should now be so different? Maybe because she didn't seem like herself. Sure she had just been covered in throw-up, but the old Evie would have laughed it off. That is how remarkable she was. But this new Evie, she was so closed-off emotionally, so harsh. Seth chalked it up to grief. "But people always find a way, you know?"

Evie smiled. That was the Evie he remembered from law school. As quickly as it appeared, the smile vanished. Evie was back to business. "What more can you accomplish by coming here today? I know you can handle a public relations crisis from afar. You do it all the time. So why the rush? And don't fuck with me, Seth. The truth. And why are they here?" Evie pointed to Tammy and Buddy, both busy unloading gear from the helicopter.

"Well, that's Buddy—"

"I know who he his. I don't know her."

"Tammy Wurser, head purser."

"What kind of a name is that? Sounds like Dr. Seuss."

"Agreed. How do you know Buddy?"

"Everyone around here knows him. NordStar has had a huge impact on Lutak. Depending on who you talk to, he's either a hero or the devil."

"Where do you stand?"

"Is there a difference?"

"Well, as archetypes, they're pretty much polar opposites."

"I realize that. But, in reality, there's not much difference between hero and devil in Alaska."

Evie wasn't making sense.

"Back to the matter at hand," she said. "What are you doing here today? Why now?" Seth looked back at Buddy and Tammy, now examining their post-flight checklist.

"Okay." Seth took a deep breath. "I have a request."

"Well that's a surprise." Evie's voice was full of contempt.

"And I need you to hear me out before you answer. Because you're not going to like this, but I think it's for the best."

"Go ahead."

"You promise to hear me out?"

"I promise to walk away from you right now if you don't get on with things."

Seth gulped and wiped a fleck of half-digested bread from Evie's nose. He had no time to waste.

"I need you to help me get that—" Seth stopped talking when he noticed Buddy, a few yards away, following their conversation intently. He hadn't wanted his first in-person conversation to be like this. He would have preferred meeting over a meal, or a drink, and exchange social niceties before getting down to brass tacks. "I need you to help me get the bear that killed the MacReary's."

Seth dropped his eyes towards the cement dock and shook his head. To Seth's surprise, Evie did not criticize him. She did not slap him. She did not ask, "Why me?"

Instead, her eyes went unfocused and she started babbling. Her eyes fluttered and her body fell to the dock. Seth lunged for Evie and caught her head in his palms just inches before it struck the hard concrete.

# 25

"Help! I need help!" Seth shouted.

Buddy ran to Seth. Tammy appeared interested, but did nothing – like a cat watching a bird through a windowpane. When Buddy arrived at Seth's side, Evie's eyelids had stopped their frantic motion and she was moaning softly. Buddy opened an aluminum canteen and poured a thick cord of water between her lips. Then she was sitting up and sputtering, water coming like a geyser from her mouth. The liquid that didn't escape her mouth forged a phlegmy stream from her nose. A large globule of greenish mucous struck Seth just below the right eye. The sputum in Evie's throat triggered her gag reflex, which then encouraged the contents of her stomach onto Seth's loafers, their careful reddish-brown luster now a muddled galaxy of corn and chunks of unidentified other.

"Touché," he said. "Now we both need a change of clothes."

Evie cracked another smile, then laughed heartily. She had always loved getting even. Seth put Evie's pale left arm around his shoulder and the pair walked off of the dock, the Beast in tow.

Once back on terra firma, Seth and Evie followed a spotless cobblestone footpath away to the dock. A worker in a blue NordStar jumpsuit swept the walkway, setting the stage for the Diana's arrival two days hence. Across the polished cobblestones was a phalanx of tall, black craftsman-style light poles. Seth imagined that the lighting made for a beautiful evening departure. He also noted that every third pole had a lipstick-sized security camera silently scanning the dock. More post 9/11 precautions, he assumed.

"I didn't mean to throw up, you know," Evie said. They were now out of Buddy and Tammy's earshot.

"Me either," Seth replied. "Sometimes you just don't have control over your stomach. You know?"

Evie smiled and shook her head. "No, this is different."

"Do tell. You have some unusual control over your gag reflex?"

Evie shook her head.

"Is this yoga-related? Pilates?"

"No, I mean—" She stopped, mid-way through the line of light poles, and took her arm from Seth's shoulder. She looked into Seth's eyes, and Seth finally recognized her again. She had dropped the pragmatic, tough-girl veneer she employed on the dock and was once again the lovely, impish Evie that Seth had loved so long ago.

"Look," she said, "I staged the whole fainting thing. I just didn't expect that old fucker to shove water into my mouth."

"I think he was trying to help."

"Right. Because I've attended a ton of CPR classes where the instructor encourages water boarding when a person is in distress. Makes complete sense."

This was a side of Evie that Seth had tried to forget. In their short romance, she regularly spouted about a vast right-wing conspiracy. While he agreed in principal — money allows the rich to manipulate the poor more than the other way round— he bristled at Evie's insistence that the privileged always meant evil. And his line of work had mostly confirmed that Evie was simply paranoid. His clientele were all members of Evie's supposed conspiracy, but they were far too disorganized to work together for any larger purpose, let alone keep it a secret. On the other hand, Buddy's response to Evie's fainting spell had been strange.

They walked past the lighted columns and underneath a giant, black iron sign welcoming NordStar passengers to "Lutak: Earth's Last Eden." Beyond that iron portal was the gleaming city that Seth had seen from above. He recognized the layout of Lutak's Main Plaza from drawings that hung in his office. The Plaza itself mirrored the Diana's town hall layout. The redundant layout, Buddy had explained, was vital to the new port's success.

"Our passengers won't have a ton of time here," he had said. "Most will spend an hour, max, in town before or after an excursion, or they'll just come down for a meal and some shopping before they head back to their cabin for an afternoon nap. So it's crucial that the town be as efficient as possible. We want our passengers to know where they can shop, where they can get a quick bite to eat, where to have fancy lunch, where to move their bowels. An efficient town means more money for NordStar."

Despite the identical layouts, the Plaza architecture was wildly different from The Diana's. Its buildings reminded Seth of those he had seen on trips to ski towns like Vail and Telluride — bases of rustic grey stacked stone and dark brown wooden beams sat beneath brightly-colored standing-seam metal roofs. The combination of rustic and modern made the Lutak port feel authentic, but safe — frontier Alaska by way of Disneyland. The town also had a number of the same stores and restaurants that Seth had seen aboard the Diana. They proudly displayed their multiple store locations — Lutak, Grand Cayman, Nassau, Aruba, Martinique, etc.

A perfect blanket of sparkling, powdery snow flanked the cobblestone path leading into the main plaza and filled the open spaces between Lutak's buildings. It was still late summer in Alaska, and while snow covered mountains matched the picture on the cruise brochure, he had not anticipated snow at any of the cruise's port elevations.

"It's beautiful," he said. Seth wanted to jump into the white stuff, make snow angels, throw balls of it at Evie. "No wonder everyone's so bonkers over this place."

"It's fake," Evie said. "It's still summer here. And did you happen to notice that it's not snowing anywhere else in town?"

Evie might have been ruining the port's magic, but what he saw next absolutely destroyed it. Not fifty yards from where he stood was the very reason that Seth, Buddy and Tammy had come to Lutak. Well, not exactly the same reason. This bear was much whiter than the grizzly that Seth sought – a polar bear. But that did not make matters any better. The polar bear reared back on its hind legs, a snarl turning its carnivorous face into a pants-wetting thing of terror. Seth looked into its black eyes and saw the soulless nothingness of a shark. He tripped backwards, his right hand cracked against the Plaza's fake snow, and the fingertips jammed against the sparkling white, shellacked illusion. He nursed his injured hand. He looked up at Evie, his eyes wide with horror.

"Get up," she said quietly.

"I-I," he stuttered. "I don't know what to do."

"You get up. That's what you do. You're making a fool of yourself."

The plaza was dotted with people in blue NordStar uniforms, each attending to some task to ready Lutak's main plaza for the Diana's arrival. Some washed windows, others trimmed greenery in the town square, a few zoomed around on Segways supervising the others. None seemed to give a second thought to the white monster.

The snarling white demon moved towards him.

And that's when Seth noticed the wheels. There were four of them, the closest two hovering nearly a foot above the ground. And then he saw the wooden platform that the wheels supported. And he noticed the bear's remarkable balance, staying atop a wooden platform that skated towards them, wheelie-style. And then he saw the man in blue pushing it along on an orange dolly that carried the stuffed bear.

"That's fake, too," Evie said. "And look, there's a scary fake bunny, and there's a scary fake bird, and over there is a scary stuffed grizzly. Nothing to be afraid of here, tough guy."

A gardener with an enormous set of shears stood laughing near a bald-eagle shaped topiary. The man turned away, giggling. He angled the shears to trim an errant branch, and lopped off the hooked tip of the eagle's carefully constructed beak. He stopped giggling, his face flushed red with fury. He turned back to Seth, now deadly serious. A second man came into view, yelling and shaking his fist at the first man. The topiary trimmer grunted.

When the second man left, the topiary trimmer grunted and looked at Seth. "Chupa me, puto," he said.

Seth reached down to push himself off of the ground and away from the man with the giant scissors, but his jammed fingers would not support his weight. As he stumbled back into a crouching position, Evie grabbed Seth's collar and pulled him to his feet.

"Come on," she said, "let's go someplace a bit more authentic."

Seth followed Evie across the plaza, happily giving the trimmer wide berth.

Evie kept a brisk pace and Seth struggled to keep up. The Beast's wheels scraped up earth on either side of the cobblestone path. Beyond the main plaza, Seth was surprised to encounter a building that he did not remember from the port's plans. It was low and long, sharing the stone, wood and metal roof combination that typified buildings in Lutak's main square. The chainsaw cut sign along the cobblestone footpath announced that this was The Inn at the End of Paradise. Calling this enormous structure an Inn, however, was as inappropriate as calling the Diana a boat. Beneath the name was an odd, but attractive logo, a vibrant yellow sunflower with propeller-blade petals. Seth was confused. "This wasn't in the plans," he shouted to Evie, who was now well ahead of him.

"What wasn't?" she shouted back.

"This 'Inn at the End of Paradise.'"

"It's not an Inn, it's an abomination."

"Exactly what I was thinking. I mean, the Diana's not a boat either, right?" An Inn made no sense here. Lutak was just a cruise stop, a place for passengers to shop, shit, and eat, then move on to NordStar's bread and butter — overpriced excursions.

She threw a troubled glance at Seth but let the subject drop and continued down the cobblestone path. As Seth approached the pathway leading to the Inn's entrance, he saw a piece of the view that would be fully available from guest rooms on the other side of the building. He finally understood Lutak's draw. The land behind the Inn fell away, revealing an expanse of crystalline-blue water uninterrupted by docks, boats or buildings. The lake — Chilkoot Lake — was ringed on all sides by stand after stand of dark green spruce-hemlock. Large birds lazily circled infinite airspace above the lake. Beyond the birds, a range of snowy mountains exploded skyward. Seth craned his neck to find their tops. These behemoths made molehills of Phoenix's dirt-clod buttes.

Evie walked right past the pathway leading to the Inn's entrance.

"Where are we going?" Seth shouted.

"Just keep up. We don't want to stick around here long."

Seth passed the tee in the footpath that led to the Inn. He looked down the long cobblestone path and spotted a gunman in familiar NordStar blue positioned at the front door. The gunman pointed his at Seth, then waved him along with a "nothing to see here" gesture. Seth hurried after Evie.

# 26

Evie was still a ways ahead of Seth. She made an abrupt right turn and disappeared behind a barrier of tall trees. Seth did not like being alone here. This was strange territory, with gunmen and a killer bear on the loose. He hurried to the tree line and turned right. When he rounded the corner, Evie was waiting, hands resting impatiently on her hips. Seth fondly remembered the excitement of putting his hands where Evie's now were. Only, in his memories, there were no jeans between his hands and her hips – just creamy-white skin on his apartment bed.

Judging by Evie's tired face, however, it was clear that the past was not prologue, not today. Seth was here on business, and Evie was not in the mood to play. Seth's eyes moved beyond Evie's comely shape and settled on the two-lane blacktop behind her. The road looked new and led all the way up the foreboding mountains to Lutak's east. About a mile away, just before the road hit the mountains, the road stopped at a collection of shacks: Old Lutak.

"Evie," he said, "what was all that about?"

"What was what?"

"You act like a dude strapped with an assault rifle is business as usual around here."

"It is. Don't you know we're all a bunch of moose hunters up here, shooting wolves from helicopters?" Evie laughed. "Look, Seth, everyone here is carrying."

"You're not."

"You don't know that. Anyway, you get used to it."

"But an AK-47 at the front door to an Inn?"

"That's no Inn."

"We covered that already. A bit too big for an Inn, right?"

"No, I mean, it's not a hotel. I have my suspicions."

Seth shook his head. More of Evie's paranoia. "Well, whatever it is, why the heavy weaponry?"

"Buddy's ruffled some feathers in Lutak. Apparently, some of the locals messed with the Inn, spray painted their names on it or something. Buddy's promising a reward to anyone who gives him 'information leading to the arrest' — and torture, I'm sure — 'of the individuals that vandalized NordStar property.' There are notices posted all over town."

"I didn't see any."

"You haven't been to Lutak."

"But we just walked through—"

"That isn't Lutak. That is an abomination. Lutak is up there." She pointed to the huddled shacks near the mountains. "Come on."

Seth wiggled his toes and felt a blister beginning to form. He hadn't expected to cover such a distance just to have a sit down with Evie. "Why can't we just drive over?"

Evie cocked an eyebrow. "No cars allowed in the port. Segways only. You know that. Some bullshit about environmental sensitivity. Probably makes it easier for NordStar to keep track of who comes and goes. Besides, it's not much of a hike to town. And a little walk will do your desk-jockey ass some good."

"I have desk-jockey ass?"

Evie looked him up and down. "You're more a pear than you were in law school. Nothing a few good walks won't take care of. At least you don't have flat ass."

"Desk-jockey ass and flat ass are different?"

"Jockey still implies cute and small, but well-worn. Flat ass is like having pie tins under your trousers. Not pleasant. A few more years riding that desk, Ozzy, and you'll be there."

A quarter of a mile before reaching the huddled shacks at the base of the mountains, Seth and Evie passed the Lutak Burger 'n' Shake. Seth was starving, and it looked like the perfect place for a conversation and a blessed meal, but Evie did not stop. She powered on until they were in the center of the assorted clapboard shacks. Once in their midst, Seth realized that the port's ugly mountainside sibling was a full-blown town. The buildings were mostly grey and unfinished-looking, with a smattering of brick here and there to give the place a feeling of permanence. There were a wide variety of businesses — markets, stores, offices, outfitters — and a good number of people milling about.

Unlike the port's cobblestone paths, Lutak's sidewalks were made of wooden planks — also gray and unfinished-looking — and elevated a few feet from either side of a muddy, rutty road. Seth made his way along Lutak's boardwalks, ducking occasionally to avoid ornately carved wooden signs hung by chain link from the businesses' small wooden porch roofs. Evie turned left into a pair of swinging doors beneath a sign that said, "Mother Chuck's."

The bar was the darkest watering hole Seth had ever seen, and it was choked with tobacco smoke. His eyes adjusted until he could just make out Evie's small figure disappearing deep into the chalky swirl. He pursued, passing a bar tended by an old man in a leather World War II bomber helmet and a black t-shirt that said "I Am a Mother Chucker" in bold white letters. The bartender's .44 sat in a bright holster on his hip. When he met Seth's stare, Seth saw an ugly, scarred ridge of skin where the man's right eye should have been. Seth stopped staring and looked for Evie, but was unable to find her in the darkness.

"Ozzy!" she shouted from somewhere beyond the bar. "Get over here!"

He headed towards the sound of her voice and soon found himself in a small red pleather booth. As he sat, a bright flash went off. He tried to shield his eyes from the blinding spark, but struck his jammed fingers against the table.

"Motherfucker!" he shouted. He put his good hand against his mouth, shocked by the outburst. When the temporary blindness receded, he saw that the flash came from a flame on Evie's Zippo, held out so that he could light the Marlboro Red lying on the table before him. He also saw the one-eyed bartender's gun, pointed straight at his temple from just a few feet away.

"It's okay, Mother," Evie told the bartender.

"In here," he croaked, "we don't talk to ladies like that." He did not lower the gun.

"Mother, I said it's okay."

"If you say so, Evie," Mother said. "But I'd keep my good eye on that one if I were you."

Before Seth realized he was gone, Mother was back behind the bar rubbing a rag across a glass mug. There were 10 or 12 other patrons in the dark of the bar. None had paid attention to the near shooting that had just taken place. Evie popped up, whispered a few words to Mother, stroked his shoulders reassuringly, and returned with two large mugs of dark beer.

"You're going to want to watch your language for a bit," she said. She smiled, seemingly enjoying Seth's near-death experience with the one-eyed man she called 'Mother.'

"Where did he get that name? Mother?"

"Why do we call anyone anything? Back to bear business."

Seth took a small gulp of beer, the head tickling his nostrils. Time for the pitch. "Look, Evie," he said, "my career rides on what happens here two days from now."

"Sounds a touch dramatic."

"It's not. I've seen my colleagues tank on a lot less: a lost motion, a typo, a misdirected e-mail. It doesn't take much, and right now Lutak is shaping up to be a monumental disaster."

"Because of the bear."

He pointed his cigarette at her, then caught Mother staring at him and rested it on the ashtray. "Right! The bear. That thing is killing people here indiscriminately. It needs to be stopped."

"Before your cruise ship gets here, you mean. So that people spend money here, I get it."

"It's not just that, Evie. That thing is genuinely dangerous. You know that. You saw what it did to Bill and his wife."

"I know it's dangerous, Seth. It's a fucking bear. Come on. And it's probably lost its fear of man. So maybe that means that people need to stay away from it until a team of hunters from Anchorage can get out here and take care of the situation. Not you and captain oldie and that ridiculous girlfriend of his from the helicopter. I don't think rushing is any sort of answer."

"I know you don't. But, I'm telling you this, as a friend. I'm sunk if I can't take care of this situation. Hell, this whole thing is so fuc—" Seth grunted at looked a Mother, whose good eye was indeed fixed on him. "This whole situation is so messed up that I haven't even told my boss how bad it looks here."

"Maybe you should take another job. Why compromise yourself like this?"

"I am your friend, Evie. I'm asking you for a favor."

"Why me?"

"Because we both know that the land around Lutak is protected. No hunting, right? But you have pull around here. You can poll the town council to let us take care of this thing and keep the town's tourist industry alive. You can help me save Lutak."

"So, I pull a few strings to let you and the A-Team wreak havoc in the mountains around here? Who knows how many bears you'll end up shooting? Who knows whether you'll even get the right one? They tend to get a little aggressive when people are shooting at them, Ozzy."

"Evie, you and I both know what happens when that Anchorage team gets here. They're going to destroy this bear, and I know you don't like that."

"So I should let you do it? Because you're my friend?"

"No!"

Mother was now standing between the bar and their booth.

Seth spoke quietly. "No. Look, I don't want to destroy the bear at all. I think we can all be winners in this thing. Even the big bad bear out there. Just hear me out."

# 27

Evie had been gone for hours, off to persuade the town council to issue Seth's hunting party a license to hunt the monster that had stalked Lutak. Things were looking up. But there was one hurdle Seth had yet to overcome — calling Thad.

"What the fuck, bitch?"

"I know," Seth said, "I know. I'm sorry I didn't call you earlier. I had to make some important decisions very quickly."

Seth was wandering old town Lutak aimlessly. It was late afternoon now, but there were still quite a few people milling about the town's wooden walkways.

"Bad answer, motherfucker. You and I both know that reasoned decisions aren't made quickly. Smart decisions are the result of thought and collaboration between partners -- like me -- and associates – little bitches like you."

"I know. But I think we're still on good ground here."

"The fuck you are. You're misleading the passengers again. And you're advising our clients without my consent."

"Buddy likes the new plan."

"Of course he does. He thinks it gets NordStar out of very hot mother fucking water. But we're not in the business of simply getting our clients out of trouble without fully analyzing the associated risks."

"I've already considered the associated risks."

"Okay, you stupid bitch. What are they?"

"Well, primarily, I am risking my own ass. Personally and professionally."

Thad huffed through the line. "I could give two shits about your personal ass. Did you think about what happens when Buddy gets hurt out there? You advised him to go on a fucking bear hunt! I don't think I've ever even contemplated the malpractice suit that comes with that."

"He's excited about it, Thad. And he's willing to put it down, in writing, that this is just a recreational hunt. Some boys' time out. A 'thank you' for getting the port opened up."

"Jesus. And how well do you think his stipulation holds up when he says he signed under duress, duress brought on by his own personal fucking attorney?"

"Thad, I had to do something. I can't let this thing fall apart."

"I appreciate your persistence, bitch, but sometimes you just have to accept the way things are. And you, you've never even held a gun. What are you going to do when you get charged by a bear?"

"Look, you want me to call off the hunt?"

"No."

"No?"

"No. I want you to go out there and cover Buddy like the secret fucking service. If there's a bullet, a bear, a rabid raccoon coming his way, I want you to get your personal ass right in front of it. That man is to have no reason to sue us, understand?"

Seth let out a long breath, relieved that Thad would not stand in his way. "Absolutely."

"And one other thing."

"Yeah?"

"If you don't come back with the bear, you don't have a job. You'll quit voluntarily."

Seth's faced flushed. "I understand."

"And we never had this conversation. You never filled me in on your plans. I just thought you were on vacation. At least do me the professional courtesy of getting the fuck out of my professional life."

"Absolutely." Seth accepted this as a quiet victory. Lutak's success or failure was squarely back on his shoulders. He could handle that.

"And Seth?"

"I'm here."

"You know, be successful. I like working with you, bitch."

Seth put his cell phone away and checked his watch. He was once again outside of Mother Chuck's, his and Evie's designated meeting place. But Evie hadn't returned.

# 28

The sun was setting outside Mother Chuck's tavern and Evie still hadn't returned. He called her cell phone but went straight through to message. He began to worry, his brain spinning elaborate theories about her absence. Suddenly, Mother Chuck's double doors opened. A swirl of smoke and chatter escaped from within. Seth turned around and saw a familiar mustache stumble out of the inky interior, a big smile on his old face.

"What a great town," Buddy said, puffing on a cigar and steadying himself against the Beast. "We're good to go, my boy. Good to go. Thanks to you."

Seth had no idea what was happening. What was Buddy doing here?

Then Tammy Wurser, The Diana's head purser, came through the doors. She had the rheumy eyes of a person who had downed one beer too many. "I'm particularly glad," she slurred, "that the Council was willing to meet in open session."

Buddy smiled and straightened his broad cowboy hat. The get-up made Buddy look like Teddy Roosevelt in his Rough Rider days. "Okay, son, we're heading back. See you in the morning, first light. Edge of town."

"I'm sorry," Seth asked, confused. "What's going on here?"

"Don't be so humble," Buddy replied, then pulled Tammy into the dusky evening and away from the flickering lanterns that framed Mother Chuck's doors. The doors opened again, and Seth was relieved to see Evie round the corner.

"You can come in now," she said. She swayed a bit and held on to the door. Seth followed Evie back into Chuck's. A light came from a back room that he hadn't noticed during his earlier visit. A motley group came out of the back room, each shaking the hand of a proud looking Mother as they left.

"You all have a good night, you hear," Mother said, winking his good eye. "Be careful out there, there's a bear about." The strangers laughed and scurried out of the bar.

"Who are these people?" Seth asked Evie. "What's going on here?"

"Mother heads the town council, Seth." She clumsily landed a hand on his shoulder. "Not everyone can afford a city hall, hotshot. Besides, last I checked, there's no free booze at Phoenix council meetings."

"And that was them? Leaving out of the back room?"

"Yup," Evie smiled. "And you got your hunting permit."

"Just like that?"

"That's how we do things here," Mother said, his hand resting on his holstered .44. "We have always prided ourselves on a distinct lack of bureaucracy. We like to keep things simple. And we have a particular fondness for little Evie here."

Evie looked down, red with embarrassment.

Seth turned to Evie. "No, seriously, how did you persuade the Council?"

"It was easy," she said. "I told them that you wanted to head out into the mountains without any slugs. The Council figured it was a win-win proposition: either you rid us of a maniac bear, or you get Buddy and yourself killed. The town appears to see both as a positive."

"But there's one condition," Mother said.

"Yeah?" Seth said.

"Evie doesn't go with. Lutak doesn't need to lose anyone else to that thing." He glared at Seth with his one good eye. "Or to your lack of experience."

Seth looked to Evie, a question on his lips.

"Seth, you don't need me out there. According to Buddy, Tammy's a tracker. She'll help you find what you're looking for. And besides, after this morning, I'd prefer not to be isolated out in the woods with that old Wilford Brimley look-alike under any circumstances."

"Can I get you something?" Mother said, now back behind the bar. Seth never saw him move.

"What were they having?" Seth asked, motioning to the back room.

"Mother's hooch. Want a snort?"

"Want or need?" Seth asked.

Mother nodded and slid a shot glass of clear liquid Seth's way. Seth took a whiff – pure lighter fluid. He walked away from the bar but was stopped by a hand grabbing the back of his collar.

"Mother's hooch ain't free," Mother said.

"But, the Council meeting—"

"Meeting's over, young man. My hooch is 15 bucks a shot."

"That's pretty fuck—"Mother's right hand traveled down to his .44 "—pretty darn expensive, Mother."

"Oh, it's not too bad, considering," Mother said, his right hand back on the counter.

"Considering what?" Seth asked.

"Considering that you'll only need one," Evie said, laughing, her eyes watery.


One had been enough. The room wasn't quite spinning, but it did take on a softer quality. Seth lounged against a booth cushion. Evie, across from him, did the same. This was, Seth believed, probably the best buzz of his life. And Mother's Hooch had made it much easier to catch up with Evie. While the two had corresponded regularly over the past two years, the discussion never really moved beyond the tasks at hand. Seth could tell that tonight would be different.

Seth filled Evie in on the events of the past few days — adopting the Beast, meeting Nan and Charlie Jenkins, Ceejay Brecht and Cliffy Clay-

Phan, his brief and frightening introduction to piloting a cruise ship, and his failed attempt to cut off communications to the ship. Evie seemed particularly delighted by Seth's retelling of the exploding safety vest story.

"I can't believe she did that to you!"

"I know. Pretty humiliating."

"But, I mean, that takes a lot of preparation."

"Just shows you how much the ship's crew likes me. Anyway, Cliffy promised to steal Tammy's remote for me. I still have the inflatable jacket, and I'll get back at her." Seth paused. "Okay, enough about me. On to you."

Evie's smiled with mock joy. "Great."

"No, seriously. I mean, I know you're studying geology out here. But I don't really have the slightest clue what that means. Or even how you ended up here. So, tell me about it."

"Okay, Ozzy. Because you are my special guest, and I have had a helping of Mother's fabulous hooch, I will tell you. Prepare to be thrilled. After I left law school—" she dropped her eyes when she said this "—I decided to specialize in a branch of geology called geomorphology. Heard of it?"

"Of course, who hasn't?" Seth laughed.

"Okay, let's work it through together. We'll do prefixes for $200. 'Geo' is Greek for this celestial body."

"What is Earth?"

"Good. And 'morph' means?"

"Well, this one I do know something about. 'Morph' used to be short for 'metamorphose,' which referred to undergoing a transformation. Nowadays, we've shortened everything to a cool buzzword –the kids all say 'morphing.'" Seth was proud of himself.

"True. Unimportant, but true. Okay, so, put those together and you get —"

"The study of earth changing."

"Exactly. And that's why I'm here in Lutak. In this one backwater, I get to study all four branches of geomorphology," Evie splayed her fingers and tried, but failed, to point at each in turn, "fluvial, hill slope, glacial and weathering." She sighed drunkenly, and then continued, "And boy are things changing quickly. If you had stayed on the Diana for another day, you would have seen passengers standing on the deck wearing only bathing suits, watching Mendenhall glacier fall into the water. That's new."

"So you're a global warming wacko," Seth said.

"Find me someone who isn't."

"I thought there was some legitimate debate here."

"Not really. Look, all scientists believe in global warming. They just don't agree on its causes or impacts. Some even argue that there are positive benefits to the changes. Longer growing seasons, greater food production, an easier life up here in Alaska."

"Doesn't sound awful."

"Nope. Not until you factor in the resulting disease, increased hurricanes and heat waves, and, finally, the onset of another ice age."

Seth considered this. "So you're not a global warming wacko. You're a doom and gloom wacko."

"I wasn't before I came out here. Back then, I just wanted to see it for myself. I wanted to know how much time is left before we ruined the Earth."

"You think we're causing it? People are destroying the Earth?"

"Maybe I misspoke. We're not destroying the Earth. The Earth is going to be just fine until it gets sucked into a black hole. Nope, we're destroying ourselves. Look, even if it wasn't global warming, take a look at the impact of vehicle and factory emissions over major cities like Los Angeles. Instances of asthma and cancer have increased dramatically. You think that's just a coincidence?"

"No. But it's no worse than black lung in turn-of-the-century Pittsburgh."

"Nope. Just the latest version. Just like this fucking port. The only reason I was willing to help you out is that Lutak is dying. It needs the influx of tourism money. Just like our world still needs fossil fuel energy to function. But, thanks to your good work and my help, Lutak as I know it is going to disappear. The local culture, native and import, it's going to go away. Lutak will be just another cruise line franchise. And its inhabitants know it and accept it."

"But isn't that just a natural evolution? I mean, it's not like Lutak was always here. The Tlingit were here before Mother Chuck's was, and they were run off in the name of progress. So, someone rolls over the Lutak that rolled over the indigenous people here — who probably rolled over someone else. I don't think I can shed too many tears over that."

"No, I totally agree. Things change. Things disappear. But there's a – what do you call it? – a tipping point, a point at which the change is not just progressive, but permanently detrimental to our environment, a point of no return. That's what I'm watching for. And when I see it, I'll take the steps necessary to deal with it."

"What are you talking about?"

"Well, it's like global warming. A lot of scientists believe that we're destroying our chances on Earth and we're probably past the tipping point. I mean, it's not like high-efficiency light bulbs are going to stop an inevitable ice age, you know? And if we stop using fossil fuels, we'll start using batteries that are full of toxic, habitat-destroying chemicals. No, to have any impact, our changes have to be bigger than that. More radical. And I don't see people voluntarily making that change. So, maybe we need a push. As smart as we think we are, we're powerless in the face of progress. Just like you couldn't make the Diana into Myanmar, and I can't — and won't — stop Lutak from becoming that new shining thing by the water. It's why Bill was right to oppose NordStar, and why I wasn't wrong to oppose Bill. It's the natural state of things."

"Wow." Seth looked at his empty glass of hooch and reconsidered the one-glass cap. "You are, like, a walking, talking buzz kill."

Evie smiled sadly. "You asked. There it is in a nutshell. I went from rebellious law student to Debbie Downer. Sometimes the stuff you don't want to know starts filling your world." She cradled her empty glass and stared at the table. "Either accept it or do something about it. I'm here to do something, I'm just waiting for the right opportunity. And if it never comes, my world will continue to be as lonely and sad as it's been for the past seven years."

Seth couldn't believe he had stumbled into such serious territory. He reminded himself not to ask any more questions about Evie's career. He tried to think of a way back into friendly conversation, but he could only think of one other topic. It loomed large in Seth's mind, and, though he tried to stuff it back down, it floated back up at every opportunity: why had she left him? She was there one day in law school, then gone the next. Words were left unsaid, questions unanswered. He knew the answers couldn't be pretty, but he finally had Evie in person again, how could he not try?

He opened his mouth, but couldn't find the words. He didn't know where to begin. How could he put into words the confusion he felt those first few months after Evie abruptly left? How could he explain the longing for her that he felt during his years with Melanie? How could he tell her that he delved into his career with a passion meant for only her? Evie stared at Seth happily, seemingly unaware of his inner turmoil. Why couldn't he just let things be? Why couldn't he be cool and simply enjoy the company of an ex-flame? Because he just couldn't, that's why. Seth opened and closed his mouth again, then squinted. Evie cocked her head.

"Evie—" he said, and then stopped.

"Evie," he tried again. "Why?"

Evie shut her eyes. When she reopened them, they were filled with tears. She leapt forward and kissed Seth, then grabbed the Beast and ran out of Mother Chuck's.

# 29

Evie dragged the Beast through Lutak's dirt streets, maneuvering around ruts and bumps with ease. Seth fought to keep up. As far as he could tell, they were headed to the imposing mountains at the edge of town. They left the maze of wooden walkways that formed the center of the old town. Town had been dark, but now things were absolutely black. For the most part, he was able to keep stride with her, despite bumping against the occasional tree or tripping over a low plant.

After several minutes, it was clear that Evie was not planning to slow their flight. They kept going up and up, into the mountains. They no longer passed roads, just foot paths here and there. Seth's drunken brain began to suspect that perhaps Evie was going to drag him into the mountains and kill him. All that talk about needing to destroy things to make a difference. Maybe she was the one responsible for violently destroying life after life in this backwater.

*Just the hooch talking*, he thought. *Stop being ridiculous.*

Still, Seth was relieved when Evie stopped at the door to a small cabin. She leaned against the wall. Seth doubled-over, breathing in long gasps of cold air and fearing that he might throw up again. Luckily, he was able to ignore the cramps in his sides, stand up, and smile. Evie reached into her pocket, fumbled for a bit, then unlocked the door. She grabbed the Beast, and then stopped with a jerk when the Beast stubbornly jammed itself in her door. Seth was relieved to learn that, despite her facility with the Beast on the trip to her cabin, it could be as stubborn for her as it had been for him. She tugged at the Beast, but it refused to move.

"It's summer," Evie shrugged. "We don't really need to close the door anyway."

Evie tore off Seth's jacket and worked through the buttons on his stained oxford. Seth lifted Evie's wool hoodie and unhooked the fasteners on her ribbed undershirt. They groped at each other's body — the thigh, the forearm, the breast, the belly — as if reassuring themselves that this was actually the person they had loved so long ago. Their intertwined bodies moved against a cabin wall. Seth unpeeled Evie's tight jeans and made his way up her legs, lightly kissing each surface. When he finished, Evie was panting. Seth stood up, satisfied with his own performance, and lazily traced the sweat-outline of Evie's breasts across her damp Henley. Evie caught her breath, pushed away from the wall, and then shoved Seth into it. The wood held Evie's warmness. She jumped onto his hips, and took him into her with one swift grab.

Occasionally, Seth would look at Evie, watching her beautiful face contort with pain and pleasure. But then watching would be too much. He would shut his eyes and lay his head against the ridged wall, concentrating on anything but the present. Still, nothing would quiet the thrill of Evie, half nude, enthusiastically using his body as a climbing wall. He couldn't wait any longer. It was over.

Evie was crying.

"I'm sorry," he said. "I wanted it to last longer."

"No, Ozzy, I'm sorry."

"Why?"

"You don't understand, Ozzy. You never really did."

"What are you talking about?"

"Forget it." Evie shook her head as if trying to force the water from her sad eyes. Evie was never one for a post-coitus snuggle. Needs fulfilled, she was back to business.

"You want a tour of the place?" she asked. She dried her eyes with the back of her hand.

"Sure," Seth said and buttoned his clothes.

Evie took Seth's hand and walked him in a circle. Evie's cabin was a one room A-frame broken into three living spaces: a tidy but unclean kitchen with outdated appliances, a living area, and a ladder that led to a raised loft. There was a dartboard with a well-pierced corporate logo pinned in place of the bull's-eye. Seth recognized the logo – a vivid sunflower with propeller-blade petals – from the Inn at the End of Paradise. But the name underneath – ST Energy – was unfamiliar.

"You got it?" she said.

"Got it."

"Up for another round?"

She walked to the loft ladder and, with a few powerful pulls, was up and out of sight. Seth shut his eyes, trying to hold the image of Evie's toned legs, their tops covered only by black lace boy shorts, mounting the loft. He gave a second's thought to the Beast, still jammed in the doorway, but quickly put the luggage out of mind. He scampered up the ladder, eager for another go.

# 30

Morning arrived rudely.

It was just after sunrise. A fiery white beam poured through the square skylight above Seth's head. Rolling away from the light source, he badly misjudged the size of Evie's loft and rolled into open air. At the last minute, he caught the rickety wooden ladder with his left hand. Fortunately, he was nearly as tall as the ladder and — with one hand holding the top rung — his toes hovered just inches above the cabin floor.

Seth rubbed the sleep from his eyes with his free right hand, the jammed fingers still swollen and complaining. He dropped the remaining few inches to the ground. Perhaps a night with Evie cured him of his clumsy oafishness, at least temporarily. Speaking of Evie, Seth did not see her in the bed, or anywhere else in the small cabin.

"G'morning, sweetheart! Don't you look cute!"

Seth didn't remember Evie having an Aussie accent.

He spun and looked in the direction of the voice. Tammy, clad in camo jumpsuit, looked through the open space between the Beast and the door jam. Then came Buddy's face, a strange-looking rifle held high. Framed by the Beast and the door, Tammy and Buddy looked like a bizarro-world version of Grant Wood's American Gothic.

"Ready, son?" Buddy asked, a maniac smile turning his mustache tips skyward. "Sun's up. The game is afoot."

Seth looked around. Where was Evie? In her living room, filling much of the braided floor rug was a large safe on a wooden dolly. Dust tracks traced the dolly wheels' path from a closet in the kitchen. It was the kind of safe Seth had seen at Sam's Club back in Phoenix, a big shiny black thing with a bronze three-spoked combination wheel. Nothing made sense.

"Must have had a big night," Tammy said. "Cheers, lawyer-man."

Seth turned red. "So, where is Evie?"

"She's in town," Tammy said, "at Mother's, I assume. That big ugly asshole told her she's not allowed to help us any. To which I say 'fine.'"

"At least she gave us these," Buddy said, then pushed a strange looking rifle through the opening in the door.

Seth inspected the gun. The label called it a "Crossman Outdoorsman." Seth had no experience with guns, but he knew enough to know that this was an unusual one. It looked less like a rifle than a knotted wooden walking stick with a black barrel at one end.

"It's an air gun," Buddy said. He and Tammy each raised theirs. "Runs on CO2, see? Comes in a canister that should do you for about 30 shots." Buddy jingled a pouch-ful of quart-sized CO2 bottles. "But, if you need that many, we're all in trouble."

"And," Tammy said excitedly, "Evie gave us a ton of these crook darts." She held up a number of nasty looking metal projectiles with yellow plastic caps on the back. "She said that they each have about 6 ccs of horse tranquilizer in 'em. Ketamine, I think. And just look at the needles on these things. They've got to be 2 inches. It's enough to stop an elephant, let alone a little old grizzly." She beamed, barely containing her excitement.

"Alright, enough talk," Buddy said. "We're heading out. Put this on." He threw a camo jumpsuit through the space in the door.

"Shouldn't we have breakfast before we go?" Seth asked.

"Yeah," Tammy laughed, "a dingo's breakfast."

"What's that?"

"A yawn, a pee, and a good look around. Get moving."

Seth looked at the new outfit. Except for the camo pattern, it was identical to the blue jumpsuits he had seen in port the day before, down to the NordStar logo on the right breast. He pulled it over his sleep-wrinkled clothes. He didn't see a need to shave or shower, and he was too nervous to use the bathroom. He took a deep breath, grabbed the dart rifle, and then climbed over the Beast and outside.

Though his air gun was nearly weightless, its shoulder strap dug uncomfortably into his skin. He tried to flex the jammed fingers on his right hand, but had little success. They were still hopelessly swollen. Buddy and Tammy remained several paces ahead of him. Buddy walked a bit more stiffly than usual, dragging his right leg a bit, but neither he nor Tammy had slowed since leaving Evie's. It looked like they were enjoying this death march, playfully hip checking one another from time to time during the endless slog.

"Hey guys," he said. "Can you give me an idea where we're going? And, more importantly, when you think we're going to get there?"

They ignored him.

He tried again, louder this time. "Buddy, Tammy, please tell me you know where the hell we're going!"

Tammy hushed him. "We're hunting, drongo. Don't you know anything about hunting? You want to talk, get up here."

Seth hurried up to the other two.

"So, where are we headed?" he asked quietly.

"To the tent," Buddy said.

"The tent?"

Buddy took out a topographical chart, and pointed to a high plateau marked with two poorly drawn skulls. "We're going to Bill MacReary's camping spot. Where Evie found him and the wife. The kill site should still be relatively fresh, so it's as good a place to start the day as any. From there, maybe Tammy can find some tracks, get some idea of what we're dealing with here."

"That's a good couple of hours off, Buddy," Seth said. "Don't you want to sit down for a second, catch your breath?" Seth made a point of looking at Buddy's stiff right leg.

Buddy just smiled. "No time, son." Buddy said. "We've got a job to do, and the Diana arrives tomorrow. If your plan's going to work, we can't spare a second."

"No, I can see that. But, I just thought maybe if we were all fresh when we encountered the murderous monster out there that we'd—"

Tammy jumped in front of Seth and stopped their forward progress. She shoved a finger into Seth's chest. Buddy walked ahead.

"Would you just stop whinging," she said quietly but firmly, "I mean, I think we've all had a gobful."

"Don't make me come back there, kids," Buddy said, now a good distance ahead.

"Cheers," she said, scurrying up to Buddy.


Seth was surprised by his own reaction to the campsite – the place where Bill MacReary and his wife had lost their lives in a most gruesome and horrible way. Seth expected to double over with dry heaves, pass out, and then need to be revived by smelling salts. But the intense sun removed any mystery or horror from the scene. It reminded Seth of a visit he and his family made to a civil war battlefield when he was a child — it was obvious that something terrible had happened on the grassy spot, but the sunny tranquility of the day removed any sense of the tragedy that befell the same spot at some point in the past.

Like he had at the civil war battlegrounds, Seth felt a detached curiosity. The shredded and bloodied tent was still staked to the ground. Nearby, a small shovel lay on the ground next to a tattered yellow sock. Seth assumed that this would have all been bagged and tagged by now, then put into evidence or something, like on television. Propriety dictated that at least the bloody tent be removed from the scene. But it was all here, laid bare.

Buddy sidled up to Seth. "What do you see here, son?" He crooked an enormous white eyebrow at Seth.

Before answering, Seth made sure that Tammy was out of earshot – she was on the other side of the clearing, inspecting the myriad footprints in the dirt and snow. "Does Tammy know what we know?"

"About Bill's gun being empty? Nope. Thought it would be a better test of her tracking mettle if she didn't have all of the info. But, looking at this, what do you think?"

"I can't imagine anything other than a bear could have done this. I mean, just look at that tent. Whatever attacked Bill tore that thing to shreds. That would take powerful hands."

"Or powerful motivation."

"What do you mean?"

"I mean that NordStar's expansion into this territory wasn't all that popular."

"Yeah, but Bill was against it. Why would they target him?"

"Doesn't make complete sense to me, either. But," he drew closer to Seth, "I should tell you, Evie might have —" Before he could finish, Tammy called from the other side of the clearing.

"Got something!"

"We'll talk more later," Buddy said, patting Seth's chest. Buddy walked stiffly towards Tammy, still dragging his right leg.


The footprint engulfed Seth's hand. It didn't take an expert to figure out that a bear had visited the campsite. More outsized prints walked out of the campsite and into the dense woods. Tammy tasted a patch of soil in the print, then tried a splotch of blackened snow, nearby. She spit several times into the grass-snow mixture around the tracks.

"Blood," she declared. "Either an injured animal walked through the campsite following the attack, or this is the bear that killed the MacRearys. I'd bet the latter."

A chill ran down Seth's spine. He was torn between relief and terror. While Tammy's deduction did not explain Bill MacReary and Rainbow

Bear's empty guns, Seth was certain there were a million other explanations for the missing ammo. As Kelly and Buddy agreed, Rainbow Bear was not prepared for the wild, and might have missed an important detail like loading a gun. And Bill MacReary hastily left his house after an argument with his wife. It was certainly possible that he forgot to take bullets with him. Stranger things had happened.

On the other hand, Tammy's discovery meant that they were hunting an actual ursine behemoth — a monster responsible for at least three deaths. Nausea coursed through Seth's stomach. Tammy dashed off into the woods, following the bear's trail.

"Okay," Seth said to Buddy, "that thing might be a bit out of our league."

"Might," Buddy said, blowing down the barrel of his air gun. "But what choice do we have? We're here to act, son. Anyway, this was your idea."

"Well," Seth stammered, "yes, but I thought we might have more than just the ship's purser for —" Seth was stopped by a tinny, techno-fied rendition of the Macarena playing somewhere nearby. Buddy huffed and reached a hand into his jumpsuit. He retrieved a tiny phone and held it up to his ear, leaning face-forward against a grey spruce bark.

"Yes. Kelly. What?" Buddy's eyes drew into tight slits, nearly disappearing under his heavy white eyebrows. "What? When? Do we have his name?" He let out a great gust of air and looked at the ground.

"What's going on?" Seth asked.

Buddy closed the phone. "There's been another attack. Well, we assume it was an attack. He's still missing."

"Who?"

"A CNN cameraman."

"Jesus." Seth slumped against a tree and slid to the ground.

"Jesus is right, son," Buddy said, and then joined Seth on the ground next to the tree.

"Maybe," Seth offered, "we should just admit that this thing is bigger than the three of us. We need to call in some help."

Buddy nodded and looked lost in thought. "Perhaps," he said quietly, absently.

Then the screaming started.

# 31

Seth had never felt a real adrenaline rush before. His ears pulsed with every heartbeat and his senses became hyper-aware. He liked the feeling.

"Help!" Tammy screamed horribly. "One of you cunts better fucking help me!"

Seth and Buddy ran in the direction of Tammy's shrieks, all the while fumbling with their respective air guns. They ran deep into the forest, amazed that Tammy got so far ahead of them so quickly. The further they wandered into the heart of the woods, the thicker the trees became, slowing their progress.

"I fucking mean it, you assholes!" Tammy bellowed angrily. "Help me!"

Buddy and Seth ran for what seemed like ages, and Tammy's cries seemed closer and closer, but they couldn't find her. After a few more frantic moments, Seth realized that Tammy's noises had grown quieter. Somehow, they had gotten further away from her. Seth put an arm across Buddy's chest, afraid that Tammy was somehow being moved against her will, away from Buddy and Seth. Tammy's shrieks fell away to a chorus of grunts.

Buddy cocked an ear, listening carefully. "Back this way," he said.

They ran back in the direction from which they had come. As before, Tammy's noises grew louder, and then faded. Panicked and confused, Seth and Buddy retraced their steps again. Tammy's voice was here, there and nowhere. Suddenly, she sounded close again. Seth and Buddy slowed their pace, scanning the forest for a trace of Tammy's blonde hair. She sounded like she was right next to them, but they could not see her.

"Fellas!" Tammy yelled, somewhere near. Now she sounded more annoyed than scared. Seth and Buddy spun in place, but Tammy remained unseen.

"Above you?" she said.

Slowly, Seth and Buddy looked up. Tammy was suspended at least ten feet above their heads, struggling against a primitive-looking net.

"Get me down, deadshits."

Seth's eyes moved from Tammy's net, to the rope holding it in place; then to the rope's pulley, attached to a tree limb a few feet above the net; then to a second pulley attached to a tree a few yards to its right; then to a coil of rope at the base of the second tree; then to a dirty bearded man standing next to the coil of rope at the base of the tree. The bearded man pointing a rifle at Seth's head.

"Guys," Seth said, calling the others' attention to the man with the gun.

Buddy drew his dart gun and pointed it at the man. A shot rang out. Buddy shrieked as his gun flew into a million pieces.

"*Dohbroye ootra!*" the man said, a broad smile on his face. "*Pozhalujjsta ponyetye vashye ohruzhye.*"

Seth and Buddy stared at him.

"*Ya skayl! Pozhalujjsta. Ponyetye. Vashye.  Ohruzhye!*" the man said, now impatient. Other armed men and women stepped out from the forest and formed a circle around them.

"What are we supposed to do?" Seth asked.

The strangers edged closer.

"I haven't got the slightest clue," Buddy said.

"Are they speaking Russian?"

The bearded man let out a loud whistle. He pointed at Seth, made his right hand into a gun, and, with his other hand, made a big show of placing his "gun" on the ground.

"Okay, okay," Seth said. He slowly put his air gun at his feet and then kicked it away. After much effort from above, Tammy's rifle fell to the ground. The bearded man collected the gun as another lowered Tammy's hammock slowly to the ground. Tammy stood up, grumbling about *dillas* and cunts.

They led Seth, Buddy and Tammy through the dense spruce. Seth was in the lead, his face flushed. The bearded man hadn't said a word. Not daring to take any chances, Seth held his hands high and marched.

"You can put your hands down," Buddy said, somewhere behind.

Seth peeked at the group walking behind him. Buddy moved along with that odd stiff walk, but looked relaxed, his arms at his sides. Tammy was further back still, hiking beside a dirty teenage girl that stared and smiled at the clean, blonde Aussie. The bearded man at Seth's side smiled. Seth lowered his hands, and the man nodded approvingly.

"*Nye stohl plokho, da?*" the bearded man asked.

Seth had no idea how to respond, and simply smiled. The bearded put his hand back on the small of Seth's back and motioned forward.

"*Bih haroshoh?*" the man asked.

Seth still had no idea what the man wanted, but smiled and nodded just the same.

"*Haroshoh*," the bearded man said, still walking. A half hour had passed since their capture. Ahead, Seth saw wisps of smoke rising between the trees. A rustic wooden encampment was just visible through the smoke, built between – and of – the surrounding spruce. Dirty children rushed out from the wooden buildings. The bearded man threw handfuls of candy and rubbed his hands through the little ones' filthy hair. He motioned to a small building at the edge of the village, where a dirty old woman beckoned through an open door. Seth smelled something familiar, but could not place the aroma.

"*Vkhohdeevsheey, vkhodeevsheey,*" the old woman said.

The old woman's house was a primitive affair, complete with dirt floors and a blazing fire-pit in the middle of the room. The woman pointed to benches lining the walls and motioned for them to sit. Stripes of soot lodged in the woman's wrinkled face and along her big nose made her look like a wizened zebra.

"*Chay*?" she asked.

Seth looked to Buddy and Tammy, who both looked as confused as he felt.

"Oh, definitely" Seth nodded and smiled, "*chay*."

"Yeah. Why not? Grande *chay* tea latte while you're at it," Tammy said, a curt smile on her face.

Buddy laughed nervously then patted Tammy's knee. "Now is not the time to make fun," he hissed. "Just be polite, and we'll get through this."

"No, I'm serious."

"So you speak Russian now?" he asked.

"Enough to know that *chay* is *chai* the world around. You pick up a thing or two working on a cruise ship. These blokes are offering us a cuppa, and I'd like mine with some milk is all I'm saying."

The old woman scurried into a room somewhere in the back of the small home, where she immediately began quarreling with what sounded like a younger woman. Then the two started laughing. The old woman rushed back into the room, along, now with a teakettle, a jar of leaves, and three mugs looped around a thick, dirt thumb.

"See," Tammy said, "just like Starbucks."

The old woman carefully extracted a handful of leaves from the glass jar, placed some in each of the three mugs, hung the kettle from a metal stand above the fire, then handed a mug to each of her guests. The bearded man came into the room. He whispered something to her.

"*Aht stahn*," the old woman told the bearded man. He nodded and left the house. She turned back to her guests. "*Ohchen preeyatna*." She waited for a response, but nothing came.

"*Harosho. Harosho.*" She paused, deep in though, and then put a hand on her chest. "*Minyah zahvoot Zoya Vladimirovich Kozlov. Baba Zoya. Da?*"

The three stared at her.

She patted her chest, "Baba Zoya." She put her hand against Seth's chest, "*Kak vas zahvoot?*"

She tried again, patting his chest gently, "*Kak vas zahvoot?*"

"Seth?" he tried.

"*Zahvoot* Sed?" she asked. She shrugged and winked. "*Woo woo.*"

The teapot whistled. The woman poured a stream of hot liquid into his mug. The familiar aroma, the smell he had noticed outside the small house, immediately crept into his nose. This time he remembered exactly where he had smelled it before: Dmitri's Luggage Shop. He immediately flipped open his cell phone and was amazed that he still got a couple of bars out here. The old woman regarded him with concern. She reached for the phone, but Seth held her off with his index finger.

"Just a minute. It's ringing. I think I can get this straightened out in just a few—"

The woman squinted her face and shouted, "*Mneh noozhnah vahshah pohmashch!*"

In a flash, the bearded man arrived at the door along with two others. "*Kak pozheevayetye?*"

The woman pointed to Seth. The bearded man signaled to the others to follow him, then rushed Seth.

"No," Seth said, struggling with the man. "Look, just a minute, I think we can —"

A bored voice answered Seth's call. "Yes," it said, "hello."

"Yes, hi," Seth sputtered, "can you please put me through to Dmitri."

"May I tell him who's calling?" the Russian voice asked, obviously uninterested in actually fetching Dmitri.

The bearded man drew his gun, and motioned for Seth to hand him the phone.

"Tell him it's Seth. Seth Sterling. I met him a few days ago. He gave me an enormous, very frustrating black suitcase. A window display, I think."

"Seth Sterling?"

"Yes, please just tell him."

"Seth Sterling!"

"Yes. Please…"

"This is Dmitri! Oh, it is good to hear—"

The bearded man ripped the phone from Seth, and put it to his own dirty ear. "*Ktoh zto!*" he demanded. Seth heard a stream of angry Russian erupt from the cell phone's tiny speaker. The bearded man pulled the phone away from his ear.

"*Da?*" the man asked sheepishly. "Vasily."

The bearded man began speaking very quickly. After a moment, the man laughed. He handed the phone to the old woman. She listened for a few minutes, then laughed. After what sounded like a pleasant conversation, she handed the phone back to Seth.

"What is wrong with you, Seth?" Dmitri demanded. "I thought you were a good guy."

"I am a good guy. What are you talking about?"

"This old woman makes you tea, and you are on the cell phone? That is very rude."

"I don't understand what's going on here, Dmitri."

"I didn't know your cruise was going to Russia. Why didn't you tell me this, Seth Sterling? And how is my luggage serving you? Good, yes?"

"I'm not in Russia. I'm in Alaska. Lutak, Alaska. And these people held us up at gunpoint. What is going on?"

"Alaska. That is weird. Okay, you put Baba Zoya back on. Let me help."

Seth showed the phone to the bearded man and said, "Baba Zoya?"

"*Nyet*," the man said, patting his chest, "Vasily." He pointed to the old woman. "Baba Zoya."

Seth nodded and handed the phone to the old woman. After a long conversation, Zoya handed the phone back to Seth.

"Okay," Dmitri said, "this is very interesting."

"Yeah?"

"You seem to have stumbled upon, like, a sleeper cell."

Seth's eyes widened.

"But, I mean, not like Al Qaeda or anything. No, this old woman, Baba Zoya, her family is here in Alaska since the late 1700s."

"Get out of here."

"She says her family settled this land, took it from the Tlingit. When Czar Alexander II sold Alaska to the United States in the 1860s, she says he told her grandfather to stay in this forest, keep an eye on American activity in this land so close to Russia. She says Alexander told her grandfather about a secret signal that would bring them out of hiding if the Russians chose to reclaim Alaska for the great empire."

"Did she tell you what the signal was? The one that was supposed to bring them out of hiding?"

"She didn't know. Other than her grandfather, no one knew. And he died in the 1890s. So her family just stays here. She told me that they go into town occasionally and trade labor for supplies. But they try to keep a low profile."

"Do they know that the Russian empire ceased to exist like a hundred years ago?"

"Yes. But they don't care. They are happy out here."

"Okay, so why did they take us hostage?"

"I don't think that has happened, Seth."

"They pulled guns on us, Dmitri."

"She says that she was told you had tiny rifles."

"Okay. That's true."

"And she said you got caught up in one of their bear traps. They've been having bear problems lately—"

"—Bear problems?"

"Right and she—"

"What kind of bear problems?"

Buddy and Tammy leaned forward.

"They said some sort of bear attacked one of the camp's children. They said someone came and told them was called a 'grizzly.' Is that right? Grizzly?"

"They were told? Who told them?"

"They say they never knew her name, just that she had hair that looked like it had been dyed in borscht."

Borscht? Seth wondered what hair dyed in borscht look like?

"Baba Zoya wants you to know that she's sorry about the trap, and she wanted to give you some tea to make up for it. And then, she thinks you are calling immigration on her."

Seth ignored Dmitri. Borscht is made from beets. What do beets look like? Those squiggly red pickled things that you avoid in the Souper Salad bar? Right! So, if you made a soup of those things, it stands to reason that hair dyed in borscht would look like – Evie! But what would she be doing up here?

"None of this makes any sense."

"I know. But these people are isolated; maybe they go a little crazy. So I told Zoya that she should come to Arizona, where it's warm. Much more hospitable for her arthritis. I could outfit her and her family for the trip, too. I never pass up a sale, you know?"

"Back to the bear, Dmitri. How long ago was the child attacked?"

"She says just two days ago."

"Did they find the bear that hurt the child? Did they kill it?"

"Oh, that. No, she says the bear was a mother, and the child accidentally wandered between it and its cubs. So, they don't kill it. Instead, she tells me a long story about this girl that marries a bear. Very strange. I tell her I don't believe her story. She tells me she never did either – that it is a story that her grandfather learned from a Tlingit."

"Anything more you can tell me about the bear that attacked the child?"

"No, just that it was big, brown, and protecting a pair of cubs."

"Can we see the child, talk to him?"

"Put Baba Zoya on the phone, I'll ask."

Seth handed the phone back to Baba Zoya. The old woman laughed, and then said "nyet." She listened some more, then laughed some more, and then said "nyet." Again she laughed, and then said, "nyet, spasibo." She shook her head with amused disbelief and handed the phone back to Seth.

"Let me guess," Seth said.

"It's a no," Dmitri responded. "Sorry, my friend. You win some, you lose some."

"Yes. Well, at least we're free to go. Right?"

"Of course! But remember, they were hospitable to you, so you will be nice to them. You will raise your tea, you will say *za vas*, which means *to you*. You will finish your tea. You will say *spasibo* — which is *thank you*. And then you will excuse yourself. Okay? These are nice people. Don't be rude, Seth."

"Got it. *Za vas. Spasibo.* Thanks for your help, Dmitri." Seth glanced at his watch. It was already after two. The day was wasting away.

"You didn't tell me how the luggage was doing."

"Can we discuss that later, Dmitri?"

"Oh, yes, sure! We'll talk soon, Seth Sterling. You and your crazy adventures."

Seth put his phone away. "Alright, folks," he told Tammy and Buddy. "I've got a lot to tell you. But, for now, just do what I do and we'll get back to work shortly."

"*Za vas*," Seth said and raised his tea.

## 32

With faces full of soot and bellies full of tea, Seth, Buddy and Tammy followed Vasily's rough directions to the site of the child's encounter with a grizzly.

Seth was worried. After the Russians destroyed Buddy's gun, the troupe was down to just two air guns. And, of the remaining shooters, Seth doubted that his swollen fingers would let him fire the weapon. Not that he had a chance of hitting a target anyway. He was no marksman.

Tammy reclaimed the lead. Seth and Buddy struggled to keep up with her. She said little as she picked her way through the brush. "Buddy," Seth told Buddy quietly, "I don't think I can shoot this animal."

"Don't go pussy on me now, son. We came to do a job, and we're damn well going to do it."

"No, it's not that. It's my fingers. I jammed them back at the port." He showed Buddy his right hand, his index finger now a yellow, puffy croissant.

"Jesus. Why didn't you mention that earlier?"

"Well, I didn't really think of myself as the shooter, you know? I thought that you two would handle that part."

"That's the problem with you attorneys," Buddy scolded, "you always think you need people for things. You might try a little thing called 'self-sufficiency,' it would probably do you some good."

"Maybe. But I think maybe I should give you my gun. I think you'd do better with it than me. I mean, I doubt I can get my finger through the little loop-thingy where the trigger is anyways."

"It's called a trigger-guard. And you'd be surprised what a little adrenaline will do for you. You keep the gun. Trust me, you'll be happier that way. Do something for yourself that you never thought possible." Seth smiled unconvincingly. Buddy strode ahead, still oddly stiff.

Suddenly, Tammy stopped. She held her index finger in the air. Buddy crouched low and Seth followed suit. Seth's heart was pounding in his ear again. The adrenaline was back, chilly at first, then a comforting warm sensation that took away his pain and anxiety.

"There," Tammy said quietly, and then pointed into the distance.

Seth tried, but saw nothing in the woods but the brown, moss-covered clutter of hemlock-spruce they had seen the entire day.

"I've got it," Buddy said.

"I'm not seeing anything," Seth said. "What is it?"

"A cub," Buddy said. "There." He pointed in the same general direction as Tammy.

Seth tried again, his eyes jumped from tree to tree.

"Nope," he said, "nothing."

"There's a trick to it," Buddy said patiently. "Stop moving your eyes. Fix on a spot, then wait for motion to enter your field of vision. Do that and you can't miss it."

Stilling his rapid eye movement involved suppressing some of the adrenaline's wonderful surge. He took a few shallow breaths, then a few deeper ones, and then his eyes stopped their frantic dance. He picked the spot that he guessed Buddy and Tammy were fixed upon and waited.

Nothing.

*Nothing.*

Then something.

It was wet and black-brown, about a foot off of the ground. A nose. He waited and saw the body connected to the nose. "I see it," he said. "And one more."

"Where?" Tammy demanded.

"To its left," Seth said. He crept forward and crouched behind a tree. "Fifteen yards, maybe? It looks like it's scratching itself against a tree stump or something."

There was silence as Tammy and Buddy confirmed Seth's sighting.

"That's no tree stump," Tammy said.

"No it's not," Buddy echoed. "Lady and gentleman, the hunt is on." Buddy tugged at his jumpsuit.

Seth looked at the ragged brown stump again. The illusion melted away, a giant bear paw in its place. A curtain of trees blocked the rest of the grizzly bear's body. The bear's paw raised and tapped the irksome cub, sending it sprawling across the forest floor.

The cub popped back up and went back to rubbing itself against the gigantic paw. Suddenly, the larger bear's face emerged in profile from behind the trees. Seth was disappointed by its expression. This was not the ferocious beast his adrenaline had promised. Its face was hangdog, more bloodhound than man-eater. Its brown jowls drooped low on its face. Above the lips, the bear's fur became a grayish white.

He could see why the Russians didn't want to hunt this creature. She was a burdened parent — the cubs' mother, Seth assumed — not a danger to their village. But, of course, that would not do today. It was, after all, Seth's idea to bring an end to this thing's "reign of terror." Returning to the ship and telling already terrified passengers to just watch their step during their Lutak excursions would not suffice.

He pulled the air gun from his shoulder and held it firmly with both hands. He wasn't sure of hunting etiquette. Should Tammy have the first crack at the sow? Should he flank the bear and flush her Tammy's way? Tammy didn't offer any help or hand signals. Instead, she was unzipping Buddy's jumpsuit. Once undone, Buddy reached in and removed the cause of his limp: a short, black nylon case. Buddy took a few tentative steps, stretching the cramped muscles in his right leg.

"What is that?" Seth whispered.

"Insurance," Buddy grunted, pulling a dwarf gun from the case. At just over a foot long, the lethal device looked like a toy.

"It's so – so, tiny," Tammy said.

"I've never been so happy to hear a woman say those words," Buddy said. Tammy leaned closer. "It's called a super-shorty. The world's shortest pump-action shotgun. Had it custom made. Look."

Seth now understood why Buddy hadn't accepted Seth's air gun when he had the chance. He had brought his own, and it looked like he was going to shoot to kill.

"We agreed that we wouldn't bring guns. Those were the rules," Seth hissed. Seth glanced over his shoulder and found the mother bear's face, still a good distance away, still partially buried in the ferns.

"Rules? Rules are the hobgoblins of little minds," Buddy said. He winked at Tammy. "To paraphrase Emerson."

"But we've got the air guns." Seth said. "And enough tranquilizer to stop an elephant. We don't need that thing."

Seth snuck a few feet ahead of the other two. He now had a clear view of the furry hill nestled among the low ferns about 60 yards ahead. Behind him, Buddy was still showing off his new toy.

"That's my name right there," Buddy told Tammy. "And there's the year of manufacture, and the inscription, 'Specially Designed For Scott 'Buddy' Tennison.'" Buddy turned his super-shorty over and, like a proud parent, showed Tammy the metal stock.

"You little ripper," Tammy told Buddy. "I knew you'd have something up your sleeve. What kind of ammo does it take?"

"All custom." Buddy reached into his bag and retrieved a handful of pencil-width shotgun shells. "The loading process is a bit tricky. They had to show me once or twice before I got it right. You slide back the action bar while holding the release button, push in the round, careful not to release the —"

The shotgun made a small popping noise.

Tammy fell.

Seth turned and saw what looked like a Three Stooges gag. It looked as though Tammy had knocked herself to the ground by slapping her own face. Then he noticed trails of smoke escaping the gun's tiny barrel. Tammy writhed on the ground, her hands glued to her face. Buddy dropped the little shotgun and rushed to her.

"Dear god," Buddy said. "Dear god dear god." He tried to pull Tammy's hands away from her face, but could not. Blood seeped through the purser's fingers. She rolled back and forth on the mossy ground, making wet, guttural noises. Buddy held her shoulders and repeated his new mantra: "Dear god dear god dear god."

Seth removed his jumpsuit and, using his teeth, tore the jumpsuit fabric into rough strips. He had no first-aid training, didn't even know CPR, but he figured that bandages couldn't hurt. Then he remembered the grizzly. With all the noise they were making, it had to be aware of them by now. Seth chanced a look over his shoulder. The cubs were still there, bouncing in and out of the ferns, but the brown hill was gone. Rockets of warm adrenaline shot from Seth's stomach, to his lungs, to his brain.

"Buddy," Seth said.

"Dear god, dear god, dear god."

Seth looked back at the cubs. His eyes darted around the terrain. The mother was gone.

"Buddy!" Seth hissed. "I don't see the bear."

"Dear god dear god dear god."

Seth held the air gun to his chest and spun in tight circles. He needed to stop, to be still, to let the bear's motion enter his field of vision just like Buddy taught him. But the adrenaline was back in a big way. Seth's body was awash with muscle ticks and the overwhelming need to take action, to move, to fight.

He blinked his eyes and licked his lips. He forced himself to stop circling, to stop moving. He started breathing. The air smelled like pine-fresheners. Bugs buzzed his forehead. He wiped them away, anxious to return his hand to the safety of his air rifle. The world slowed. Seth allowed his eyes to defocus and look back to the place where the bear had been. Still nothing. He reached into his pocket and pulled out an lengthy yellow dart.

Seth had no idea how to load the dart into the gun. He examined the rear of the gun and, not wanting to end up like Tammy, carefully pointed the barrel away from his body. He found the bolt and slid it back, revealing an empty chamber. This was easier than he thought. Seth put the dart into the chamber, pushed the bolt shut, and told himself that everything would be okay. He wasn't sure if he could manage to get his swollen finger through into the trigger-guard, but it would be okay. It had to be.

Ferns snapped in the near distance, accompanied by the sandpaper scrape of matted fur against tree. The sounds came from a dense thicket of trees to Seth's left. The snapping and scraping grew louder. Then he saw her. The sow was pushing through the trees at full gallop, her claws throwing clumps of plant and soil in her wake. Seth raised the air gun's scope to his eye, but he saw nothing. The bear was too close for the scope to be any help – it was s pointless as watching your own hand through binoculars.

Seth heard the sound of his own fear. It started as a flutter in his stomach, forced its way through his lungs, then wrenched itself free from his lips. It was a horrible and oddly feminine din, like a yodel mixed with a snarl. And it went on forever. He screamed and shook the rifle over his head. He did not know why he was doing this, only that his lizard-brain thought it was his best and last chance at survival.

The grizzly skidded to a halt so close that Seth smelled her sweaty-sweet breath. She regarded him with a mixture of fury and curiosity. He kept shaking his rifle and bellowing, his strange sing-songy growl became raspy but did not stop. The sow shook her head violently as if asking him to stop the racket. But Seth could not help himself.

The bear pulled its mammoth head back and reared on its hind legs. Its enormity overwhelmed Seth. He could no longer comprehend the bear as a whole, instead seeing the monster as a series of horrifying parts: the taut jowls; the snarling black lips; the yellowed teeth, dulled and chipped; the fetid breath; the horrible roar. The Roar. It reeked of death and rage. It filled the forest and swallowed Seth's cries. No matter how much he shouted and shook, he could not make himself more horrible than the grizzly bear.

But he *could* shoot it.

He could make it sleep.

Seth brought the rifle to his eye once again. The glass showed an endless field of brown — the sow's fur. He tried to close the fingers on his right hand, without luck. His right index finger was still hopelessly swollen. No matter, the adrenaline made him immune to pain. He squeezed his overstuffed sausage of a finger through the trigger guard. His finger was big enough to push the little metal semi-circle against the metal stock without pulling.

Then CLICK. Then nothing. Time slowed.

Seth remembered Bill MacReary and Rainbow Bear. Both prepared to shoot bears, but neither had ammunition when the moment came. Seth knew he had the ammo. He had loaded it himself. He had popped it in the chamber and pulled back the bolt. He was ready to go. Maybe the CO2 canister was empty? It was then that he remembered: he hadn't attached a CO2 canister. The canisters were still in Buddy's pouch. Seth's shoulders slumped. The bear closed in. Seth's right index finger was helplessly wedged in the air rifle's trigger guard. Even if there had been time to grab a canister from Buddy's satchel, he wouldn't be able to reload the gun and pull the trigger. For all his schemes, plans, angles and arguments, Seth Sterling was finally out of options. He was going to die.

And for what, he wondered. His career? An over-leveraged cruise line? Why did he choose this? And there it was, the worst of it: worse than losing a fiancé for the sake of a career; worse than losing a partnership for the sake of ambition; worse, even, than being swallowed by an angry bear. The worst of it was that this had been his doing — his choice. Seth dropped his right hand, rifle still attached, and surrendered to fate. The bear slapped his chest with a flat paw, sending Seth through three young spruce. Bigger than saplings, but still green, each tree bent and thwacked Seth's head as he passed. The blows dulled his senses and turned the world into a gauzy blur.

Whistling objects whirred past his face. Three distinct thumps hit a brown cloud. Voices shouted in English and Russian. Nearby, an old voice cried for help. There was an intense red flash. Seth thought of cinnamon Jolly Ranchers and cherry Kool-Aid.

"Ozzy," it said. "Ozzy, you're going to be okay."

Then there was nothing.

## 33

Seth sat up and regretted it immediately.

His head felt like a cracked egg and his mouth tasted like metal. He looked around. The room was dark except for a ribbon of light spilling into the room from the hallway. The door was open, the Beast again stuck in the narrow jamb. A blanket hung from the top of the door, covering the space between the top of the jamb and the Beast. He smiled. He was home — back in his cabin. He lay back down and the pressure in his head lessened. Something stirred next to him. He was not alone.

"Hey there, Rambo," Evie said. She watched him intensely.

"What time is it?" Seth asked.

"Six."

"In the morning?"

"Yes."

"Jesus. Okay." Seth rose again, more determined this time. His body screamed. A hand gently pushed him back towards the mattress.

"You're not going anywhere," Evie said.

"I need to check on things."

"Everything is fine. You need to stay in bed." She snaked a warm leg over his waist.

He pushed his head back into the pillow and nodded. "So what now?"

"Breakfast." Evie withdrew her leg and popped out from under the blankets. She wore only one Seth's wrinkled blue oxford, her bare knees poking out beneath the long shirttails. As enticing as she was, there was another need competing with Seth's libido. He was, he realized, very hungry.

"I could do breakfast," he said enthusiastically. "In the room?"

"Yes," she answered, then pulled open the drapes. Sunlight flooded the dim room, the sunlight making Seth's head throb anew. His eyes slowly adjusted and found themselves fixed on a sight he would just as soon forget: the Lutak port. They must have arrived while he was out. Nightmarish memories of the day before filled his head.

"I thought I was done for," he said sheepishly.

"Me, too," Evie said, "but I'm glad you weren't."

"How's Tammy?"

"Pissed off. Luckily, Buddy loaded that stupid little gun with birdshot. Old fucker couldn't even kill a bear right. Anyway, the ship's medic spent like an hour plucking little pellets out of her face."

"What about Buddy? Is he okay?"

"Haven't seen him. I think someone said he headed off into town to drink his sorrows away."

"You should have seen him, Evie. After he shot Tammy, it's like he just fell apart."

"I did see him, Ozzy. First time I ever saw the old man show some real emotion."

Then he remembered that she had been there. The Kool-Aid red flash, the voice shouting in English. That had been Evie. "What were you doing there, Evie?"

"Why does anyone do anything?"

"No, seriously. You weren't allowed to be part of the hunt. Why were you there? Are you affiliated with that Russian cell?"

Evie laughed off the question.

"I'm serious."

"I can be pretty sneaky when I want to." Evie opened the sliding glass door. "I couldn't let my sweet Ozzy go native without any backup, could I? Anyway, what were you three going to do with a bear? I mean, if you had actually been successful."

"I didn't really think that through."

"That and about a million other little things."

"And how did I get back here? The Russians?"

"That's right. They carried you, Tammy and the bear out to the port yesterday afternoon. From there, it was just a hop, skip and a jump to the Diana."

Evie grabbed the ship's in-room menu from the dresser and headed for the small table on the balcony.

"And the bear?"

"In the wine tower, just like you wanted." Her eyes widened. "Jesus, Ozzy, you should have seen the passengers. They were thrilled to death. I mean, imagine this huge grizzly bear being brought in on a stretcher, with all these fat, rich folks watching and sipping wine. I would have though the bourgeoisie would be a little freaked out, afraid that the grizzly was going to pop off the stretcher and attack them. But no. They definitely trust that this ship is a safe haven."

"Just like I trust you, Evie. You said those darts could take down an elephant, and you were right. If only I had screwed on that stupid canister. So what happened when the bear came to?"

"The whole ship was there to watch. I tried to keep the idiots from banging on the glass, but what can you do? And I'm not going to kid you, Ozzy. She is not happy. She roared and gnashed her teeth and did all of the normal aggressive bear shit. I didn't think the tower would hold up. But it turns out it would take a lot of pressure to crack that thing." Evie was paused for a beat, then continued, "After a while, she just got all depressed looking.

"But, Seth, the worst of it was her poor little cubs. The cruise director's up on deck showing them off like they were another of the ship's features. He was feeding them and treating them like pets, and all in front of their Mommy. While I wish they could stay with their mother, it was a total relief when the Anchorage Zoo folks took the little ones away. At least the sow won't have to watch that travesty any longer." She grabbed Seth's hand. "Promise me that NordStar will turn her over to a zoo after a few days."

"That's pretty much the plan," Seth sat up, became woozy, and laid back down. "She'll stay in the tower for the rest of the cruise, then we'll turn her over to the Alaska Zoo until NordStar can outfit the tower appropriately. Once NordStar's done, it'll be no different than the lion habitat at the MGM Grand in Vegas. And she won't have to stay there the whole time. Just while the Diana's up here. Like I told you, it's a win-win." Seth felt suddenly sleepy.

"Everyone's a winner," she agreed. "The passengers seem happier than ever, that bear is getting a second chance, and you're going to make partner. You got what you wanted. Looks like you made exactly the right choices."

*Choices.* Seth vaguely recalled something about choices. Something from the day before. Trying to fish that memory out of last night's blur was like trying to get a tiny speck of eggshell away from its yolk. He gave up.

"Take another one of these," Evie said, shaking a pill loose from a brown plastic bottle.

Seth swallowed it with a gulp of stale bedside water. Whatever was in that pill was fantastic. Any lingering doubts about his choices disappeared. Evie was right: his scheming had paid off. The cruise was safe, the bear in custody. That big to-do about the bear disarming its victims was pure speculation. There would be no more big decisions to make. From here on out, he would be a vacationer and nothing more. Evie kissed Seth's neck, and then ran her fingers over his eyelids, gently closing them.

# PART III

# Tina Paloski

I hate that Skinny Bitch Nancy.

Four months ago, I would have told you I'd never get caught dead doing one of these marathons. I never even thought someone like me could have the guts to do it. I mean, I was a solid McDonald's-for-breakfast, Arby's-for-lunch, Wendy's-for-dinner kind of gal. As for exercise, I paid my dues at a month-to-month sweat chain in Anchorage, but hardly ever went.

It was a terrible cycle.

I'd get up the nerve to go to the gym, then I'd feel great for about a week. Then I'd get a cold, or I'd feel depressed about something, or I'd have to work late, and I'd skip the routine for a day or two. Then two days would become three. When Sunday came around, I would tell myself that I'd get back to the grind on Monday, make a fresh start of it. Then a month would go by and I'd be back to my old friends: McDonald's, Arby's and Wendy's. No weight lost, no muscle gained, just a marked decline in self-worth and an increase in muffin-top.

But in every mediocre life, there comes a moment when one has to take a stab at glory, right? For me, that meant sticking to a workout routine. But there had to be some goal in it. Not just losing weight, that had never worked before. No, I needed something tangible. I needed something I could put on a t-shirt and show Nancy and the other skinny bitches of the world.

I saw that Skinny Bitch Nancy thumbtacking the poster to the billboard in the break room. It advertised the "Grizzlathon," a stupid-long run that started in Haines and followed footpaths all over the Passage. I looked from the poster to that Skinny Bitch Nancy. She had to be like 45, but had no waist — I mean zero — and I never saw her sweat. And I got it into my head that I wanted people to look at me exactly the way I looked at Skinny Bitch Nancy. So, I asked that Skinny Bitch Nancy how I could get involved with the run.

She told me, "Tina, I am so glad that you asked me how you can help. We need volunteers like you every two miles to pass out water bottles and cheer on runners like me." Can you believe that skinny bitch? Like no one else is allowed to get a leg up in this world!

So, I told Skinny Bitch Nancy, "No, you skinny bitch, I want to run, not volunteer."

"Honey," she laughed, "I don't think you're cut out for it. I think maybe you'd be better off volunteering."

Then you know what that skinny bitch did? You won't believe it. She pinched my waist! She reached right over and wedged my pudge — my muffin-top — in her skinny bitch fingers.

So, you know what I did, right? Yup. I slapped that Skinny Bitch Nancy.

Afterward, my supervisor Grace told me, "I'm glad someone finally slapped that Skinny Bitch Nancy." Then she called a temp agency and gave me a positive reference.


When I showed up for my temp job the next week, they told me my cubicle was right next to the break room. And, get this: on the wall outside the break room, just visible through my cubicle opening, I saw another poster for the Grizzlathon. And I was like, this is a sign, right? Then I looked closer at the poster, and it said that if you wanted to run in the race you had to call the team leader.

Guess what her name was? Yup. Nancy.

Whatever, I figured, maybe this was a cosmic do-over or something. So, I called the new Nancy, and she was nothing like that Skinny Bitch Nancy. She was nice and even more out-of-shape than me. Fat Friendly Nancy was realistic and convinced me to run a half instead of a whole marathon. She said I might even need to walk part of it. She wasn't mean about it or anything, she was just being honest. And we trained together.

So, for the past four months, we trained four days a week. And you know what? I didn't get a damn bit skinnier. I think I lost some weight maybe, but I look pretty much the same, muffin top and all. But I feel better, so that's something. And I stuck to it, which is unbelievable. And the best part — I was going to wear the same t-shirt as that Skinny Bitch Nancy – even though I was just doing a half marathon. So that's something, too. And that kept me on schedule. Until I started getting the blisters.

Oh, they were awful. Big pus-filled pockets right on the backs of my size 9s. I'd want to pop them, but everyone would give me different advice: don't pop 'em, you'll get an infection; pop the thing with a heated-up safety pin, or else you won't be able to run any more. Neither way worked. The blisters became so painful that I told Fat Friendly Nancy that I was going to have to stop running. That's when she took me to a running store. The guy there told me that that the problem wasn't so much what to do after the blister but how to stop getting the blisters in the first place. The solution? New shoes. Turns out I supinate or something and my clearance-rack Nikes weren't stopping it.

The new shoes did the trick. I had no more blisters in the weeks leading up the race. I was going to show Skinny Bitch Nancy.

Then you know what happened? Yup. The Grizzlathon was cancelled. And on the night before I was supposed to run!

The organizers said it was too dangerous, something about a bear attacking people on the course. That was it, I decided. The world was conspiring against me. I was never meant to be healthy, in shape, or happy. I made the rounds that day for lunch: a McDouble at McDonalds, a large Frosty at Wendy's, and a Beef 'n Cheddar with horsey sauce at Arby's. I sat in my car, opening each little food package and crying. It was definitely a low point. I drove back to work fast and reckless. I thought maybe I'd get myself killed on the way back and wouldn't have to worry about whether I'd ever show up Skinny Bitch Nancy. Unfortunately, I made it back to work in one piece.

Fat Friendly Nancy came up to me as soon as I got back to my desk. "Guess what?" she asked, all excited.

"What," I said.

"It's all back on! Somebody got that bear. We're going to run after all!"

I put my hand over the horsey sauce stain on my shirt.

"It's time to show that Skinny Bitch Nancy," I said.

The morning of the race, all that fast food was rooting around in my belly. When we started running, my stomach rolled and gurgled. It was so much harder than it had been while we were training. About a half hour into the Grizzlathon, I lost sight of Fat Friendly Nancy, which made things even harder. She pulled ahead a little bit, then a lot, and then I just couldn't see her any more. I looked around and realized that I was now running alone, just me and the woods. I was freaked out, but decided that being alone gave me time to focus on my rhythms instead of keeping up with the others. No distractions. No excuses.

At mile six, I hit a sort of groove. I just thought about putting one foot in front of the other. I was actually counting how many times my feet struck the footpaths. I estimated how many more times my feet would have hit that path before I could stop. Turned out it was about 60,000 more times. I was going to have to start thinking about something else.

Guess what I thought about? Yup. I thought about Skinny Bitch Nancy.

I imagined that every time my feet pounded the ground, I was hitting that skinny bitch right in the face. I started laughing and moving faster. I must have looked totally crazy, but I didn't care. It was working, and I stopped feeling so tired. But then around mile 8, mentally slapping that skinny bitch with every stride, I got a blister right on the back of my left heel. The pain was so intense, it felt like someone was holding a Zippo lighter against my heel. But I was 8 miles in, so I couldn't just give up. Right?

Then I felt another blister on my right heel. I got so mad. Still, I pushed on. I had worked too hard to just stop. But then I did — stop, I mean. And I didn't want to. It didn't make any sense to me. I was just on the ground, my palms on the trail. I pulled my right leg around to try to massage my calf, then I threw up. You know those two bones in your lower leg? The tibia and fibula? They were sticking out, with nothing between them. I could literally see the needles along the path through the hole in my leg. Around them was a jagged flap of skin and whatever tissue was left clinging. I didn't dare look at my other leg, but I could feel the blood soaking through my new running shorts on that side. I tried to put together a plan, but then I was up against a tree. I think my back broke.

It all happened so quickly that I never got a good look at it. I mean, I saw enough to know that I'd never seen a bear like it. But it didn't look like a grizzly or a black bear. I saw a cable show about the Yeti on a double-bill, maybe it was more like that. Maybe it was an albino Sasquatch or something. Truth is I didn't give a cold fart about what it was. It didn't matter. It was dragging me into the forest and I was going to die and I didn't care about that. What I was really mad about was that Skinny Bitch Nancy. She was going to get to wear the race t-shirt tomorrow and I wasn't. I wasn't going to get to show her up.

I hate that Skinny Bitch Nancy.

# 34

"What up, bitch?"

"Oh, hey Thad." Seth struggled to pull himself from sleep's warm embrace. The room was swimming. He braced himself against the bed and found Evie, still asleep next to him.

"Were you asleep?" Thad asked, a hint of accusation lingering on the word "asleep."

"No." Seth wiped sleep crumbs from the corner of his eye and cleared his throat. "Uh, no, just watching the news."

Thad said nothing. Normally, the pause would have made Seth sweat. But this time Seth had the pain meds, and they made everything better. "Looks like I won't have to resign, after all, huh?"

"We'll see," Thad said. "The cruise isn't over, bitch. This is no time to get cocky."

Seth smiled. He felt like this was the perfect time to get cocky. His head still hurt slightly and he felt woozy, but he felt well enough to try one of those cruise dinners he had heard so much about. This was about to be one Seth's finest days. His plan had worked.

"So, you're watching the news?" Thad asked.

"Yeah." Seth switched on the TV. Evie opened her eyes. She was about to say something when Seth hushed her.

"So you know CNN's on the Diana's promenade deck right now?" Thad asked.

Seth fumbled with the remote and flipped to the news channel. It showed The Diana's wine tower, now emptied of spirits and containing a sedate bear skulking about her glass cage. Passengers stood around the glass, pointing and smiling. The occasional camera flash obscured the depressed sow.

Seth stifled a yawn. "Yeah, can you believe it? This could be a very good thing for NordStar. Good publicity."

Evie propped herself on her elbows and watched the television.

"Maybe," Thad said. "Did you look at the ticker?"

Seth blinked his eyes a few times, and then focused on the tiny text rolling across the bottom of the screen. There was an item about Angelina Jolie's next baby, and then a blurb about a CNN cameraman in critical but stable condition.

"You see that?" Thad asked.

"Yeah, who's Chuck Tucker?"

"Part of the CNN crew assigned to Lutak."

Seth remembered Buddy telling him that a cameraman went missing, presumably the victim of the monster-bear that was now entombed in glass aboard The Diana. "Is he the one who—?"

"Yes, bitch. That's him. And it looks he's in critical condition, probably won't ever poop normally again. But he might make it. He wandered into port this morning with a battered camera and a handful of guts hanging loose. Pretty nasty."

"Oh my god."

"And Seth, check this out."

An anchorman came onto the screen. A graphic behind the square-jawed talking head showed the cameraman smiling — a stock photo from better days — next to a picture of an angry-looking grizzly. Evie turned up the volume. "— Tucker," the anchor said, "is not speaking and remains heavily medicated. CNN recovered his camera and plans to review its footage. It is believed that Tucker may have captured the attack on tape. We will update you as we learn more, but would like to emphasize how happy we are to have Chuck back. We wish him all the best and a speedy recovery." The man looked off-camera. "He's one of the best in the game. Really is." The channel went to commercial.

"Holy shit," Evie said.

"You get that?" Thad asked.

"I heard it," Seth answered. "This thing is going to be bigger than I thought."

"Yes. Very big. You better cross your fingers."

"Why's that?"

"Well, they're going to look at Tucker's camera footage. An old hand like him, you can bet he wasn't going down without getting everything on film."

"You're probably right. But I don't see what that has to do with me."

"Maybe nothing. But you better hope that the bear on that tape looks a lot like what you've got caged up on the Diana."

Seth hadn't considered that. His lip felt heavy with sweat. How had that not occurred to him?

"Well, bitch," Thad said. "I have to go. One of your colleagues just shouted 'fire.' Apparently I'm the only one with a hose. Enjoy the cruise."

There was a click on the Phoenix end of the line, and Thad was gone. The next thing Seth heard was a strange thumping outside the cabin door. It sounded like an inexperienced hand beating a cheap bongo. After a few slaps, Seth realized this was what passed for knocking when you had luggage for a door.

"Everyone decent?" Before anyone could answer, Cliffy's head appeared through the curtain draped above the Beast. Evie had just fastened the last button on her pants, but wore only a bra on top. "Er. Sorry there, Evie." His head retreated.

"It's okay, Cliffy," Evie said. "I'm sure you've seen these before." She pointed to her chest.

"Don't be so sure about that," Seth said, then realized that Evie had addressed Cliffy by name. "How do you know Cliffy?"

"Oh," she said mischievously, "I got to know him while you were sleeping off your meds. He's been in and out all day, if you know what I mean."

"Shut it," Seth said.

A plate of cookies and milk lifted the curtain and slid along the top of the Beast. "I brought you an afternoon treat," Cliffy said from the hallway.

"Still creepy," Seth said.

"Good to have you back, Ozymandias," Cliffy said.

Evie threw on the oxford she had worn earlier, tying it fashionably mid-waist. She brought the tray to the bed, plopped down, and tore into a cookie. "Ooh," she said, "Cliffy, these are great. Fresh-baked." She pushed one into Seth's mouth.

Seth chewed, remembering the calming effect Cliffy's cookies had on him just a couple nights before. Then he remembered that Cliffy was still patiently waiting out in the hallway. "Cliffy, get in here."

Cliffy clambered over the Beast and rolled into the room. The flesh around his eye was still purple from running into Ceejay's iPhone two days before. "Oh, Evie, I have that thing you wanted." He reached into his pocket and pulled out the remote control that Tammy had used on Seth during the Welcome Aboard drill.

"What do you want with that?" Seth asked.

"I plan to get revenge on our Aussie friend," Evie said, her face utterly serious.

"The woman is recovering from a gunshot wound to the face, Evie. Don't you think that's in poor taste?"

"No mercy, Seth. It was just a flesh wound."

Seth's stomach's continued grumbling caused him to prioritize his own hunger above whatever sympathy he had for Tammy. "Hey, I think I'm up to strolling over to the buffet." He turned to Evie. "Want to make it a date?"

Evie dunked her cookie in milk. "That's just the Vicodin talking. And it's time for another one. Anyway, you're not getting out of here so soon. You will stay in bed today. Cliffy has agreed to bring you whatever you need."

Seth swallowed another pill. He had no idea how many he had swallowed in the last 24 hours, but he knew he enjoyed them tremendously. He closed his eyes and shivered as it swept through his nervous system. His muscles loosened.

"But he's so snide," Seth slurred. "I don't think I can eat if I know he's the one who brought the food. It's just one of those things."

"Yeah. Something tells me you boys will do just fine."

Cliffy showed Seth his pack of 555s.

Seth waggled his eyebrows. "Want to?"

Cliffy nodded and pulled two cigarettes from the pack.

"Obviously in fighting form," Evie said, heading for the Beast.

"Where are you going?" Seth said.

"I have some mischief to make," she said, pumping the remote control in the air. She put her hands on the Beast and turned back to Seth, suddenly wistful. "And, Seth?"

"Yeah," Seth answered.

"I'm sorry."

"What for?" he asked.

"For everything." Evie disappeared through the curtain and over the Beast.

"I don't know why she keeps saying that. She is so complex." He rested his head in his hands.

Cliffy nodded and lit his cigarette. The 555 flew out of his mouth as Seth's body collided with his. Seth hugged Cliffy tightly.

"I couldn't have done this without you, buddy," he said.

"You need to let go of me." He tried to push Seth away.

"And you need to get comfortable with hugging men, because this is what man-friends do. They hug. And you have a pretty mouth."

Cliffy wrinkled his nose.

"Hug time," Seth said, blissfully.

"I'm comfortable with hugs." Cliffy wiggled free. "I'm just not comfortable with setting the ship on fire."

Seth noticed the smoke coming up from his feet. "Oh my."

Cliffy grabbed a pillow and beat the spot where his cigarette smoldered on the carpet. The smoke soon died out, leaving a miniature ashen crater.

Seth's cell phone rang. It was Matt Schott.

"Seth Ozymandias St —" Matt shouted, Modest Mouse's "Dance Hall" blaring in the background.

"I know who I am, Matt. Take it easy. My head hurts."

"You're lucky that's all that hurts. *Mierda*! I'm surprised you didn't shoot yourself."

Cliffy lit another cigarette and headed for the balcony.

"Me too," Seth said.

"Well, you know what they say, *perro que no camina, no encuentra hueso*."

"No, I don't. Who says that, Matt?"

"Your mom." Matt giggled. "Look, I'm calling to say I'm glad you're still with us. Among the living, I mean. I'm also calling to make sure you didn't hook up with Evie, because that girl is loco. I mean, she is complex. I'd stay clear of her."

"Huh?"

"You should see the scary shit she put on her Facebook page this morning. I mean, I always thought she was a little into the conspiracy theories back in school. But I thought it was in the college activist vein. Peacenik bullshit. But this stuff is *desmadre*, bro. It's freaky."

"What is it?"

"I'm not sure how to put it. It's like the Unabomber manifesto mixed with a last will and testament. It has her life history, then this treatise on resource exploitation and the Gaia theory, the world changing, and how no one is innocent and how humans deserve what they get. I've never seen anything like this."

"Are you serious?"

"Serious as a heart attack. I'm serious enough to think she might try to hurt herself. And maybe others."

This was killing Seth's buzz. He tried to snap his fingers at Cliffy, who was out on the balcony, but only succeeding in making a brushing noise with his thumb and middle finger. Cliffy pretended to snap along, and bobbed his head like he was in a jazz club. Seth covered the phone's mouthpiece and yelled at Cliffy, "I'm serious, man. I need you to get the fuck over here."

Cliffy rushed over. Seth fumbled with the phone for a bit, then finally found the tiny button that activated the speakerphone.

"It's just, I don't know," Matt continued. "It's just that it seems like the kind of thing a suicide bomber would say before they boarded a public bus. You know? I think Evie might be on tilt."

Cliffy's eyes widened. "What do we do?" he whispered.

"I need you to follow her," Seth responded, his hand over the phone's mic. Cliffy nodded.

"And, Seth?" Matt said through the speakerphone.

"Yeah?" Seth asked.

"She said something else. And I thought maybe you might want to hear it from me before you heard it anywhere else."

"Yes?" Seth was losing his patience.

"She had an abortion."

Seth felt completely sober. "What are you talking about?"

"Oh man," Matt said. "Right after she left law school. She said she aborted your baby because the world was too fucked up or something."

Seth dropped the phone and looked at Cliffy.

"Go!" Seth yelled.

## Evie Kramer

The hallway was empty save a few stragglers on the way to afternoon tea. I bumped past them and nodded "hello" — cool as a cucumber-and-cream-cheese sandwich. They smiled back, obviously thrilled with the idea of gorging themselves with crumpets before heading off to the buffet. That's when it hit me. I was actually doing this!

The promenade was as Seth described it — Mayberry *sur le mer*. The bourgeoisie were milling about, their cheeks fresh pink from the strong Alaskan sun. I was glad that the crowd was so diverse, a nice mix of old folks, teenagers, families and couples. More ages and backgrounds make for a better story. I walked through the town square, passing people on benches sipping cappuccinos and cocktails. I passed the fountain and let my fingers dabble in the water for a bit. Every sensation has a new vitality when you know it is your last day.

I followed a footpath to the tower. There was still a thick crowd gathered around the glass, watching the sow. The CNN crew sat in a cafe nearby, eating and laughing. It was good that they were near. I hoped they would have their wits about them and manage to get some of this on camera. I elbowed my way through the crowd and ran my hands along the circumference of the tower until I found its hidden entrance. There was a square membrane just to the right of the door. Seth said it was a biometric scanner and PIN pad. He didn't know the combination and I didn't care. Fingerprints and combinations were superfluous.

It didn't have to end this way. I blame myself. I have a PhD in geology and I totally forgot about a key principle: encroachment. Encroachment is one of those words we scientists bandy about when we want to say something has grown beyond its limits. Usually, we're talking about floods or sea levels. But the one that concerns me the most, the one I should have realized was unmanageable, was human encroachment. Humans are far too clever to be confined – how could I forget that? Buddy. That's how. I made the mistake of going to Buddy first. I let him whisper in my ear.

I thought it was the only way to protect them. And then it became our little ruse, a bit of slight of hand. People would be allowed to encroach — to enter their territory — but only when and where we wanted it to happen. Sure, it meant allowing NordStar to take control of Lutak, but that was a small price to pay. Buddy convinced me that we — he and I — were the next step in an ongoing evolution. He said that we could make conscious decisions to shape growth and manage encroachment into their environment. We didn't have to step out of the game altogether. All we had to do was be smarter than the masses and one step ahead of the growth curve.

But Buddy was always one step ahead of me. He had something bigger in mind. How could I not see that? And he thought he still had me by the shorthairs. But there's nothing left of me any more. Not after Bill MacReary. Not after Lois. Not after Rainbow Bear.

I aborted my own baby in the name of principle. I killed it because I believed that the world didn't need another person to spoil its precious resources. Another person to encroach. If Buddy knew that, he wouldn't think I cared enough about myself to avoid desperate action in the name of what is right.


I pulled the yellow, inflatable jacket from my pocket and bent over, acting as if I was going to tie my shoes. The subterfuge didn't really matter. Most of the crowd was watching the bear, not me. Those that looked my way seemed more interested in my butt than what I was doing with the length of yellow rubber. There was a small slit between the bottom of the tower's glass door and the surrounding panels. I slipped the life jacket into the small gap, then turned and stood before the hidden door.

"Excuse me," I said. No one turned.

"Excuse me," I repeated, louder this time.

A few people looked my way, and then turned back to the sad-looking grizzly. They must have thought I was talking to someone else. There was no way I was going to get everyone to notice me just by talking. The sun was setting. I was going to have to make my move before it became dark. I wanted this to look good on tape.

"Well, I'm sorry," I said. No one paid attention. "For everything."

I pressed the button on the remote and heard the inflatable jacket struggle against the confines of the slit. Then the glass gave.

I smiled, relieved. Let the abortion begin.

# 35

Cliffy was out of breath when he reached the promenade deck. He scanned the crowd — it was quite busy now, just before dinner — but couldn't find Evie. What could she be up to? The man on Seth's cell phone likened her to a suicide bomber. That meant she would be looking to make an impact. She probably wanted to make the news. That was it. She would be near the CNN crew. Cliffy ran to the promenade's restaurant quadrant. He stood there, searching the faces, when something tugged at his belt.

"Heya Cliffy," Ceejay said. She sat at a table with her parents in a fenced patio outside the quadrant's coffee shop, DownTown Grounds. The patio was busier than Cliffy had ever seen it. "Mom, Dad, this is Cliffy."

"Oh, hey Ceejay," Cliffy replied, his eyes still darting here and there, looking for Evie. "Nice to see you, Mr. and Mrs. Brecht."

Doug and Linda Brecht gave Cliffy a polite smile.

Ceejay frowned. "Are you okay, Cliffy? You look nervous."

"I hate to be rude, but I have some work to attend to. We'll talk soon?" The CNN crew was a few tables over, their microphones and cameras on the floor, leaning into their lattes and scones. Where was Evie?

"Sure," Ceejay said, her face wrinkled with concern. "I guess. And maybe we'll–" she mimed puffing a cigarette. "I'll even roll you one if you can get some loose tobacco."

Cliffy shot a glance at her parents, if they knew he was sneaking her cigarettes, it could mean his job. Thankfully, neither seemed to notice Ceejay's display. The bear in the glass tower opposite the coffee shop had their full attention.

"Uh, sounds good, Ceejay," Cliffy said, slightly relieved.

"And tell Seth that I'm glad that—" she trailed off and pointed to the wine tower.

There was a loud cracking sound, like dry wood popping in a hot fire. Cliffy spun. Glass veins shot up from the tower's base. The sow moved towards the noise and sniffed at the splintering glass — its cracks steadily branching and growing. A CNN crewmember grabbed his camera and inched closer to the cage. The rest of the crowd edged away from the glass, unsure what was happening. Soon, there was only one other person left standing before the habitat. The grizzly stood directly behind her, distorted by the broken glass. The woman's red hair contrasted brilliantly with the grizzly's dark-brown. She stared at Cliffy, her eyes glassy, and a strange grin on her face.

"Evie!" Cliffy shouted. "Evie, get away from there!"

The popping noises stopped. The glass veins had pushed themselves into a perfect door-sized rectangle and spread no further. Cliffy sighed, relieved.

"Okay, Evie," he exhaled, "thank god. Just walk forward. It's okay."

Evie raised her right knee and kicked the fractured glass behind her. It fell away easily, leaving only inches of air between her and the confused bear. The grizzly stood on its hind legs and let out a series of hoarse, angry barks. An old woman in flip-flops and stonewashed jeans screamed. The bear tore into Evie.

Suddenly, people were everywhere.

Cliffy was glued to his spot beside the coffee shop, not believing his eyes. Evie was on the ground – that much was obvious – but he couldn't decide where her red hair ended and the blood began. Then the bear was past Evie, working through anything that stood in the way. Its massive haunches propelled sharp claws at faces and torsos, a cloud of gore and panic consumed everything. And now the monster headed his way. Cliffy froze as the bear closed in on him. He closed his eyes.

A shot rang out.

Captain Michael Kelly stood a few feet away; his right pant leg rolled up to the knee. The air next to the small revolver in his right hand quivered from the heat of an escaped bullet. The bear regarded Kelly with curiosity.

"Get off my ship!" Kelly growled. The Captain looked past the bear to the passengers huddled in the patio. He winked at them involuntarily. The bear sniffed the ground but did not retreat. Kelly lowered the revolver and took aim.

"I said. Get—"

*BANG!*

"Off—"

*BANG!*

"My—"

*BANG!*

"Ship!"

The bear's fur was dense with fresh red clumps. It stumbled backwards towards the coffee shop's patio railing. Cliffy jumped the small fence and ran squarely into Ceejay and her parents. Inside the railing, passengers fought their way into the coffee shop. The bear found its footing and moved away from the railing and back towards Kelly. Kelly emptied his last two bullets into the sow, snapping its head back with the first, and taking off much of its right ear with the second. The bear howled with hurt and anger. Captain Kelly shook his gun at the sow and repeatedly squeezed the trigger, but no more bullets came.

The grizzly lowered its head and fixed its gaze on the Captain. Dark-red droplets fell from its damaged face. It stiffened its back legs and stood, swaying slightly, then jumped. Kelly disappeared into a thrashing mass of black, brown and red. Seconds later, the bear turned its tortured maw back towards the coffee shop patio, where Cliffy and the Brechts huddled behind a small table. They were still several feet from the coffee shop entrance when the shop's door slammed shut. In addition to Cliffy and the Brechts, there were at least twenty others stranded outside, staring in horror as the bloodied grizzly headed their way. A frustrated cruiser in a straw hat pounded at the coffee shop's door.

Ceejay's father grabbed Cliffy. "Keep them safe," he said, and then ran to the railing. To the bear.

"Daddy, don't!" Ceejay yelled.

"Doug!" Linda Brecht screamed and grabbed for her husband.

Doug met the bear at the short fence. Its paws scissored around the railing and trapped Doug, constantly adjusting their purchase on Doug's torso and crushing him against the fence's rod-iron posts. "Get them away from here," he groaned.

Cliffy heard dull snapping noises.

Before Cliffy could stop her, Linda ran to her husband, whose arms and legs were splayed awkwardly along the fence. Linda grabbed for one of the bear's immense paws, but was flung away immediately. Her neck struck a metal chair. She lay on the ground motionless. Doug stopped struggling against the bear's embrace and closed his eyes, his breathing labored. Ceejay screamed and shook her head.

"We need to go," Cliffy said. "Now!" He yanked Ceejay's arm with a force he didn't know he possessed. Ceejay did not protest. Together, they jumped the railing and ran past the bear, past the Captain's ravaged body, past newly closed storefronts jam-packed with terrified passengers. The bear released Doug from the fence and followed.

"We can't outrun it!" Ceejay shouted, running full speed through Restaurant Row. She wiped her cheeks free of tears as she ran.

"I know," Cliffy said, holding Ceejay tightly. "But I think we can out stop it."

"What?"

"Inertia," Cliffy said, then grabbed Ceejay's hand and pulled her towards the double doors leading to the kitchen at the end of Restaurant Row. He heard the bear panting behind him, its pads hitting the floor as it galloped in pursuit. There was no way they were going to beat the sow to an exit, but

Cliffy knew that if they could get close to the double-doors they'd have a shot at getting out alive. He didn't dare look back. The panting was getting closer. They were almost there. He released Ceejay's hand and surged ahead.

"Don't leave me!" she shouted.

"I won't!" he responded, then looked back to see the grizzly hot on Ceejay's trail, its nose nearly touching the back of her sneaker. Cliffy caught Ceejay's wrist, and, using all of his strength, threw her against the wall adjoining the double doors. He then spun and deposited himself against the opposite wall. The bear scrambled to slow itself, but its claws helplessly clacked against the brick floor. It tumbled through the swinging doors and into the Diana's kitchen. From inside came a chorus of clanking metal and startled yelps.

Ceejay tried hard to ignore the sounds in the kitchen. "What about the people working in there?"

"At least they have knives," Cliffy said.

# 36

Seth swallowed another pill.

An abortion? Is that what he said? It was hard to think clearly now. His cabin intercom crackled to life.

"Attention all passengers," a vaguely European accent said, "This is not a drill. If you are in your cabin, please lock your cabin door and remain where you are. If you are elsewhere on the ship, proceed in an orderly fashion to the nearest stairwell, where a NordStar crew member will give you further directions."

Seth sat in his bed, unsure how to proceed. He was certain he was still in his cabin, but he had no door, just the Beast. And he was in no condition to make his way to a stairwell. Each step sent the world spinning around him. He surrendered to the bed and pulled the blanket over his head.

A loud crash came from somewhere in his room. He pulled the blanket from his head and saw Cliffy, sprawled on his cabin floor. Then another body flew between the Beast and the top of the door. It was Ceejay. She was breathing hard but there was something strangely vacant about her expression. Outside, a horse galloped by. Why was there a horse in the hallway?

"Seth!" Cliffy yelled.

"What is it?" Seth complained.

"We need to go."

"No, the little speaker-man said we have to stay and shut the door. I got a bit hung up on that one."

"He was wrong. You're not safe here. That thing is tearing through these cardboard hallways like an angry bee trying to get out of a car."

"That's a terrible simile," Seth said, dropping a half-full pill bottle onto the nightstand. He heard another horse gallop down the hallway. "It's like the Preakness out there. See, that's a good simile." He giggled to himself, then said, "horsey, horsey, horsey."

"God damn it, Seth," Cliffy said. "How many pills did you take?"

"Yes," Seth said.

"Great," Cliffy said, exasperated.

"Well, it's good to see you Cliffy. And you, iPhone attacker. And you, horsey face."

"Horsey face?" Wonderful, you're hallucinating now."

Ceejay backed away from the doorway. "He's not hallucinating," she said, her emotionless voice hollow.

The sow's black nose peeked out from under the door/curtain, its wet nose expanding and contracting. It huffed and then pushed its entire head through the gap. The right side of its face was a congealed black-red mass dotted with spiky clumps of dark-brown fur. Its right ear hung by a thin string of tissue. It opened its mouth, allowing globs of pinkish drool to fall onto the Beast. Ceejay screamed. The sow screamed back, then surged against the Beast. Thankfully, the Beast held.

"So," Seth said, "it looks like its time to go." He threw off the sheet and grabbed the pill bottle from the nightstand.

"Yes," Cliffy said, eyes wide. "The balcony."

Cliffy half-carried Seth through the open sliding glass door, and onto the balcony. Cliffy pulled the door shut and all three looked back into the room. The bear rammed itself against the Beast again and again. Its head pushed further into the room with each attempt. The doorjamb splintered. Finally, the bear dislodged the Beast and bounded into the room. It groaned, obviously frustrated by being trapped in yet another glass cage. It sniffed at the glass door, fogging the pane.

"Move," Cliffy insisted. He unlocked the plastic partition that separated Seth's balcony from Nan and Charlie Jenkins'. Nan appeared at her cabin's sliding glass door. She threw the door wide.

"Get in here!" she hissed, then slammed and locked the door once all three were through.

The Jenkins' cabin was the mirror image of Seth's. Unlike Seth, however, the Jenkins had kept their space much neater. The seasoned travelers had found room for their clothing and luggage in the small room's various cubbies. The only thing that looked even slightly unkempt was Charlie. He sat on the bed grimacing. His hair was a mess and he held his right foot in his hands. He flinched in rhythm with a series of crashes coming from Seth's cabin. Seth laughed hysterically.

"What's wrong with him?" Charlie asked, nursing his foot.

"Too many pills," Cliffy said. He pointed to Charlie's foot. "What's wrong with your husband?"

"He sprained his ankle running back to the room," Nan said, trembling. "Look, we can talk all day, but that monster is going to come through here any second. We can't stay."

"Relax, Nan, we need to stay here and stay calm," Charlie said.

"No, she's right," Cliffy said. "We need to get out of here. It'll break out onto the balcony and walk over here. It'll see us — a prepackaged TV dinner just begging to be eaten. We should go."

"Wait," Charlie said. He put his finger to his lips. "Listen."

There was a scratching sound, from next door – Seth's cabin. It sounded like the world's largest cat begging to be let back in. Then the bear thudded across Seth's cabin, left, and thundered past the Jenkins' door. Somewhere in the hallway, a woman screamed. Ceejay grabbed Cliffy and quivered. After a few seconds, her screaming stopped.

"Good Jesus," Nan said.

"I vote," Charlie said, "that we just hole up here until your people can subdue that thing." He threw Cliffy an angry glance.

"My people?" Cliffy asked. "What are they supposed to do? Shout it off the ship? Attack it with brooms?"

"Don't you have guns and stuff to defend the ship from pirates?" Charlie asked.

Cliffy snorted. "Since 9/11, the only person on a domestic cruise that gets a weapon is the Captain. And I think he's out of bullets."

"Bringing a bear onto a crowded ship was a stupid idea from the get-go," Nan said, furious.

"Agreed," Cliffy said. He glared at Seth. "But here we are. We need to think of a solution."

"Can't we call for help?" Charlie said. "Can't someone in the port get an army in here to put it down before it hurts anyone else?"

"There are guys in the port with AK47s and blue jumpsuits," Seth said.

"That's the pills talking," Cliffy said. He ran his index finger in small circles around his temple, the international sign for cuckoo.

"So what do we do?"

"I have an idea," Seth said.

"God, please, no more ideas from you," Cliffy said.

"Yeah. You've done enough," Charlie said. "We need to stay put."

Ceejay's phone vibrated in her pocket. She pulled it out and found a message from Laura, the one-time love of her life.

"I want to hear him out," Ceejay said.

"Honey, I can tell you've been through a lot. But he's clearly not with it," Charlie said.

"Charlie," Nan interrupted, "none of us have come up with anything feasible, other than hiding in here until that thing busts in here and attacks us. The girl is right, we should hear him out."

Charlie threw his hands in the air. "Nan, he's high on whacky pills. He's just going to tell us something loopy, like we need to let loose the purple unicorns. Or maybe we should call Batman. Or maybe, just maybe, we should put on a show! Like in those old Judy Garland Mickey Rooney movies. How about that, Nan? Would that help?"

"That last bit would," Seth said.

The others stared at him.

"The bit about the show. That would work."

## 37

Cliffy snuck back onto Seth's balcony. The bear was gone. He waved Seth and Ceejay forward. Despite a multitude of aches and pains — still present, but bearable with the pills — Seth now propelled himself past his ruined cabin. Inside, the Beast lay discarded by the door, its ballistic-nylon body badly shredded.

"Poor guy," Seth said. "Beast, I hardly knew ye." He giggled.

"Hush," Cliffy said, and pushed Seth forward. The Jenkins stood by their sliding glass door, where Charlie offered a weak thumbs-up.

"You all better be in one piece the next time I see you," Nan whispered. "Be careful now."

Seth and Ceejay nodded to Nan. Cliffy quietly unlatched the partition aft of Seth's balcony then led the Seth and Ceejay to the rear of the ship, balcony by balcony. Most of the cabins they passed were empty. Of the few that held passengers, only one person dared to come to the sliding glass door.

"What do you people think you're doing?" an old man in a golf shirt and herringbone pants asked through his sliding glass. Behind him, a television was tuned to CNN. On it, a reporter talked to the camera, The Diana just visible in the background.

"Stay put," Cliffy told the old man. "This will all be over soon. I hope."

"Did you find a way off the ship? Someplace safe?"

"We're going to put on a show!" Seth said.

The man stared at Seth. "Is he okay?"

"Just stay here, and keep this door shut," Cliffy said, pushing Seth past the man's balcony.

Finally, they reached the last balcony. The attached cabin was empty, save an unmade bed and clothes strewn about on the floor. Cliffy tried the sliding door handle, but the room was locked from the inside. He kicked at the glass until it gave, scattering tiny shards across the carpet. The three crunched across the glass and into the room.

"This was your idea, Seth," Cliffy said quietly. "You check."

"I'm the idea man, not the action—"

Ceejay slapped Seth's head.

"Ow! What was that for?"

"Time to act," she said. Seth's plan of action seemed to bring Ceejay back to life.

Seth dry-swallowed another pill. In seconds, medicinal bravery coursed through his system. He knew that the situation was incredibly perilous, but it was also so silly. He shook his head and laughed, then went to the cabin door. He opened it a crack, half expecting the grizzly to leap through the gap and kill him on the spot.

*Now, that would be funny*, he thought.

But there was no bear waiting for him, just a hallway with a dark smear of red on the opposite wall. He swung the door open further and saw that the room was cater-corner the entrance to the Starlight Theater. They were almost there. Then he looked in the other direction to make sure the path was clear.

The Vicodin could not mask what he saw. While the rest of the evening's events would become a vague blur in the months to come, this scene would remain vibrant and clear in his memories. Most of the hall's sconces were on the floor, crushed. The light fixtures that remained on the walls were either off or flickering. Bodies were scattered across the floor, limbs lying at awkward angles to the bodies. The walls were covered in lines and splashes, strange calligraphy describing the massacre that had taken place here. At the other, dimmer, end of the hall, was the sow. She hunkered low, tearing at something Seth could not identify. Seth felt bile in his throat. He quietly closed the door and leaned against the wall, his head down. The pills were already wearing off.

"Well?" Cliffy said.

"We're close enough, but the bear's on the other end. Thankfully, I don't think she heard me. She was busy." He swallowed again.

"Busy?" Ceejay asked.

Seth ignored her. "Remember," he said, "the Starlight's to the right. Don't even bother looking left."

"Okay," Cliffy said.

Ceejay nodded, her eyes darting from Seth to Cliffy and back again.

"Are we ready?" Seth asked.

"No," Ceejay said. "How can we be? But this is, like, a moral imperative or something." Cliffy put his hand on her shoulder and squeezed.

A moral imperative. That was something Seth had never, in his adult life, seriously considered. He was an attorney, a paid facilitator, a hired hand. He acted in accordance with his client's needs, and, as long as it did not violate legal ethics, did not ask why. But acting of his own will – simply because it was the right thing to do – that was new. "You're right," he said, "it's a moral imperative or something."

They bunched up behind the door. Seth held his swollen index finger in the air, then his middle finger, and then the ring finger. He pulled the door open and they moved, swiftly and quietly, to the closed Theater door. Seth tried to open it, but it was locked from the inside.

Ceejay, Seth and Cliffy huddled together.

"You didn't tell us that the door was closed," Ceejay whispered.

"I figured we could open it when we got here," Seth responded. He looked over his shoulder; the bear was still on the other end of the hallway, still busy. It carried on with its meat, and Seth assumed that it hadn't noticed them. He yanked on the Theater door handle again, but had no success.

"Didn't you think it was kind of important that we know whether the door was open or not?" Ceejay asked.

"I'm doing my best here."

"Your best needs to get better."

Seth took a deep breath. "We have two options. We can knock on the door and hope someone is on the other side to let us in. But that means that we make more noise, and maybe she—" he jerked his thumb over his shoulder "—hears us. Or we just head back to the room and wait it out. Personally, I vote for the latter. We were already taking a risk, but this is too much."

"I can't see giving up now," Ceejay said. "That thing's going to come after someone else sooner or later. I can't have that on my conscience if we can do something about it. I vote for knocking."

"That's one vote for knocking, and one vote for retreating." Seth looked at Cliffy. "Well?"

"I vote for neither." Cliffy pulled his universal access key card from a coat-pocket and swiped it through an electronic reader. The reader beeped. Behind them, Seth saw the bear's good ear perk up. Then its whole head turned. An amber light flashed. The bear reared up and set itself on its paws. It huffed and lowered its head.

"Shit," Cliffy said.

"Okay, open the fucking thing," Seth said.

"It didn't work."

"Try again, try again," Ceejay insisted.

Cliffy swiped the card again. The grizzly sniffed the air, and then galloped towards them. The reader beeped and flashed amber. Seth felt the bass-thump of the grizzly's footfalls as it hurtled through the hallway.

"Okay, we need to get back to the room," Seth said.

"Wait," Ceejay said.

"No, no more tries," Seth said.

The bear was now halfway to them.

"No!" Ceejay yelled. "The card on arrow's the wrong way. Look."

Cliffy's eyes went wide. He turned the card around, swiped it, and the reader turned green. He turned the handle and pushed, but the door only opened a few inches before closing against itself.

The bear was close now.

"Help me!" Cliffy yelled.

Ceejay and Seth put their shoulders against the door, and the three heaved it open. They jumped through the door, and watched it close again, smashing into the bear's cheek as it tried to power through the opening. Five large men in NordStar uniforms shut the door against the bear's massive head. The bear continued to pound against the metal on the other side of the door, but the NordStar strongmen managed to hold the door tight enough to latch it shut. After a few moments, the pounding on the other side of the door stopped.

"How could you not tell us that the door was closed?" Cliffy demanded, grabbing Seth's shirt.

"How did you," Seth shoved pointed his swollen index finger at Cliffy's nose, "not tell Ceejay and me that your key card worked in that door?"

A man in a torn tuxedo walked up to the group. It took Seth a few moments to realize that this was Stevie Bruebecker, The Diana's cruise director. The left side of his face was purple with bruises and he was scowling.

"You could have killed us all!" Stevie shouted.

"Us all?" Seth asked, then looked around. At first, he saw only the spectacle of the Diana's Starlight Theater, its three levels and its enormous electrochromic window, the glass now transparent and looking out onto the ship's rear deck and the Lutak port beyond. But then he saw them: the bedraggled passengers and crewmembers all around him, staring at him and his friends with something akin to hatred. Most were in groups, seated in the orchestra section or on the stage, their legs dangling into the pit. A few wandered the aisles alone, lost in what Seth hoped was thought, but was probably trauma. Some lay across multiple seats, their faces and bodies bloodied.

"What the hell do you think you're doing?" Stevie demanded.

"We were," Seth gulped, "going to put on a show."

## 38

When Seth was done explaining, Stevie looked disgusted. "You want to let that thing in here?" The theater crowd grumbled and circled, shark-like, around Seth and his co-horts. The strongmen who had been guarding the door gave up their stations and drew closer.

"Yes," Seth said, attempting the practiced confidence that came from years of contract negotiation. "Yes, that's what I'm saying."

"Why take the chance?" Stevie asked. "We've got injured people in here, old people, whole families. They're safe right now. Why not just let things be?"

"Because," Seth said, "because—" he trailed off. The pills were making it difficult to think clearly.

"Because," Ceejay said, "there are a lot of people on this ship that aren't safe. And they deserve our best efforts to get them home alive."

"Right," Seth said.

"And because," Cliffy continued, "NordStar hired us to help everyone on the ship, not just the few that managed to make it to safety. We're here to be sure everyone has a safe journey. You're the cruise director, you know better than anyone."

"Hold it," Stevie said. "I didn't come here to risk my life. I'm just a college student – okay? – a theater Arts major, and a bad one at that. I was the understudy for Tevya in Fiddler, for crying out loud! NordStar hired me because I'm white, I have nice teeth, I sing and dance a little, and I'm not self-conscious. In return, I get measly pay — mostly thanks to this guy." He pointed at Seth. "No, I'm just here to lop off a tiny, itsy-bitsy fraction of my six-figure student loan. And I think I speak for everyone here when I say that we did not sign up for this cruise intending to put our lives on the line."

The crowd mumbled its agreement. The strongmen from the door now stood between Cliffy and Stevie.

"Does Mr. Bruebecker speak for everyone here?" Seth asked. "No one here wants to lend a hand to those that may not be able to help themselves?"

The crowd was silent.

"Okay," Seth said.

"Okay?" Ceejay asked, bewildered.

"Okay, plan's shot. If these people want to turn down their chance at greatness — hell, even goodness — I say we let them. It's not every day that we have a chance to save other people. But if they want to pass it up—"

"We just don't see the point in committing suicide for other people," a woman in the orchestra section said. "We're safe here, I say we leave things be." Those around her nodded.

"Totally," Seth said. "I totally understand. It's much easier to follow the understudy here, to choose cowardice over heroism. It's—"

"It's pragmatism," an old man said. "It's not cowardly. We're making a decision to stay put."

"—Your choice," Seth continued. "Why get involved? That CNN crew out there won't know the difference, anyway. They'll just report that a hundred or so people survived by hunkering down while a thousand others remained in peril. I get it. It's easier to be scared."

"We're not scared!" Stevie said. "It's just that this is the wise thing to do!"

"You're scared," Cliffy said.

"Given the chance to be a part of something," Seth said, "the selfless opportunity to save another's life, you would all rather live with cowardice and regrets. It's all very modern."

"Shut up!" Stevie said. "You're just confusing things." He gestured to the strongmen. "Make sure they stay put." One of the big men put his hands on Cliffy's shoulders, another grabbed Ceejay, and two more made their way towards Seth.

"No, you're right. Makes sense." He ducked out from the strong man's grasp. "Lots of German families said nothing about the Holocaust. That was much worse that this, and who's judging them? What's a little spinelessness among friends, right?"

The strongman who had been grasping for Seth's shoulders put a hand to his lips. "I think he's got a point there, Stevie," he said.

"No, he doesn't," Stevie said. "It's all hyperbole. It doesn't mean anything."

"I don't want to be part of this," he said. He looked at Seth. "I'll help however I can."

"Good," Seth said, "I could use some help with the glass."

"On it," the strong man said. He waved to the other hulks and the group followed Seth, Ceejay and Cliffy towards the theater's stage. The crowd parted ways and allowed them through.

"Wait!" Stevie shrieked. "You can't be serious."

"Okay, Cliffy," Seth said, "you're going to be up in the producer's suite, right?"

Cliffy nodded.

"I thought we had an understanding here, people!" Stevie cried. "We can't let that bear in here!" Stevie said. He tried to stop one of the big men from going on stage, but was thrown to the floor like a used rag.

"Okay," Seth said, "we need to get everyone out of here. Ceejay, please make sure everyone gets up to the mezzanine level. Cliffy, you sure this will work?"

"I'm not sure of anything, Ozymandias. But it's worth a go."


"Is everyone clear?" Seth asked.

He shielded his eyes from the harsh stage lights. Cliffy was in the producer's booth, above the third level of seating, his thumb in the air. Except for the strongmen, the crowd was now safely seated in the mezzanine.

Piles of theater chairs blockaded stairways to that level. Night sky poured onto the stage through a big, jagged hole that the strongmen carved out of the electrochromic glass. The portion of the window that remained intact was now a dense, milky-white.

It was time. Ceejay stood before the theater entrance; her jaw was set with determination.

"You sure you really want to do this?" Seth asked.

"What else can I do?" Ceejay responded.

"Don't answer a question with a question."

"Smart ass," she said, her jaw loosening slightly. "Yes. I really want to do this. My parents would have wanted me to."

"Well, good. Because no one else here has the balls to try it. It's a real bonsai kind of move."

"It's a death relay," Ceejay said, deadly serious.

"Wow, hadn't thought of it that way. I guess that makes me the anchor of the team."

"Yep," Ceejay said. "But only if I make it back here in one piece."

"You will. You've got to." Seth put his hand on Ceejay's shoulder. "Now, I want you to know that it's a little, well, awful out there."

"Nothing I see out there can be any worse than what happened up top. When that thing got loose—" Ceejay shuddered, then welled up.

"I can't even imagine," Seth said.

"No, you can't." Ceejay's heavy black mascara ran down her eyelids and onto her cheek.

"Oh, you shouldn't cry," Seth said. He awkwardly patted her back.

"Why not? I was terrible to them. I was terrible to my parents for the past few months, and now they're gone."

"I'm sure you weren't terrible, you're just, I don't know. You're just a kid. Your parents wouldn't want you to be so hard on yourself."

Ceejay cradled her head against Seth's chest. His awkward pats became a full embrace. They held their hug for a minute, then Seth pushed back and looked down into Ceejay's face.

"You're a good kid," he said. "But if you don't stop crying, I'm going to have to call you 'zebra face' again. And I know how that hurts."

Ceejay cracked a smile and sniffled.

"Actually," she sniffled, "I think Zebra Face would make an excellent name for a superhero." She smiled through her tears.

"What you're about to do definitely qualifies for superhero status."

"Or a Darwin award." She walked away from Seth and drifted towards the theater's double doors.

"Hey Ceejay, can you do me a favor?"

She turned around.

"As if becoming human bait for a psycho bear wasn't enough?" She shook her head, bewildered. "Absolutely, Seth, I'd love to run an errand for you. What's on your mind?"

"If you happen to see Evie out there, and she's still in one piece, can you tell her I'm sorry? I may not have the chance."

"Sorry?" Ceejay asked, incredulous. "What in the name of crazy psycho bitch do you have to be sorry for?"

"I didn't think things would turn out this way. I thought it was going to be best for—"

"Seth!" Ceejay shouted. "Evie's gone. And I'm glad. That redheaded coose is responsible for all of this. She let a bear loose on a crowded ship. She killed my parents!"

Until now, Seth's pills had done a remarkable job of erasing his earlier conversation with Matt Schott. But now it all came crashing back. He went pale.

"I thought you knew!" Ceejay said.

"This is all my fault," he said. "I'm so stupid."

"Maybe," she answered. She tapped one of the strongmen holding the door. He nodded to the others, who opened the door. Ceejay looked into the hallway and gave the men a thumbs up. "But now you get to make up for it." The men in blue threw the door wide.

Ceejay disappeared into the gloom of the hallway.

## 39

All was quiet in the corridor.

There was no sign of life in any of the bodies littering the beige carpeting. Ceejay looked through the gloom to the other end of the hallway, but the bear was not there. She flicked her lip ring nervously, certain that, at any moment, the bear would explode from one of the hall's closed doors and tear her to pieces. It would kill her, just as it had her parents. She was certain. And this conviction — the sheer fatalism of it — gave her the reckless bravado of a kamikaze pilot.

She looked back at the open theater doors and signaled that she was going to keep moving. Seth, just visible through the open door, nodded. Ceejay made her way to the central staircase. The extent of the devastation was overwhelming. It was amazing that one creature could have destroyed so many people in one fell swoop.

Her foot landed on something squishy. She looked down to find her right sneaker atop a large, flappy, arm. Its wrist was adorned with gold bangles, a turquoise-and-silver watch the size of a basketball hoop, and a charm bracelet featuring tiny bejeweled shoes. She stepped off of it as though she had stepped in a wad gum. As she lifted her foot, the arm's gold bangles clanged against one another. In the quiet of the hallway, the rattling jewelry sounded like a symphony of bells. Ceejay clenched her fists and shut her eyes. She held the lip ring in place with her tongue. She was certain this small misstep had summoned the monster. She listened for the sow's approach. But the bear did not come. She opened her eyes and looked back to the theater doorway. Seth pointed to the roof, a questioning look on his face. She nodded and walked up the broad stairs as quietly as possible.

When she reached the promenade deck, Ceejay again paused and listened. Still nothing. The town square appeared deserted. On second glance, however, she realized that the buildings ringing the square were filled to the brim with people, unfortunate throngs pressed against glass windows — and occasionally jutting through. There were still plenty of derelicts crouched outside, hiding behind planters, tables and benches. The whole scene reminded Ceejay of the old Westerns she watched with her father when she was small: the small town deserted save the cowboy with the white hat and the one with black, the townspeople nervously awaiting a shootout. She very badly wanted a white cowboy hat.

She carefully entered the faux town. Still no sign of the bear. She walked past CJ McDoodles, a gift shop with a display window that usually displayed high-end watches — Omega, Breitling, Corum, Suunto, all the best. Tonight the window showed only the people crushed inside the building, pressed uncomfortably against its outside walls. On closer inspection, Ceejay noticed a number of cracks in the shop window where the pressure of those inside had been too much.

"Hey!" a nearby voice said. Ceejay looked down to find a man, crouched alone and shirtless, partially hidden under a wrought iron table. He pressed a bloodstained polo against the side of his head. A woman lay across his knees, unconscious.

"Get down here!" the man hissed.

"Where is it?" Ceejay asked.

"Get down here and stop making noise. You need to hide."

"Where is the bear?"

"It's not here. Not now anyway. You need to hide. You're going to give us away. It'll come back." The man was trembling.

"No," Ceejay said. "You don't get it. I'm here to save you."

The man looked confused. "Are you hurt?" he asked.

"No, seriously. I have a plan. I just need to know where it went."

The man shrugged and pointed to Restaurant Row. Ceejay nodded and headed to the Row, studiously avoiding the spot where her father was still pinned, lifeless, against the coffee shop rail. Like the town square, the ship's restaurants were overloaded with passengers and crew, with others still caught hiding in plain view. Ahead of Ceejay were the swinging double-doors that led to The Diana's main kitchen. Ceejay shuddered when she remembered running towards those doors with Cliffy just a short time ago. A pair of jeans-clad legs held the kitchen's right-hand door open. Ceejay edged closer, daring herself to peek through the partly open door, daring herself to look at the thing responsible for her parents' deaths. But before she could get close enough, something violently yanked the legs back into the kitchen. She jumped back behind an oversized park bench and stumbled over a family of four.

"There's no more room here," the father whispered, hugging his young son and daughter to his chest. "Find another spot."

"I'm not planning on staying long," Ceejay said, nervously flicking her lip ring.

"Well, good," the mother said softly, using her hips to push Ceejay from the makeshift shelter and towards the kitchen doors.

"You need to get out of here," the father said.

There was a loud clattering in the kitchen. The mother yelped. "It's coming back again."

"Again?" Ceejay asked.

"It must think the kitchen is its cave or something," the father said. "It keeps pulling people in."

"Why don't you run?" Ceejay asked.

"You saw those jeans?" the man asked. "That was the last runner."

"So you're just going to wait here to die?"

"Help will come soon," the mother said, patting her youngest child, a blond girl. "We just need to stay put." She tried to force a smile, but her lips betrayed her.

"Look," Ceejay said, "I don't see anyone coming to help, at least not soon enough. But I think I can get that bear out of here and take care of it. I just need to stay here for a bit before I make my move. Can you four be cool for a couple more moments? Then I'll be on my way."

"No," the mother said, and shoved Ceejay out from behind the bench.

With no place to hide, Ceejay saw no sense in delaying. But she still needed to know where the bear was. She needed to know how much of a head start she'd need if she was going to survive the relay. Ceejay moved up against the double doors. The bear was still in there, she could hear it, but it was further away than before. She bit her lip ring and peered through the door's small inset window. She saw the bear's mangled head — a brown, black and red blob set against the kitchen's endless stainless steel. It was licking something yellow from a jar that had been knocked onto the floor. The jeans-clad legs were on a counter just above the downed can. Ceejay called on her track training. From the bear's position in the kitchen, she'd need a lead of at least a city block. That would make her close enough to look obtainable, but far enough to avoid teeth and claws. But how could she get the bear's attention from so far away? Then it came to her. She dashed back to the family's hiding place behind the bench. She grabbed the father's hand.

"You need to help me," she told him, looking directly into his eyes.

"I, uh…" he mumbled.

"Don't you do it, Billy," the mother said. "You need to stay here with your family."

"I thought," Billy said, his eyes darting between his wife and Ceejay, "that you were going to get the bear. You don't need me to get mixed up in this thing."

"Plan changed. I need you to pull that door open for me. That's all. Then you can go back into hiding. I promise."

"Billy," the mother pleaded.

"Lady," Ceejay said to the mother, "there's no time. We need to do this before it hurts anyone else." She turned back to Billy. "I watched my parents die. Right—" her eyes found the coffee shop railing, then jumped away, "—

right over there. I don't want your little boy and girl to see something like that. No parent wants that. Help me."

He stood.

"Billy, you can't," his wife said, sobbing.

"Phyllis." He kissed her cheek. "I have to."


Ceejay took her mark at the end of Restaurant Row, her back to the kitchen doors. She stretched her calves and pulled her head against her shoulders. She was as limber as she was going to get. She told herself that this was just like a high school track meet, like she was back in Ann Arbor trying to make All-Region. She wondered how she would have done in her time trials had a bear been chasing her.

She smiled despite her terror.

She was ready.

She gave Billy the signal, her thumb high in the air. Billy flung the door open, then hid behind it. She saw his face through the door's small window, white with fear. The bear lifted its massive head, but did not move. It looked confused, unsure of the source of the commotion. It sneezed, a stream of yellow sauce sprayed from its bloodied nose. The sneeze must have been very painful, because the bear shook its head violently from side to side like it was trying to exorcise a demon from its nasal passages. When it stopped shaking, it reared on its hind legs and stared at Ceejay. She felt warm liquid spread through her blue jeans.

"Come on," she peeped at the bear. She wanted to yell, but her vocal cords would not to cooperate.

The bear stared at Ceejay for such a long time without moving that Ceejay was convinced it had not seen her at all. Perhaps its face had been so damaged by the Captain's bullets that it couldn't make out much of anything. The bear dropped back down to all fours and licked at the yellow sauce once more.

"Bring it," she whispered, vocal cords still denying her a proper tone.

The bear looked up again. This time it walked to the open kitchen door. Billy — still visible through the small window — began to shake. Ceejay noticed for the first time that his shoes, protruding from underneath the door, were shuffling back and forth. The bear watched them for a beat, and then roared. Billy screamed back, his shout fogging the glass, mercifully hiding his terrified expression. His children cried out for their father.

"Billy!" Phyllis yelled, leaving the relative safety of her hiding place. The grizzly fixed on Phyllis.

"No," Ceejay said, her fear still quieting her, "no. You are supposed to come after me." But the bear paid no attention to Ceejay.

Instead, it shook its head and ran in toward Phyllis. She shut her eyes and hugged herself. Then, as it had earlier, the bear slipped, its paws scrambling for purchase against the slick man-made stamped concrete floor. The sow's mammoth body slid past Phyllis and into the park bench, where her children hid. Phyllis opened her eyes and turned in slow-motion horror to see her children cowering beneath the giant bear.

"No!" Ceejay yelped, finally able to corral the vocal power that had so far eluded her. She was yelling now, louder than she ever had before. "You are supposed to come after me, bitch!" The grizzly looked at Ceejay, outraged. This time, Ceejay believed the bear — only twenty feet away — could see her just fine. It started towards her.

Ceejay ran for her life.

# 40

In the Starlight Theater, Seth stared through the open door, looking frantically for Ceejay. The pills had worn off. He shook the nearly empty bottle in his pocket, badly wanting to take another but knowing that he needed his wits about him — at least for a little while more.

"This is working out really well," Stevie Bruebecker complained, hidden behind the NordStar strongmen. "She's not back yet. Doesn't that bother you? Aren't you an attorney or something? Does the word negligence mean anything to you?"

"More than it means to you," Seth shot back. He motioned to one of the strongmen. The strongman nodded and crammed Stevie's black bowtie into his mouth. Stevie let out muffled protests. The strongman glared at Stevie until he became quiet, then moved back into formation.

"Thanks," Seth said.

Seth chewed his nails, blinked and licked his lips. What if the worst had happened? What if she wasn't coming back? In a dark, secret part of his brain — a part he would never share with another human being — he realized that her failure to return might not be so awful. After all, if she didn't return he didn't have to run. If he didn't have to run, he didn't have to outpace a killer bear. And if he didn't have to outpace a killer bear, he'd probably survive this misadventure alive – ashamed, jobless, and sad, but alive. He shook his head. Of course he wanted Ceejay to return alive. He wanted her to drive the bear right down the hallway and into the theater so that he could lead it to its death.

No sooner had he though this than he heard a series of bleating, deranged noises coming from somewhere in the hall. They sounded like the hollering of a psych ward — laughs and screams, yells and rants. Then he saw the source of the noises: it was Ceejay, loping down the stairs and streaming across on the hallway's bloodied carpet. She was a whirling and howling dervish. Her arms spun and her legs pumped in a great blur through the corridor's flashing lights.

"Thank god!" Seth shouted, waving her to the door. "Come on, Ceejay! Come on!" He clapped his hands at her, as though she were a dog. Anything to make her move faster, to arrive safely in the theater. He needed to start his leg of the race.

Then came the bear, galloping at full run down the stairs and into the hallway. It was right behind Ceejay now, threatening to overtake her with every powerful push of its legs. Ceejay's shoe had come off at some point in the relay, but she held her head down and raced forward, her nose pointing at the floor, her eyes scanning the floor's gruesome hurdles. She had a wide, maniac's smile. Seth had no idea how she managed to stay ahead — or how he would when his time came.

Ceejay was only a few doors away now. She lifted her head, her mascara-splattered eyes stared at Seth's, unwavering. Somehow, maybe it was seeing the finish line, Ceejay pulled further ahead of the sow. Seth signaled the strongmen to get into position around Seth, ready to receive the exhausted runner.

"Seth!" Ceejay shouted, her eyes breaking contact with his, suddenly confused. Just steps from Seth, her feet struck an abandoned leather handbag. She was tripping, falling forward, as though her torso had outrun her legs. Her irises contracted into tiny black dots and her forehead flung back. Her arms pin wheeled and her body lurched towards the carpet.

Before he knew what he was doing, Seth leapt towards Ceejay. He grabbed her and forced both of them towards the oncoming bear. Together, they rolled at its mountainous body and underneath its still-moving legs. The sow's claws grazed Seth's cheek, loosing a small stream of blood that ran into his right eye, as they barreled under it its 800-pound body. Seth blinked frantically and waited for the sow to steamroll over him and Ceejay.

But the bear was already past them. It was almost at the theater's open doors. Ceejay and Seth jumped to their feet. Seth's mind raced: his grand plan was ruined; there was no way to get the bear through the glass now. The best thing he could do now was save the people inside the theater from having to fend off a pissed-off grizzly. "Shut the door!" he shouted to the strongmen. He and Ceejay would have to find another way out of an already bad situation.

The strongmen ignored him, instead jumping aside as the bear charged into the theater. Seth ran to the doors and looked into the Starlight. He blinked the blood out of his eye and tried to make sense of what was happening inside. The bear was halfway to the stage now. It had covered an amazing amount of distance in the time it had taken Seth to reach the theater doors. Even without him leading the way, baiting it, the bear was still making a beeline for bear-sized hole in the electrochromic window. It made no sense.

Then Seth saw him — the tuxedoed man emitting a series of high-pitched screams as he ran down the theater aisle, towards the stage and the crack in the gigantic electrochromic glass window.

Stevie was baiting the bear!

# 41

Cliffy had been in the producer's booth for what seemed like hours, his hand resting on the little silver lever. He was roasting in that small space surrounded by banks of buzzing electronics. He mopped his forehead with his shirt. The stage below him was dim, save a carefully positioned line of spotlights. At any moment, Seth would leap onto the stage, bear in tow, and break through the spotlights. That was Cliffy's signal to pull the little silver lever.

Cliffy ran his hand over the controls one more time.

*Okay*, he told himself, *you flipped the main electrical toggle. The LED is green, which means we're good to go. The selector knob is pointing at "CHROM. GLS." Perfect. Now all you have to do is pull the lever when Seth crosses the row of spotlights. The glass goes clear, the bear gets zapped. Everyone is safe, the bear is dead. Simple.*

Simple in theory, anyway. Cliffy knew that his timing was going to have to be perfect. If he pulled the lever too soon, he'd fry Seth. If he waited too long, the bear would live, and Seth would be dinner. He put his shirt to his forehead again and peered out the glass window at the front of the booth. Still nothing. People milled about nervously in the mezzanine below.

Then Cliffy heard Ceejay's voice.

There was a flurry of activity at the mezzanine railing. Cliffy could not see the theater doors from his position, so he fixed his eyes at the front of the stage, waiting for Seth to break through the darkness. Sweat poured from Cliffy's forehead and into his eyes, but he would not blink. He would keep his hand steady and his eyes on the stage. He would get this right. He would be patient. After an eternity, something leapt up onto the stage, screaming. Instead of Seth's blue oxford, it wore a tuxedo. Cliffy's mind reeled. It couldn't be. But Cliffy was certain. Stevie Bruebecker was running and waving his arms as he ran for the hole in the glass. The bear trailed close behind.

"Now, now, now!" Stevie shrieked from below. He ran through the stage, barely evading his pursuer. "Turn on the goddamn window NOW!"

What on Earth would have motivated that coward to do this? Cliffy was lost in thought. Where is Seth?

"TURN ON THE GODDAMN WINDOW NOW, GODDAMNIT!" Stevie yelled, breaking through the row of spotlights, and entering hole in the electrochromic window. Cliffy snapped to and yanked the small lever that controlled the stage window. The milky, opaque stage window cleared, becoming completely translucent. Stevie had just made it through when the sow entered the opening in the glass. The house lights flickered as the window shorted. Streaks of electricity exploded from the ragged glass edges and burrowed into the bear's fur. It howled in pain and swept its right paw forward in a last, vain attempt to catch its prey. The bear connected with Stevie's right ankle. A blue bolt of electricity shot from the bear's paw and into Stevie's leg, sending the cruise director flying across the rear deck beyond the window. The sow's legs went limp as its body rolled through the window-crack, at last coming to a stop, belly-up. Cliffy smelled burnt hair.

The theater was silent. Seth bounded onto the stage and examined the enormous brown mountain that lay just beyond the hole in the glass. Smoke rose from its great brown body. Seth carefully approached. The bear did not move or breathe. Seth poked it. It did not respond. He waved to Ceejay, who hesitantly came forward. She tapped the bear with her sneaker. Still nothing. Emboldened, she kicked the monster. Still nothing. She kicked it again, and again, and again, now beating the sow and screaming at it. Seth pulled Ceejay away from the bear, back through the glass, and into the theater. There, the bedraggled crowd stared at him and Ceejay.

"It's dead!" Seth shouted to the mezzanine. The crowd greeted him with uncomprehending silence. Seth pressed his hand against the cut on his cheek.

Cliffy turned on the house microphone. "Somebody ought to check on Stevie."

# 42

Seth peeked out from between his fingers. He wished the man on the television would just go away. His cell phone rang again, this time it was Thad. Seth pressed the device's "ignore" button, sending the call to voice mail. He had received a non-stop parade of calls since leaving the boat — Matt Schott, his parents, his secretary, even Melanie had called — but he hadn't answered any of them. He just sent them through to his voice mail, where a greeting told them, "The bear didn't get me. Please leave me alone."

"We have informal reports," the man on the television said, "that there are at least ten casualties from today's bizarre attack aboard a NordStar cruise ship in Alaska's Inside Passage." The man's perfectly coifed hair looked like a hard, plastic shell. A graphic behind him showed a growling brown bear, The Diana, and the words, "Cruise in Crisis." "I repeat, however, that we have no confirmation at this time of any final tally."

Seth groaned. He took another sip from the ice-melt at the bottom of his jack-and-coke. He was slumped over the bar at FD Munday's, a TGI Friday's rip-off that had opened for business that morning in Lutak's new port. The place was packed with The Diana's refugees. Those who were awake were glued to the flat screen above the bar. The port had turned into a Casablanca of sorts — everyone was trying to get out of Lutak, but the port remained sealed off. Cliffy was next to him, his face pressed against the bar and a nearly exhausted 555 dangling from his right hand. Ceejay dozed against Seth's left shoulder.

Those who were still awake watched the endless coverage on the bar's little television. "We go live now," the plastic-haired man said, "to Anna Lourdes in Haines, Alaska for more information. Anna, what's the situation on the ground?"

"Hi Jack," Anna said, "we're still unable to get the KIMO news team into Lutak. The roads are closed, and emergency personnel are blocking the waterways." She hooked a thumb over her shoulder. "As you can see, the Department of Homeland Security has arrived. According to a DHS spokesperson, they will deploy a team later tonight or tomorrow morning to determine whether the maulings were a freak accident or a deliberate act of domestic terrorism."

"Do we have any evidence suggesting that this is actually a terrorist attack?" the plastic-haired man asked, incredulous. "These were bear attacks, rights, Anna?"

"At this point there is no evidence linking the attacks to terrorism. But there has been speculation based on reports from The Diana's passengers that one or more individuals may have acted in concert to release a dangerous grizzly bear in a crowded part of the ship."

The man shook his head. "Thanks for that report, Anna. Stay with us as we continued to report on the Cruise in Crisis." The image cut to a commercial for some sort of vacuum.

Seth buried his head further in his hands. "I'm going to jail," he said.

"You're not," Cliffy said, handing Seth a pre-lit 555. "Here."

Seth took a long drag, exhaled and watched the smoke filter through the Munday's crowd and out into the brisk night. Ceejay stirred. Seth petted her long blonde hair until she settled back into a steady snore on his shoulder. Seth calmed himself, then put his head back in his hands.

"I slept with a terrorist," Seth said. "Did you know that?"

"Quiet," Cliffy warned him. "Other than us, nobody here knows about you and Evie. Let it alone. Keep a low profile. I can't save you from a lynching if they think you were in on it."

Seth rubbed his eyes and took another puff.

"You weren't in on it, right?" Cliffy asked.

"No! God no. What would I have to gain from this? My life is shot. My career is ruined. I'm probably wanted on criminal charges of some sort. Oh, god."

"At least Stevie's okay."

"Yeah, good for Stevie. They think he's a hero, you know."

"I know." Cliffy shook his head. "I still can't figure out why he did it."

"He was pushed. No other explanation. Those big dudes blocking the door didn't want the bear coming after them, so they threw him out there."

"Some hero."

"Yeah."

Suddenly, the Munday's crowd began murmuring loudly, waking Ceejay. Seth lifted his head from his hands, but saw nothing unusual, just wall-to-wall people. He looked at the television, still on commercial, this time for some sort of epoxy, a man shouting about its benefits. Before the commercial ended, the crowd parted, allowing something small and dirty to make its way through to the bar. It looked like a walking potato sack. As it came closer, Seth made out the thing's filthy, soot-striped face and ragged grey clothes. It was Baba Zoya. This was part of the nightmare that Seth desperately wished he'd left behind. He turned back to the bar, pretending not to notice.

Cliffy elbowed Seth. "Do you know that woman?"

"What woman?"

"That old, dirty woman behind you, she's trying to get your attention."

"I don't know what you're talking about."

Cliffy spun Seth's bar stool around so that he faced the old woman, who now had her hand to her ear as though she was talking into a telephone.

"That woman," Cliffy said.

"Everyone's staring," Ceejay said groggily. "I think she wants your phone number or something."

"She doesn't want my phone number," Seth said. He tried waving her away, but she just stood there, pretending to talk to her hand.

Cliffy huffed. "What does she want?"

"She wants me to put her in touch with my luggage salesman."

"Makes total sense," Ceejay said.

Sensing that he would be unable to get her to leave without making a scene, Seth hopped down from his stool. Baba Zoya immediately began walking back through the crowd and out of the small restaurant.

"You guys coming?" Seth asked Cliffy and Ceejay.

"Any chance it'll be dangerous?" Ceejay asked.

"Almost definitely," Seth answered.

"Then we're in," she said, pulling Cliffy from his chair and following Seth outside.


Seth, Ceejay and Cliffy watched the old woman engage in a long, animated conversation on Seth's cell phone. Finally, she took a long breath and said, "Pakah, Dmitri. Spaseeba." She handed the phone back to Seth and arranged her yellowed teeth in something approximating a smile.

"Yes, Dmitri, what does she want?" Seth asked.

"Always business first with you. You don't say 'hello, Dmitri.' 'How are you, Dmitri?' You need to slow down a bit, Seth. Understand?"

"Dmitri, you have no idea what kind of day I've had."

"No excuses, Seth. Slow it down or I won't talk to you. Pleasantries first. How are you doing?"

"My ex-girlfriend just committed mass-murder. It's all over the news."

Dmitri laughed. Seth decided not to tell him that he wasn't joking.

"And how is the luggage?"

"A lifesaver, just like you promised."

"Good! See, not so hard. We talk, we make a couple jokes, we drink some good tea, then we make serious talk."

"So, serious talk time, then?"

"Yes. Okay, what do you want to know?" Dmitri asked.

"Are you serious?"

"It's serious talk time, of course I'm serious."

"I want to know what the old woman told you. What does she want from me?"

"Ah. Yes. The old woman. Well, I think maybe she's suffering from dementia."

"What did she say?"

"Well, these things didn't make a whole lot of sense to me, so you'll have to forgive me if I get them wrong."

"Just try."

"Okay, first, she tells me she knew your girlfriend very well. But this makes no sense, because she is in Alaska and you are from Phoenix, and you did not bring your fiancé with you to Alaska. So, you know, crazy, right?"

"Did she mention any names?"

"Yes. She says your girlfriend is named Effie. But that doesn't sound right, either. Wasn't your fiancé named Melody or something?"

"Melanie. I'm following so far. Go on."

"If you say so. Okay, so Baba Zoya says this Effie told her that she was probably not going to live past today, and that she wanted Baba Zoya to deliver a message to you on her behalf."

Seth's mind was reeling. How long had Evie been planning her attack? Had she slept with him just to get onto the ship? No, that made no sense. After all, it had been his idea to capture the bear and put it in the glass tower, not hers. Her decision to free the bear could not have been the result of some master plan. And what message could she possibly need to give him? Didn't killing and maiming dozens aboard a cruise ship send a strong enough message? Nothing made any sense any more. "Tell me the message, Dmitri."

"This is where what she says gets really weird. There are two parts. First, Zoya said that Effie wanted you to know that it's Effie's fault that the

Russians misled you about the bear attacks. Effie wanted you to know that none of the Russian's children had been attacked by a bear. She asked the Russians to tell you that story so that you wouldn't know what was really happening."

"What did the old woman say was really happening?"

"That's the second part. I told you this was weird, and maybe it's the translation. You know, some words in Russian you can't just say in English. So, you know, there's that. But there's always dementia. I think that's the simplest answer."

Cliffy pulled on Seth's shirt.

"Stop it," Seth whispered to Cliffy.

"But Seth —" Cliffy said.

"Give me a second," Seth said impatiently. Then to Dmitri, "Will you stop trying to understand what she meant and just tell me what she said?"

"Okay, okay," Dmitri said. "Touchy, touchy. She said Effie instructed the old woman to tell you that she was trying to save the white bear, whatever that means. The old woman said Effie thought the white one was special. It needed protection."

"White bear? What did she mean by white bear?"

"That's all she said."

"We need to get you back on the phone with her. I need to know more. This doesn't make any sense."

"I told you it wouldn't. I think that Russian family has been in the bush too long."

Seth pulled the phone from his ear and started to hand it back to Baba Zoya, then realized that she was nowhere to be found.

"Where did she go?" Seth asked.

"I was trying to tell you," Cliffy said.

"Tell me what?" Seth asked.

"She ran off," Ceejay said. "She was awfully fast for an old lady."

Seth craned his neck, but there was no sign of her. "Christ," he said, then pulled the phone back to his ear. "Dmitri, she's gone."

"Don't worry about it, Seth. She was a crazy old bat."

"She didn't tell you anything else? Think."

"Nope, just that no bear attacked a little child and that she wanted you to know about some special albino bear."

"Bizarre," Seth said, shaking his head. Another burst of noise from inside Munday's caught his attention. "Dmitri, I think I need to go. I'll talk to you soon." He folded the phone and pushed his way back into the busy bar.

"What's going on?" Seth asked a man near the door.

"They didn't get anything," the man said.

"What are you talking about?"

"The stuff that the CNN cameraman captured just before he was attacked on Ripinski yesterday morning. He didn't get anything."

"Nothing?" Seth forced his way through the crowds, trying to get a view of the flat screen. The crowd quieted when the news anchor spoke.

"Anna," the plastic-haired man said, "you're saying that there's no video of the actual attack?"

"That's correct, Jack," the reporter replied, "what you are about to see is the only footage that Mr. Tucker captured. Following this footage, the image becomes static, leaving only the audio portion of the tape. For obvious reasons, CNN refuses to release that portion of the tape."

"Well, that's certainly a relief," the anchor said, mocking concern. The news station cut away from the news desk to a beautiful nature scene, a sunny shot of the lake outside Lutak framed by an open glade. Suddenly, the camera zoomed to the left and found two small grizzlies playing among the ferns. The Munday's crowd involuntarily cooed at the little bears. The scene pulled away from the cubs and scanned the surroundings. The jerky camera movement nauseated Seth, but he couldn't look away. The camera bobbed back and forth and then stopped when it found what it was looking for.

There was no mistaking it. It had the same disappointing face – the drooping, grayish-brown jowls, the same look of irritated boredom that Seth remembered from the day before. The camera kept a shaky long-zoom on the bear. He was certain that it was the same grizzly that he had encountered near the Russian encampment — the bear that they brought aboard The Diana. Some of the Munday's crowd left the bar, apparently unable to sit through video of the same animal that rampaged through The Diana earlier that evening. Most, however — Seth included — were transfixed.

Suddenly, the bear looked right into the camera. The footage became even shakier as the cameraman scrambled away from his open position. Occasionally, the camera turned back to where the bear had been, but it was so wobbly that Seth couldn't be sure whether the sow was still in the shot. Then there was a crunching noise. The camera spun, cycling between green and blue color fields until it finally washed out in a sea of white. Then there was nothing. The television cut back to the reporter's frowning face. Seth looked away. The Munday's crowd resumed its normal murmur. Cliffy and Ceejay were at his side now.

"I guess that settles it," Seth said sighed. "We had the right bear. I just wish I had known what Evie was planning. But how could I have known?"

"You couldn't," Cliffy said. "But at least this proves you did your best for NordStar."

Seth shrugged.

"What did that old woman have to say?" Cliffy asked.

"She said she knew Evie somehow. But most of was nonsense. Something about a special bear."

Seth wanted to believe that the women was crazy, that there was simply no explanation for what Evie had done on The Diana. But his brain couldn't let go of the puzzle. The old woman had said that the bear was white. He flashed to the image at the end of the videotape – the field of white. It still made no sense. He was tired. He would think about her cryptic message after he had some much-needed rest. Until then, he needed to get through tonight without any more trouble.

Cliffy elbowed him. "Check this out."

The crowd quieted once again, listening intently. The TV showed the kind of candid, happy snapshot that local news shows reserve only for really terrible things. The photo showed a smiling, chubby woman, probably in her mid-thirties, the name "Tina Paloski" underneath. "You're saying another mauling occurred in the same area early this morning?" the plastic-haired anchor asked.

The murmur in the Munday's crowd grew into an angry buzz.

"Wasn't the bear on the ship all this morning and last night?" Cliffy asked.

"Yeah," Seth said. "It was." He looked back outside, and saw hundreds of passengers still milling about the port's main square. He thought about the video again. Then it hit him. "We have to get everyone inside."

# 43

"Okay, but how likely is it that the thing that attacked that woman is going to charge into a big, loud crowd?" Cliffy asked, hurrying to keep up with Seth.

"It happened on the ship," Seth answered. "I don't see why it wouldn't happen again."

"Yeah," Ceejay answered, running alongside, "but it's not like it had a choice on the ship. That red-haired bitch basically threw it at a crowd. I'm no expert, but I can't imagine any grizzly's going to voluntarily put itself in the middle of a crowd."

Seth stopped and Ceejay nearly tumbled over him.

"I don't think we're dealing with a grizzly bear," Seth said.

"What?" Cliffy and Ceejay asked simultaneously.

"You saw the video, Seth," Ceejay said.

"I didn't see anything. And what Evie did doesn't make any sense if it was a grizzly."

"Okay," Ceejay said, now furious, "first of all, there is no reason for what Evie did. She was crazy. It makes zero sense to drop a bomb on people, and that's exactly what she did. Crazy."

"No. I don't buy it. She had a reason. She told me something about doing something drastic if she saw the need. There's something bigger here. I'm not saying that what she did was justified, but don't you think it would be a mistake to just dismiss what she did as pure lunacy?"

Ceejay slapped him. "Just because she slept with you," she said, and then welled up.

Seth put his hand against the hot spot where Ceejay had slapped him. She flushed red, then ran away.

"Ceejay!" Seth shouted after her. She ran out into the dark beyond the brightly lit square.

Cliffy shook his head.

"We need to go after her," Seth said. "She won't be safe alone."

"Stop it," Cliffy said. "Let her go. She's been through enough tonight."

"No, you've got to understand. Something that old woman said is bothering me. Look, we can definitely agree that someone was attacked while we thought the situation was under control, right? While the grizzly on that tape was sealed away on our ship."

Cliffy nodded.

"You've got to believe me. There's something more here, and I don't want to have another scene like we had on The Diana. Neither of us wants to go through anything like that again."

"Okay, Ozymandias. But tell me, what do we do about it?"

"Well," Seth said, "getting everyone back onto The Diana is not an option. Nobody's allowed to board until the emergency crew and DHS finish up. And the port buildings will be like the stores on the Diana – not enough room."

"What about the old town? I've heard that some folks headed that way, looking for a way out."

"Too far for a lot of these folks to walk."

"So what's left?"

Seth thought for a moment, then it came to him. It was so obvious, he was angry he hadn't thought of it earlier. "The Inn at the End of Paradise."

"The what?"

"I'll get these people moving, you find Ceejay."

# 44

The Inn at the End of Paradise was how Seth remembered it — low and long, more like an enormous warehouse than a quaint bed and breakfast. He stood at the edge of the long footpath leading to the Inn's door. A mass of people — The Diana's refugees — was close behind him. He felt like Moses leading his people to the Promised Land. As before, gunmen in blue NordStar jumpsuits blocked the door to the Inn. They looked at Seth dispassionately, but kept the barrels of their automatic weapons pointed straight at his head. Seth broke from the throng and walked straight towards the Inn's doors.

The gunmen had dark complexions, probably Latino, and were quite short. One of the men dropped a cigarette on the ground and squashed it beneath his boot. Seth showed them a pack of Zoran's Croatian cigarettes. The men stared at him, but said nothing.

"You gentlemen running low?" Seth asked. He kept walking towards them, ever mindful of the guns aimed his way. He shook his cigarette pack until a smoke poked its way through the pack's cellophane wrapper. He pointed the free cigarette at them, but they still showed no interest. Seth reached into his pocket.

"Whoa!" yelled one of the armed men. "*Cogelo suave!*" yelled the other. They simultaneously cocked their weapons.

Seth threw his hands in the air, tossing the free cigarette in the process. The hand that was previously in his pocket now held a Zippo lighter. He pointed to the lighter with his pack hand. "Just a lighter, guys." He flicked the lighter a couple of times to give them the right idea.

"*Pendejo,*" one said, then restored the safety on his gun.

"*Ese tipo se conseguirá disparó. Pendejo,*" the said, then spit on the ground.

Seth smiled and brought his hands back down. He wasn't sure how he was going to convince these men to let his people into the safety of the Inn. Maybe he could call Matt Schott? Matt seemed to have a good grasp of Spanish. Then again, Seth could never really be sure that Matt knew what he was saying. That could cause more trouble. He decided to stick to universal currency – cigarettes. He put one in his mouth, lit it, then offered one to each of the gunmen.

The first man shook his head. "*Tengo todos los canceres que necesito, gringo.*"

The second man laughed and said, "*Y no necesitamos esa mierda extranjera.*"

This was going nowhere. Maybe he should just try the direct approach.

"Can I go in?" Seth asked.

The men stared at him.

He made his fingers walk across his palm, and then pointed into the hotel.

The first man smiled with understanding, then shook his head. "*Prohibito,*" he said, then looked at his colleague and stuck his thumb at Seth. "*Mudo.*" The other gunman laughed.

*So much for straightforward*, Seth thought. He started for the doors, but was pushed back by a pair of gun barrels.

"*Dije prohibido, y yo lo signifiqué,*" the first man said.

So they hadn't let him in, but they hadn't put at holes in him, either. The previous day, standing before the Russian's rifles, Seth had learned what it looked like a person was prepared to pull the trigger. And these jump-suited buffoons didn't have it in them.

"Thanks guys," he told the two men. "Be back in a few."

He walked back to the trailhead. Cliffy had just arrived and he was breathing hard. Seth pulled him aside.

"No sign of Ceejay," Cliffy said.

"We can't wait for her to show. We need to get everyone inside."

Cliffy nodded.

"You see those two men?" Seth asked.

"The ones with the automatics?" Cliffy asked. "Yeah."

"They might look scary, but they're not going to stop us. Do you think you can convince the crowd to rush the door?"

"Yeah, I've got it." Cliffy hopped up on a nearby tree stump. He shouted to the crowd, "Okay, everyone. We can all go in, but we have to move very quickly."

The sea of people stood still. Seth shook his head. He pushed Cliffy from the stump and jumped up in his place.

"Bear!" he shrieked, pointed past the crowd, and ran for the Inn's door.

Cliffy ran after him, the panicked army of passengers and crew following suit. The gunmen's eyes widened, white showing all the way around their irises. They abandoned their posts and ran for the sides of the building.

Seth and Cliffy were the first to reach the hotel's massive wooden doors. They pushed through and ran into the hotel's grand lobby: a large, dimly-lit space adorned with all sorts of rustic touches — stuffed bears and foxes, antler chandeliers, rugs made of various hides. To their left was a giant stacked-stone fireplace with a crackling blaze. To their right was an immense wood-and-stone staircase leading to metal doorway. Straight ahead was a long granite reception counter. Behind the counter, a small, bespectacled receptionist blinked his eyes. A security camera above the little man's head swiveled towards Seth and Cliffy, a red light flashing beneath the lens.

"Can I help you gentlemen?" the receptionist asked, then smiled and looked up at the camera. A crush of passengers and crew filed in behind Seth and Cliffy, filling the Inn's lobby. There were still a great number outside, trying to push their way in. The receptionist looked at the growing crowd behind Seth and Cliff. "Oh, no. I'm sorry, no. We don't have room for—"

"You'll find room," Seth said. "Or we'll take it. We need to get everyone in here, where it's safe."

"You don't understand, we just don't have any rooms available." He shrugged and wrinkled his nose.

"I'll need to see a manager."

"Yeah, we're not set up that way."

Seth leapt over the counter and grabbed the little man by his tie. He scanned the small, carpeted space behind the reception counter. It held none of the customary hotel accoutrements: no little key-card folders, or, for that matter, key-cards; no printers, no pens, no paper; no computers and no monitors; nothing to suggest that the little man had any way of checking hotel guests in or out. The only piece of equipment was a small, black walkie-talkie, that suddenly squawked to life.

A distorted voice from within barked a command that Seth couldn't comprehend. Then came a short, electric buzzing noise from somewhere else in the reception space, followed by a sliding click, like an airplane lavatory becoming vacant. The little man nodded and felt along the dark wood paneling lining the wall behind him. The man pushed the paneling and a door-sized section of wood popped back towards him. He pulled the panel-door wide, revealing a rectangle of blinding white.

"Follow me," he said.

Seth followed the little man through the doorway and into the whiteness beyond.

## 45

Seth squinted and threw a hand before his eyes.

Before him was a blinding field of white punctuated by the occasional blue dot or smear, depending on how fast the blue things moved. His senses were bombarded by fresh paint and an annoying clacking sound, like a thousand chopsticks striking bare, concrete walls. He stumbled forward and hit his shin against a low obstruction.

There was snickering nearby. Seth guessed it was from the receptionist, but he was still unable to make him out in this bright space.

He bent down to comfort his bruised leg and smacked his head against something else. The colorful fireworks that erupted before his eyes provided some relief from all of that white. He felt for the thing that whacked him in the head. It was cylindrical, a tube of some sort. His hands worked across the tube, searching a few feet to either side for a beginning or end, but found neither. He slumped to the floor and sat against the tube, resigned not to move until he could clearly see the obstacles around him.

Finally, the room came into focus. Seth was in a warehouse-sized space, lit by hundreds of intensely bright circles hanging in neat rows from a white corrugated-metal ceiling. He sat on a white linoleum floor, leaning against a white pipe that fed into a jumble of the same. The pipe led in and out of white cylinders and spheres and passed through gauges and interconnects – all things about which Seth knew little or nothing. To him, it looked like a giant robot's esophagus. Smokestacks jutted through holes in the metal roof. Men in blue jumpsuits walked about the space, staring at glass instruments and making adjustments with enormous wrenches. The waxy imprints of their work boots occasionally interrupted the linoleum's blinding sheen.

The smiling receptionist stood a few feet to Seth's left. Before Seth could say anything to him, the little man straightened his tie and yanked open the hidden door to the reception area. A thousand angry voices spilled through, then disappeared with a whoosh as the door shut. The little man was gone. Seth nodded, grabbed the pipe, and pulled himself to his feet. As he stood, his nose nearly touching the pipe, Seth saw that the tubing was dotted with something small: a vividly-colored sunflower with propeller blades for petals, the same logo he had seen pinned to Evie's dartboard and on the chainsaw-cut sign outside. The words ST Energy were printed in a sterile font underneath.

Just above Seth's head, C-clamped to the pipe, was a sign that read, "Prohibido Fumar! No smoking! Smoking in area REF T-1 is a violation ST Energy Policy." Below the warning was the familiar sunflower made of propeller blades. Suddenly, Seth saw the little sunflower logo everywhere: on the back of the reception door, in the middle of the glass gauges, stamped on the side of the metal cylinders and balls, even in the waxy work boot imprints on the white linoleum floor. What was this ST Energy doing at a cruise stop? And why all the secrecy?

Seth figured that he was standing in some sort of factory, maybe a refinery of some sort. Even though the equipment looked unused, Seth guessed that the unknown corporation had been here for some time. He didn't recall ever hearing of ST Energy, however. Just the same, something about the name sounded familiar. Seth thought about the company name, and what the old woman told him about the white bear. He thought about Evie trying to protect something here, saying that she might have to take drastic measures, then doing so. She wasn't doing it to protect the grizzly bears, or she wouldn't have set one loose only to face certain death aboard a cruise ship. She was trying to stop something. Something big. And, here he was, in the middle of a big something that made no sense, something that had been left out of the plans, something that was unexplained and unexplainable. Somehow, Seth knew, this place was the key to everything. He slowly ran over the pieces again, searching everything he knew for some sort of clue.

*Okay,* he told himself, *Buddy ran NordStar Cruise Line in his charismatic brother Lord's place. NordStar was on the brink of bankruptcy.*

*NordStar was gambling its survival on a new stop in Lutak and a brand new ship called The Diana. As The Diana began its maiden voyage to Lutak, news networks learned about an unusual number of fatal bear attacks in the vicinity. Unbeknownst to the news networks, the killer bear had also somehow disarmed its first two victims. Buddy decided to take his lawyer – me – and the ship's head purser on a hunt for the animal that threatened to destroy his company. I slept with Evie. The next morning, instead of finding the bear, we were captured by an ancient Russian sleeper cell run by a dirty old woman named Baba Zoya. She told us that a bear had attacked one of the cell's children. We found the bear that had attacked the child, but before we tranquilize it, Buddy shot Tammy in the face with a tiny shotgun. Evie and the Russian sleeper cell tranquilized the bear, then helped NordStar stow it in a giant glass tower aboard the Diana. Evie let the bear loose into a crowd. We killed the escaped bear by shorting out a giant electrochromic glass window. The real bear, or whatever it was, was still mauling people near the new port, as evidence by a recent attack on a jogger. The dirty old Russian lady told me that Evie and the Russians had purposefully misled us because Evie was protecting some sort of rare, white bear. And now I am in some sort of secret refinery built inside an Inn and operated by a mysterious company called ST Energy.*

*Okay, so how do these pieces all fit together?*

*They don't.*

And then, as often happened to Seth the night before a motion was due, when he was lost deciphering the most difficult of legal ambiguities, the disparate factoids and random events pulled together into something that resembled actual, logical sense – at least enough to make Seth very, very angry.

"Scott Tennison!" he yelled.

# 46

The old man's voice wafted down from somewhere above Seth. "Up here."

Seth mounted a white metal staircase and found an open door at the top. A piece of paper was taped to the door: "ST Energy General Services Office." Seth walked through the doorway and was into the small, spare room beyond. It had just enough room for two white plastic chairs, a folding table with beige plastic top, a small grey filing cabinet, a black torchiere lamp, and Buddy. Buddy sat behind the desk, a blank expression on his face and a beer in his hand.

"ST," Seth said. "Scott 'Buddy' Tennison. You're ST Energy."

Buddy took a swig of beer, the foam drawing up into his enormous white mustache. "I always preferred Scott to Buddy. James got 'Lord' and I got 'Buddy.' Lord got NordStar and I got to watch. At least that was the plan. The old man knew I was smarter than James, but he just didn't like me much — said I left a bad taste in his mouth." He took another drink, spilled a few amber drops onto his shirt, then wiped them away with a thick thumb.

"So," Seth asked, "all of this because you're mad at daddy?"

"You know that's not true."

"Maybe. But none of this was really supposed to work out, was it?"

"I think it worked out beautifully." Buddy drained the beer and put the empty bottle on the desk.

"Why, because you only planned to bankrupt NordStar, not to mire it in scandal? Is that what you mean?"

"The Lutak project was never going to save NordStar. It was too damned expensive. You would have known that if you weren't so concerned with impressing me — and making partner. Just look at the money NordStar dropped into that ship. Virtual steering technology? A town square on a ship's top deck? The glass wine tower? The world's largest electrochromic window? Seriously? Not to mention the money NordStar dropped into Lutak itself. 'Telluride in Alaska' — that's what the architects called it. A drowning company shouldn't be spending money like that. Ridiculous."

"But these were all expenses that you authorized."

"Not authorized, son. Approved and suggested. And I didn't exactly do it in a vacuum. Lord was drunk on the idea of building in Lutak. He wanted the electrochromic window and the fancy promenade, too. And Captain Kelly, that conservative, cautious fart? He wanted the new nav tech. He said that it would make for an interesting tour. And who's to say he was wrong?" Buddy smiled. "Anyway, I'm not NordStar's CEO. Final approval fell to Lord. I was just a consultant. Hell, I don't even own stock in the damned company. It's not my fault if Lord was more rubber stamp than CEO. He never did enjoy working much."

"So, no legal ties. No fiduciary duties."

"Good. That's right. I knew you were smart."

"And no ties to Lutak, either. Nothing tying you to the town that poured its hopes and resources into a new port to provide much needed employment and money to a struggling town? You killed two birds with one stone, didn't you?"

"I can't take all the credit. Most of this just fell into my lap." He shook his fat index finger at Seth, "But I take advantage of every opportunity, always have. You'll learn that about me."

"I've learned more than I want to already." Seth dropped into the remaining chair.

"Oh, don't act so shocked."

"People died."

"Little people always fall prey to progress."

"Little people like Tammy Wurser?"

"Exactly," Buddy said. "A complete mistake, I assure you. But, yes, she fell in the service of something greater. Anyway, she had her hand out, too. It's not like shooting her was the worst mistake I have ever made."

Seth shook his head in disbelief.

"Don't act like you didn't play a part. As you may recall, it was your idea to keep an entire ship in the dark about the maulings. Your idea to bring a bear — a grizzly bear! — onto a ship full of passengers. And to put it in a glass case! To make matters worse, you brought your bleeding heart, eco-extremist ex-girlfriend — a woman who was literally in league with Russians — into the place where she could do the most damage. And those were just the things you did after you boarded my The Diana!

"Before that, you spent two years looking for ways to squeeze money from a budget that had none. I never thought The Diana would launch. I thought it would rust away in some Holland shipyard as NordStar's remaining assets were sold off to other cruise lines. But you found the money. And how did you do it? You took it from NordStar's crew: a bunch of third-worlders who make nothing off-ship, who send the majority of what they make home to their impoverished families. I'm guessing a few of their mothers, brothers, sisters, or children won't survive their next illness or poor crop. They're going to die because you took from them and gave to your client. Don't kid yourself, son. You bear responsibility here." Buddy laughed grimly. "Bear."

"You used me."

"We used each other, son. You wanted partnership, so you advised your client to do stupid things that swept a very dangerous situation under the rug. You used Evie, too. You teased the dying embers of a failed relationship into full blaze in order to get approval for our port — and then to obtain a hunting license on protected ground."

"Not true," Seth said. "I didn't use you or Evie. I did what you hired me to do. I never knew your end game. Or hers."

Buddy ignored him. "And let's not forget Cliffy," he said. "Your oddly-named sidekick. You told him he had only one option to save the cruise line and his job. When all of this is scrutinized — and I assure you it will be — his role will come to light. If he's not detained in the United States, he'll be deported back to Vietnam. And you know what his opportunities will be there. You, Seth, let ambition cloud your morality. Not to mention your legal ethics. Discussing legal issues with a subordinate without management's permission? Why, that alone is enough to get you disbarred in most states."

Seth reddened.

"I'm not judging you, son. We all make our own choices. Maybe you didn't know where yours would ultimately lead, but it didn't take a genius to realize that it might not be good. So you took a gamble. The least you can do is own it." Buddy sucked himself out of his chair and walked to the office door. "But guess what? There's a silver lining. Walk with me, son."

Reluctantly, Seth rose and followed Buddy down the white metal stairs and onto the refinery floor.

"You see these men?" Buddy pointed to the blue-jumpsuited employees dotted here and there throughout the space. "Dominicans. I brought them in to get things going. And they're doing a fine job. A fine job."

"They don't make great security guards."

"Oh, they would. Believe me. But I don't let them shoot anyone. I don't want ST Energy to get into the sort of trouble NordStar's about to face. And I never thought that anyone would have the balls to test them out!" Buddy laughed and clapped Seth on the shoulder. "Caught your shenanigans on camera. I didn't think you had it in you."

"It's been a surprising few days."

"It surely has. Anyway, back to the good news. Look around you. It's after midnight, and there are still more than 50 Dominicans working here. Do you see what I'm getting at?"

Seth thought about this for a moment. "Once the place is up and running, you'll have Dominicans here around the clock? I'm not sure I see a silver lining."

"Not Dominicans, son. In about a week, the Dominicans go home for good. All of the ones working in the port, and all of the ones here in the refinery, they all vanish. And guess who replaces them?" Buddy raised his snowy eyebrows.

Seth began to understand. "The good people of Lutak."

Buddy smiled.

"But only if they're willing to play ball. Right?"

"Good. That's right." Buddy patted one of the vast networks of pipes. "It'll be just like the army. We're breaking Lutak down to build it back up."

"Let me get this straight. You encouraged Lutak to put all of their eggs in the cruise line basket with the intent to ruin the town's economy? That's why you had to hide your refinery in an Inn. You wanted to keep the town from knowing where all this was really headed. Then, once you've put NordStar in bankruptcy and ruined the Lutak's chances at becoming a viable tourist destination, you offer them an olive branch called 'drilling.' Is that it?"

Buddy smiled. "Drilling, mining, whatever. The feds seem to think we're sitting on vast natural resources here. But most of the other towns along the Passage — Haines, Skagway, Ketchikan, even Sitka — wouldn't dream of upsetting their precious tourist dollars by investigating natural resources. But Lutak will. I've seen to that." Buddy's eyes became glassy. He no longer looked at Seth. He walked ahead of Seth to the rear of the enormous refinery.

"Lutak will play ball," Buddy continued. "We've already lined up exploratory contracts that will last for decades — even if we never find a damn thing. Just think about the money this will generate for the town. The employment! This goes far beyond what any cruise line can offer. This is a chance for Lutak to become the energy-producing capital of the United States. What I've done — what ST Energy has done — is going to be a very good thing for Lutak."

"And a very good thing for Scott Tennison, right?" Seth asked.

"Oh," Buddy said, still in a daze. "Very. And it can be good for you, too, Seth."

They reached an immense rolling door at the back of the refinery. Buddy hit a green button and the door rolled up into itself. White light from the refinery spilled out into the moonless night, illuminating a small parking lot and part of the road leading to Lutak. A few people wandered along the road, pilgrims moving in a slow column towards town. Seth guessed there was no more room at the Inn. One of the pilgrims stopped to look at Seth and Buddy standing in the bright doorway but quickly lost interest and continued on his way.

"I don't want any part of this," Seth said. "I'm done."

"I don't see that you have any other choice." Buddy walked into the dimly lit parking lot. "You're going to lose your job at Radley. I'll see to that. And, Seth, the appearance of impropriety is pretty strong here. At least enough to get you disbarred. I'll see to that, too. Come on, let's have a drink at Mother's. We can discuss your options."

Seth didn't move.

"You lawyers are all the same. Okay, I'm buying. Now can we go?"

"It's dangerous out there," Seth said. "We both know that."

"There are plenty of people on the road. And we both know what we're dealing with here — the 'white bears.' I know that the old woman visited you in the port."

Seth still did not move.

"Look, son, there are people all over the road. No polar bear is going to attack a crowd on purpose. Come, let's drink to your new job."

Buddy marched across the parking lot with his chest puffed outward and then disappeared into the black road beyond the lot. Seth stared into the darkness beyond the lights, looking for ominous shapes. He ignored his gut and chased after Buddy. The road ahead was lit only by the occasional orange sodium light atop a tall wooden pole. Seth caught up with Buddy quickly.

"I thought so," Buddy said. "How does ST Energy General Counsel sound?"

"You'll pay me to keep my mouth shut."

Buddy drew so close to Seth that their noses touched. "I'm going to tell you exactly what I told Evie. If you don't want to work with me, if you want to blab to the press or whoever will listen to such madness, fine. But I will do everything in my power to discredit you. And, after everything you've done over the past three days, that won't be difficult."

"Why not just have me killed?" Seth asked. "You were more than willing to kill the people on The Diana?"

"That wasn't my decision, son. You know that already. Evie acted alone."

"And why would she do that?"

"I can only guess."

"Then guess. You want my silence, I want to understand. That's the price."

Buddy considered this for a moment. "My best guess is that she thought it was the only way to get to me. That things were so far out of her hands that she could only stop me by hurting NordStar."

"So, what, you got Evie to back NordStar's presence in Lutak by promising that you'd protect polar bears? I don't buy it."

"You've really put some thought into this, haven't you? The answer is 'no,' Evie was on board long before we knew anything about polar bears. Hell, she was with us even before they went on the endangered species list."

"Then how did it happen? How did you fold her into your web?"

"I paid her off."

"Not a chance."

"You're awfully naive for a seasoned attorney, son."

The two continued along the dark path, careful to stay out of the earshot of the groups of cruisers walking to Lutak.

"No," Seth said. "I don't buy it. I saw her cabin. She wasn't exactly living high on the hog."

"Oh, I didn't give her the money. It went to MacReary. His grant was exhausted and the economy was tanking. He was having difficulty finding funding. Picking up clumps of soil around the passage and declaring them either 'too loamy' or 'too silty' was exactly the kind of pork Washington was looking to eliminate."

"So, you became his benefactor."

"In a way. MacReary refused to take money from me in exchange for his support. I tried. He said he would have rather see his project disappear than give NordStar an inroad to Lutak. But Evie wasn't willing to let MacReary's research die. And she thought the port could be a boon to a struggling town. So, we set up a shell corporation to fund the grant and she backed NordStar. Easy."

"But then she came across the polar bear."

"Not her, the Russians."

"You knew about the Russians?"

"Son, everyone around these parts knows about the Russians. They've been living in the bush for years. Evie and Bill even paid them to take soil samples from time to time. They told her about the polar bear last year."

"Then why didn't she tell Bill about them?"

"Again, I can only guess."

"Go ahead."

"She must have thought telling me would get me to stop NordStar's work in Lutak until we could figure out how to lessen our impact on the migrating polar bears. And I'm sure she didn't want Bill to know more about her involvement with NordStar than she had to."

"Wait. I'm confused. Didn't MacReary already know that Evie was backing NordStar?"

"He knew she was backing NordStar's expansion in the port. He knew they had a difference of opinion over its impact on Lutak. But he had no idea that we were the source of his new funding. And this new discovery made their geological research even more important. Maybe Evie thought — correctly — that if NordStar had to stop building altogether, Bill would lose his funding. Maybe she thought — incorrectly — that talking to me could get NordStar to stop building without stopping the funding, at least temporarily. I don't know why she would have thought that. Hell, I don't know why so many people think I'm some sort of Good Samaritan. I'm told I look like Wilford Brimley. People seem to trust that man."

Lutak wasn't far away now. Seth thought they had covered the better part of a mile, and he couldn't believe he was still talking to this awful man, that he hadn't yet tried to strangle the man proudly responsible for so much devastation. He wanted to take another pain pill — and maybe a sip of Mother's hooch.

"So, what then? Did you threaten her?"

"I deserve more credit than that. No, I asked Evie to keep the bears to herself until I got back to her. Amazingly, she did, and somehow she got the Russians to keep it quiet as well. Again, easy. After a few calls, I found out that there had been polar bear sightings just north of the Passage and all along the same latitude in Eastern Canada. Polar bear migration was putting the animals in serious consideration for placement on the U.S. Department of the Interior's endangered species list. If that happened, it stood a good chance of ruining ST Energy and NordStar. That wouldn't do. So, I contacted some of my friends in DC. They came through, at first. They even got Alaska's governor to write an op-ed for the New York Times, discouraging the government from putting Ursus Maritimus on the list – in exchange for a call to the RNC about her viability as a VP candidate, of course. Ultimately, though, none of it made a lick of difference. Ursus maritimus still made the endangered species list. So, I went to plan B. I had to make sure that no one knew that polar bears were in Lutak."

"So, you threatened Evie."

"No. I told her the truth."

Seth laughed. "I can't wait to hear your version of the truth."

"You should never fear the truth, Seth. I don't. I told Evie that Lutak sat on natural resources. I told her that there were interests that wanted to tap into them. I told her that those interests would kill the bears. I told her that they might be willing to kill her, too, if they had to. They wouldn't let her or an endangered animal stand in the way of development – the future of our country's energy supply is far too important for that. No, they'd make the town an offer it couldn't refuse. They'd find their way in and drill somehow. Unless—"

"Unless NordStar was successful in Lutak."

"Precisely. I told her that a cruise stop would have little or no affect on the polar bears, and it would keep the town flush with cash. The bears sleep most of the day and hunt only at night. The likelihood that a bunch of day-tripping cruisers would ever run into one was pretty remote, and entirely manageable. I still believe that. I told her she just had to keep the polar bears a secret until NordStar had a successful foothold in Lutak. Then we could go public with the polar bears. Might even make Lutak a new eco-friendly travel destination."

"She fell for that?"

"More than fell for it. She agreed to take responsibility for the bear population. It wasn't hard. Very few of Lutak's residents camped out, and most visitors stayed in town. If she thought someone was going to enter polar bear territory, either she or the Russians made sure they posed no threat. Like I said, it was all very manageable."

"Until people started dying."

"That actually made things easier. Look, when Evie took the bullets from Rainbow Bear and he wound up dead, she was now killing people in the name of preservation. It turned her into an extremist, a killer, and she needed my silence as much as I needed hers. I mean, she was a murderer now, and I could hold that over her head if need be. Things were working out splendidly."

"Until Bill died, I guess?" Seth said.

"No, things changed before the MacRearys were killed. It was that Inn. It was a little too clever, a little too big. Evie became suspicious. She thought I was violating her trust by expanding the scope of NordStar's development in Lutak; that I was planning to exploit the polar bears without her consent. One night last summer, she broke in. That was back before I gave the Dominicans guns. She called me, furious over what I'd built. She insisted that I tell her what ST Energy was doing in Lutak. I told her she wasn't entitled to that information. That's when she started threatening to blow the lid off of the whole thing. She said she would tell the world about the polar bears in Lutak.

"So, I reminded her of what I told her when we started working together. The fact that I was the interest that wanted to explore Lutak's natural resources made no difference. Unless she towed the line, I would kill the local polar bear population myself. I also reminded her that she was responsible for Bill and Lois's deaths, Rainbow Bear's, too. And maybe others, who knew? I pushed hard. It made her desperate, I think. Her prank on The Diana didn't really surprise me. She was coming unglued. But like I said, she badly misjudged my attachment to NordStar."

They passed the Lutak Burger 'n' Shake, a ghostly, late night silhouette. There was a sign for "Ol' Fashioned Root Beer" written in big, black marker against orange poster board. Seth wished in vain that he could take back the last week, maybe the last two years. That he could sit here in full daylight, have a meal with Evie, and warn her about the troubles to come.

"You really have everyone wrapped around your little fingers, don't you?"

"I give people rope. Just like I did with you. But I'm doing something different for you — I'm giving you an out. This is an opportunity to live very comfortably with our little secret. Or you can do what everyone else seems to do with their rope. It's your call."

Seth stopped walking. Buddy came to a halt a few feet ahead of him. Lutak loomed large behind Buddy. Its buildings crowded either side of the muddy road, like a rickety, wooden set of teeth waiting to swallow Buddy whole. Seth had no idea what to do.

"It's go time, son," Buddy said. "We can walk up to Mother's and toast our future success or we can part ways. I'd wish you luck, but I know it won't do you much good. You're not the lucky sort. So, what's it going to be?"

Seth's lawyer brain went into hyper drive. He had never had rigid morals, but an alliance with Buddy was clearly wrong. He knew that. Then again, if he took Buddy's carrot, he had a clean way out of the mess he had caused —

he just had to keep one little secret. Everything that had gone wrong in the past week, from the MacRearys' deaths to the catastrophe aboard The Diana could be pinned on someone else: Evie. As for the other attacks – the maulings in Lutak that happened while his grizzly was imprisoned on The Diana – he figured that they could just pin the blame on yet another grizzly. Anomalies occur. They could keep the polar bear population a secret. The Russians could be bought. The only witnesses to the polar bears had all perished. It was all doable. Manageable. For the first time in days, Seth felt like he could take a breath. There was a way out. All he had to do was work with this man who everyone seemed to trust. All he had to do was let things be. He shook his head.

*How low have I fallen?*

"Buddy," he said, "I just —"

Something slammed into Seth's shoulder, hard.

# 47

"Run!" Ceejay shouted. She raced by, a blur of limbs and blonde hair. Her knee brushed Seth's arm, leaving a splotch of bright, red blood. He looked back down the road to towards the port, trying to see where she had come from, why she was running, but all he could see was Cliffy's terrified face. It came to a stop inches from Seth's.

"At the edge of the port," he panted. "Near the woods, bleeding but okay."

"What are you talking about?"

"Ceejay. I found Ceejay. But I wasn't the first. Let's go. It's coming."

Seth spun around. The column of people that had been around them just minutes before was now gone, replaced by a chaotic jumble running every which way, screaming. Panicked passengers pushed through Seth and knocked Buddy to the road. Buddy's glasses flew from his nose and were crushed under foot against newly laid asphalt.

"We need to go!" Cliffy insisted.

Seth did not move. He knew what was coming, but needed to see it for himself. He needed to know what his work amounted to. What it meant in physical, concrete terms. He had always thought of himself as a facilitator. Someone paid by a client to help the client meet its own goals. He was a stand-in, a proxy. He knew the rules and the language, but he never actually did anything. But here was something that he did. Something he had allowed to happen. And he had a perverse need to see this for himself.

Cliffy punched Seth hard in the shoulder then threw his arm around Seth's waist and forced him towards Lutak's lights. Seth looked back towards Buddy, who now stood in the middle of the road, looking confused. A trickle of blood divided his white mustache. He put his fingers to it and smeared black-red across his snowy, white hair.

Buddy clearly needed help. They should turn around and bring him with them. This would be the right thing to do. But then there was a speck of dust hovering in the darkness behind Buddy. The speck turned into a shimmering drop — a pure, white dot of falling snow. The drop grew until it became a hole in the night, a galloping mass of white fur. It did not growl or drool. Its padded footfalls were silent. It was the perfect predator — the perfect hunter. It was built for a role, and it performed its role without concern for outcome – all that mattered was that it moved forward.

*Just like me*, Seth thought.

Cliffy doubled the pressure around Seth's waist, forcing him ever faster away from Buddy and towards the town. Seth knew it would be easy to explain their choice not to stop, not to turn around and pull Buddy with them to safety. That meant risking lives — Cliffy's and his own. But that wasn't the real reason Seth didn't try to help Buddy. He didn't go to Buddy because saving the old man just wasn't the right solution. That polar bear — the terrifying and powerful ursus maritimus, its body tilting and surging towards Buddy — that was the right solution.

But, to Seth's surprise, Cliffy pulled him to stop just steps from town.

Before them was a tall, lean figure, standing at the town entrance. It wore a leather bomber helmet. Its knees were relaxed. The fingers on its right hand wiggled inches above the .44 slung over its right hip, like a Hollywood gunslinger. Seth recognized the man immediately. It was Mother. He said nothing. He just worked his fingers over that .44, waiting for the right moment.

Seth looked away from Mother and towards the approaching bear. It was closer now, but Buddy hadn't moved and inch. He just stood there wiping his bloody nose into his mustache. The bear's powerful back legs slowed its glide. It took halting steps, like a basketball player preparing for a lay-up. Then it was up above Buddy, a sublime slab of yellowish-white fur punctuated by coal-black eyes, nose, mouth and claws. Its muzzle knotted with anger, the black roots and grime layered throughout its face formed a striking contrast to its fur. Its ears flattened against the back of its head. Its lips turned down at the corners and its jaw unleashed a tangle of white, mangled knives, chipped and torn by a lifetime of difficult eating. Its paws framed Buddy's trustworthy face.

It roared as it descended on Buddy. Unlike the grizzly bear's hoarse, barking yawps, this was the sound of ten thousand lions roaring, the guttural boom of The Diana's air horns. Seth covered his ears and stumbled backwards into Cliffy. It was a sound that Seth felt as much as heard, making his stomach drop, sickeningly, towards his groin.

Suddenly, another burst of noise answered the bear's call.

It was quicker, crisper — a ferocious snapping noise, echoed in the trees, buildings and mountains. Seth instinctively knew that it was Mother's .44. Immediately, Buddy's body jerked and dropped to the road, barely escaping the bear's killing embrace. The polar bear's mammoth paws clutched the air. Its face was confused by its missing prize. It looked at Seth, angry. A second shot cracked the air. Seth chanced a look towards the town and saw Mother, his gun held high, smoke trailing up from its tip.

The bear regarded the barkeep.

"Hyaw!" Mother yelled. "Yaw! Hyaw!"

He fired another round into the night sky.

The bear dropped back onto all fours. It sniffed at Buddy's body, motionless on the asphalt. It nudged the body with its nose, then walked away, slowly and silently, through the brambles and into the dense, black woods beyond. Minutes passed. The bear did not return. Seth cautiously approached Buddy's still body. The neat dot on Buddy's forehead made him an unlikely Hindi. He put his ear to Buddy's mouth and his fingers to his neck. Seth turned to Mother's silhouette.

"He's dead," Seth said.

"Fucking depth perception," Mother said, then rubbed the wrinkled flesh where his right eye once was.

# 48

It was still way too hot.

It had to be at least 100 degrees. It was, what, mid-September? But Phoenix didn't let up until at least late October these days. Summer hadn't lasted so long when he was a kid. Sweat made its way down Seth's neck and across his back, soaking his undershirt. He straightened his coat, adjusted his tie, and wrestled the duct-taped Beast through the big glass door and into the Radley offices. A blessed blast of air-conditioning splashed his face, instantly drying forehead sweat and stiffening previously damp hair. His body, engulfed in a dark suit, refused to slow its salty waterworks.

"Gloria!" he said to the woman at the front desk.

"Just a second," she said, busy instructing one of her many assistants. She held her index finger towards him, and Seth studied the age-spots on her hand's flesh. Finally, Gloria turned and gave him her full attention. "Yes, dear, how can I..." Her eyes widened.

"Hi-ho!" she yelped. "Hi-ho" was Gloria's pet name for Seth — it had something to do with his last name being Sterling, Sterling being related to silver, and her love for The Lone Ranger. It was a bit of reach, but Seth had learned to like it.

He smiled sheepishly.

She rushed out from behind the desk and hugged him. As they embraced, she whispered into his ear. "I hear things didn't go so well in Alaska, Hi-Ho."

"It's not exactly a state secret. You can't turn on the TV without seeing something about Lutak."

"No," she said, "I mean, I heard that you didn't do so well there." She scrunched her nose.

Her knowledge didn't come as a surprise. Gloria was the administrative muscle that kept Radley's firm humming smoothly. She was also Radley's *de facto* gossip clearing-house. She had seen Radley's greats from their first year through to partnership, and served as equal parts den mother, journalist, and savvy businesswoman. Still, Seth wondered how she knew, and — more importantly — what she knew. The news stations had kept Seth's name out of things. And why wouldn't they? On the surface, he had almost nothing to do with what had happened aboard the Diana. According to them, and just about everyone else, NordStar had made a fatal miscalculation when it allowed both a grizzly bear and a domestic terrorist aboard its newest ship. But none of the reporters drew a line between these mistakes and Seth, and no one else was talking.

Cliffy had returned home to his mother's house. He told Seth that he needed to get as far away from cruise ships as he could for a while. He was concerned that someone investigating the incidents aboard The Diana would figure out that he had shut down her communications. Seth thought he was probably right. He promised that he wouldn't tell anyone about Cliffy's involvement, and Cliffy promised the same in return.

Ceejay wasn't speaking to anyone, either. She had suffered a few bruises and cuts, but was otherwise in fine shape. Seth had recommended a few good attorneys to help her settle her parents' affairs. She told Seth she'd call them, but she really just wanted to get back to Laura and Ann Arbor. She said that the members of the press that had been harassing her could all go "fuck themselves." And Seth believed that she meant her. They promised to keep in touch, but Seth wasn't so sure he'd ever hear from her again.

As yet, Tammy hadn't spoken publicly. Luckily, she never knew the whole story. Just the same, Seth was shocked to hear she wouldn't speak with the press — after all, her role probably could have netted her a good deal of money if she played her cards right. From what Cliffy was able to find out from other staffers, the Aussie was actually heartbroken by Buddy's passing and refused to discuss his affairs with anyone at all.

Seth wasn't sure how much his neighbors — Nan and Charlie Jenkins — had overheard. But he imagined it hadn't been enough to make trouble for him. He ate with them in the Anchorage airport before they said their goodbyes. They were both in fine shape, Charlie just had a bit of an ankle sprain. Their spirits were high, as always, though Nan promised that she was going to put a bad review of the cruise online. She said that, at best, The Diana would get two of five stars. They were already discussing their next adventure — a Royal Caribbean 14-day in the Mediterranean. They were excited to see Malta.

As for Mother, Seth never really figured out how much he knew. Mother told authorities that the hole in Buddy was a ruined attempt to save him from a dangerous bear, nothing more. And nobody could, or would, say otherwise. Others on the road that night mentioned the polar bear to the press, but that story seemed to pale in comparison to the rest of the night's events. A few bloggers suggested a link between NordStar's grizzly bear and a conspiracy to conceal its knowledge of the endangered animal, but no one took them seriously. Even stranger, when Alaska's governor resigned shortly thereafter, no one seemed to connect the dots.

As far as Seth knew, only one other person had any real knowledge of Seth's place in the whole fiasco: Thad Wilson. And Thad had ordered him to come straight to the office when he returned from Alaska.

"Thad took a meeting with the partners last night," Gloria said. She shook her head. "Didn't go well."

Seth nodded. "I figured."

"I really liked you, Hi-Ho."

"I still like you, Gloria."

"Oh, you know I'll always like you. It's just too bad, is all."

She pulled him tight again.

"Well," he sighed, "better head on up."

He walked to the elevator bank and felt the hot stare of each person he passed. He looked back to Gloria, who was now whispering to an associate Seth had never seen. When she caught Seth's gaze, the whispering stopped. She smiled and shrugged. He shrugged back.

Seth didn't stop at his 15th floor office. There was no point in postponing the inevitable. Instead, he headed directly to the 23rd floor – Thad's floor. The scene there was the same as that in the lobby. Secretaries, paralegals, visiting associates and partners all watched him intently, but said nothing. When he reached Thad's office, he found the door wide open. Thad was in the doorway, a sly cat's smile on his lips.

"Come on in, bitch."

Seth walked into the large sunny space, his palms sweating. Despite floor-to-ceiling windows letting in the harsh Phoenix sun, Thad's office remained cool. Thad's big oak desk was perfectly placed in the middle of the room, the monitor facing away from the door. The desktop was neat, as always: just a few stacks of documents, a notepad, his favorite pen, and a brochure from a local bakery. Thad curled up in his chair and studied the brochure.

"Sit," he said, not looking up.

Seth deposited himself on the other side of the desk and fought an urge to fidget. For an unbearable minute, Thad said nothing. Seth stared at the top of Thad's head, trying to read its contents. Finally, Thad spoke.

"Good," he said, and drew three perfect oval circles on the brochure. He turned it around so Seth could see. He had circled three cakes out of the ten in the glossy flyer. None of the chosen cakes were chocolate.

"Okay," Thad said, "pick one."

"What for?"

Thad studied Seth's face. "For you," he said, "it's your cake."

"I'm not a cake fan."

"Pick one. Not chocolate. I circled the ones I like."

"Why do I need to pick a cake?"

"Because if you leave Radley without a cake, people are going to talk. They'll think you were fired. And you're not being fired, bitch."

"So cake will make people think I left here on good terms? Who would believe this?"

"Everyone. Cake is fucking powerful. So, do it. Choose your cake."

"Don't you even want to talk about this? To yell at me or something? To discuss what's happened?"

"Yelling is motivational. Discussion is for improvement. I won't pretend for you. This is the end of the line. You fucked up. You knew the consequences."

"Well maybe I want to hear what you think about all of this. Some closure, maybe."

"I don't doubt that, bitch. We'll have lunch sometime. Choose your cake."

Seth crossed his arms.

Thad stared at Seth with his big cat eyes. "It won't change anything," he said.

"I know," Seth said. "I don't need to change anything."

"It's not going to make you any happier."

Seth said nothing.

Thad sighed. "Okay. Here's the deal. What's the worst that could have happened?"

"What do you mean?" Seth asked.

"What's the worst that would have happened if you hadn't pushed so hard? If you hadn't worked here every night and weekend for the last two years; if you hadn't pulled every trick out of the bag to keep The Diana project afloat; if you hadn't figured out a way to deny information to the passengers; if you hadn't come up with a solution for every problem that damned cruise threw at you; if you had just done your job as a facilitator. What then?

"What's the worst that would have happened if you had just let NordStar's problems be their problems? What, another year before partnership? Maybe two? Maybe no partnership? Attorneys are supposed to be risk averse, Seth. We guarantee conservative advice. We don't gamble. We tell our clients what they refuse to tell themselves. We don't sell them dreams or far-fetched plans. That's their job. So, what's the worst that would have happened if you had just let things be?"

Seth thought for a bit. "The Lutak project would have died. I couldn't let the business fail. I couldn't let everything fall apart."

"Then you shouldn't be an attorney," Thad said.

Thad got up, walked around the desk and patted Seth's shoulders.

"I told you that you didn't want to hear this," Thad said, his sleepy eyes somber and his voice grave. Then he brightened. "But there's a silver lining here, bitch."

"I've had enough of silver linings," Seth said.

"Well, you asked, so I think you should listen. The thing you need to learn about business is that the fruits of business follow the law of the conservation of energy: none of it can ever truly be created or destroyed. NordStar was always in trouble. But that port they built in Lutak? That crazy ship? Someone will buy all of that stuff and make use of it. NordStar has already contacted us about negotiating the sale of NordStar's assets to a new cruise line called Mother Seas. The new company wants to turn Lutak into some eco-destination. And NordStar is taking over a new land-based tourism business. So, you see, nothing really dies. And you — you're not going to go away either. You probably won't be disbarred. We won't file a complaint against you — as long as you don't file one against us — and we're not sure who else knows enough about what you did. You'll walk away from this, figure things out, and be back better than ever. You'll fight another day. But maybe you should rethink the attorney thing."

Seth didn't know how to respond.

"But you know the best part? After today, I don't get to call you my bitch any more. That's a good thing, right?"

Thad smiled his big feline smirk.

Seth smiled back. Thad was right. Thad was always right. Seth laughed a little, then his eyes welled up and he started sobbing.

"That's right," Thad said. He put an arm around Seth's shoulder. "Let it out. It's natural." He handed Seth a tissue.

Seth wiped his eyes and blew his nose.

"You done? You feel better?"

Seth nodded.

"Then pick your cake, bitch."

# ABOUT THE AUTHOR

Jonathan E. Hauer is an attorney living in Scottsdale, Arizona with his wife, two daughters, two dogs, and two frogs. This book is only tangentially related to his experiences practicing law. The events in this novel are wholly unrelated to his status as an "inactive" member of the Arizona State Bar. He's saving that story for the sequel.

Visit Jonathan Hauer online at http://www.jonathanhauer.com.

Made in the USA
Lexington, KY
20 December 2010